The mistress knelt
helped Vi to turn he
There seemed to be no sign of life in her. She lay
there, still, grey and to all appearance, dead!

Mary-Lou at the Chalet School,
Elinor M. Brent-Dyer, 1956

First published in Great Britain
by Bettany Press, 2007.
8 Kildare Road London E16 4AD.

Text © Liz Filleul 2007.

Quotations from the works of Margaret Biggs
and Elinor M. Brent-Dyer are used by permission
of Girls Gone By Publishers.

All characters in this novel are fictitious, and any
resemblance to real persons, living or dead, is
purely coincidental.

The right of Liz Filleul to be identified as the
author of this work has been asserted by her
in accordance with the
Copyright, Designs and Patents Act 1988.

British Library Cataloguing in Publication Data.
A catalogue record for this book is available
from the British Library.

This book is sold subject to the condition that it
shall not, by way of trade or otherwise, be lent, re-
sold, hired out, or otherwise circulated without the
Publisher's prior consent in any form of binding or
cover other than that in which it is published and
without a similar condition including this condition
being imposed on the subsequent purchaser.

All rights reserved.

ISBN 978 0 9552973 5 9

Printed and bound in Great Britain
by CLE Print Ltd, Huntingdon, Cambridgeshire.

CONTENTS

CHAPTER		PAGE
	ACKNOWLEDGEMENTS	vi
I.	OFF TO THE SCHOOL-STORY CONFERENCE	1
II.	COTTERFORD MANOR	11
III.	THE FIRST NIGHT	21
IV.	VALERIE CREATES A SENSATION	34
V.	A BUSY DAY	42
VI.	THE FOLK DANCE	51
VII.	A SHOCK FOR THE CONFERENCE	59
VIII.	THE DELEGATES GET A GRILLING	71
IX.	QUIZ NIGHT	80
X.	RHIAN MAKES A SUGGESTION	89
XI.	SALLY ON THE TRAIL	102
XII.	A DISCOVERY	110
XIII.	A STRANGE ALLIANCE	119
XIV.	A GOSSIP WITH BRIDGET	127
XV.	FIONA FINDS THE LINK	135
XVI.	A SPOT OF DECEPTION	143
XVII.	WHAT SALLY OVERHEARD	151
XVIII.	MORE PIECES OF THE JIGSAW	159
XIX.	AN UNEXPECTED DEVELOPMENT	167
XX.	WHO DID IT?	176
XXI.	A STARTLING REVELATION	186
XXII.	ANOTHER CLUE — AND A QUARREL	195
XXIII.	A DAY IN THE COUNTRY	204
XXIV.	THE MYSTERY UNRAVELS	215
XXV.	SALLY IN PURSUIT	227
XXVI.	SALLY UNFOLDS A TALE	235

ACKNOWLEDGEMENTS

Lots of people helped, either directly or indirectly, with the writing of this book, and in particular I would like to thank:

My publisher, Ju Gosling of Bettany Press, for saying yes to the book, for making so many brilliant suggestions, and for being so enthusiastic about the project from the moment I first mentioned to her that I was writing a murder mystery set at a school-story conference.

Helen Prevett and Mandy Proctor for taking the time to read and comment on one of the early drafts.

Roz Mountain for coming up with the idea for one of the twists in the tale.

Helen Barlow, Kirsty Lowson, Helen Aveling, Heather Edmonds and Sera Roberts for giving me an insight into what it's like to attend a school-story conference in real life, and Amrita Balachandran for kindly lending me *The Chalet School Revisited* (BP 1994). Helen Barlow also gave me an insight into all things Abbey, and Kirsty Lowson supplied details about public transport in the Dulwich area.

Gill Bilski, for advice on book prices.

Sisters in Crime Australia, especially Lindy Cameron, Carmel Shute and Viv Colmer, for always being so supportive of my writing.

My husband Grant for always believing in me, especially during those times when the words just wouldn't flow.

My little son Gabriel for inadvertently reigniting my interest in the books I loved as a child.

My mother Vera for keeping Gabriel entertained while I finished off the book during her 'holiday' in Australia.

Liz Filleul, 2007

For Grant and Gabriel

CHAPTER I.

OFF TO THE SCHOOL-STORY CONFERENCE

"Look here, I *do* think this is a bore."
  So it was, rather. This was the first time they had gone back to school from Trennels; and though, by road, school was barely forty minutes away, by train it took three hours — most of it spent mooching on Platform 7, Colebridge Junction.

Antonia Forest, *End of Term*, 1959

SHE definitely should have hired a car. When Sally had left the UK, more than 20 years ago, British Rail had not been too bad. True, trains had run late and Sunday services had been best avoided, but at least catching a train had been a relatively straightforward matter. Now British Rail was no more, different lines were owned by different companies, and you could reach your destination by any number of routes — the cheaper ones tending to be the most meandering, the direct ones hellishly expensive. And whatever route you chose, if you needed to change trains you were in for a ridiculously long wait. Like this current one, over one-and-a-half hours at Clinton Manning station for what would be a mere eleven-minute train journey to Cotterford Dene.
  Sally had already hauled her backpack into the village and checked the high street for second-hand bookshops. There was only one — a disappointingly

run-down shop, specialising in cheap sci-fi, crime, horror and romance, with hardly a children's book in sight, let alone a vintage girls' school story of the type that Sally collected. So she'd left the shop and, eschewing the familiar high-street offerings of W.H. Smith, Boots, Lush, and craft and tea shops, trudged back to Platform 2 at Clinton Manning station.

Plonking herself down on an uncomfortable old bench, she opened her backpack and took out a bottle of water. Then she grabbed the programme for the Tales Out of School conference and examined it for about the hundredth time.

The front cover of the programme was nostalgically decorated with black-and-white sketches of tunic-clad schoolgirls reading, chatting, or wielding hockey sticks. The inside pages promised a busy time for those attending the conference. Today, Friday, was the opening day, with everyone arriving in time for a seven o'clock supper. Saturday comprised a full day of talks and discussion groups, as well as the afternoon book sale which would no doubt tempt Sally to part with way too much money. Folk dancing — a staple activity in many vintage school stories — had been arranged for Saturday night; Sally, who had no interest in folk dancing, rather hoped there would be other reluctant dancers among the delegates who might be willing to accompany her to a pub instead. More talks and discussion groups followed on Sunday, followed by a grand dinner and quiz night, then on Monday there would be a conference overview before everyone went their separate ways.

Sally had found out about the conference via the internet. Throughout most of her adult life, she'd believed that she was the only woman in the world who still turned to the well-thumbed pages of the

Chalet School or Malory Towers when she felt unwell, stressed or depressed. But a couple of years ago, Sally had keyed 'Chalet School' into the Google search engine and had discovered several websites and discussion forums devoted to girls' school-story authors and their books — most with a solely adult membership. Sally had quickly become a regular visitor to two forums — Chalet Girls, and the enormous Jolly Hockey Sticks message board, colloquially known as 'the JHS', which covered the works of all girls' school-story authors.

Earlier in the year, someone had posted on the JHS asking if anyone else on the list planned to attend the Tales Out of School conference, a bi-annual conference organised by the Tales Out of School school-story fan club that was being held this year in the Warwickshire village of Cotterford Dene. Sally had followed a link to the home page for the conference, studied the draft programme, and wondered whether she might attend it ... After all, both her children were virtually grown up now and, although they still lived at home, didn't need her around; plus she hadn't visited the UK since she'd emigrated, and it would be great to catch up with her old friends and what was left of her family in England. Added to that, it would be fun to meet the school-story collectors she'd met online ... and, she'd quickly realised, she could combine the trip with work.

Work for Sally was editing a monthly magazine called *Australian Collector*, which covered collecting of all kinds — though mainly antiques and old wares. Since taking over the editorship two years ago, Sally had introduced a regular books feature, but so far hadn't indulged her own interest, concentrating instead on running articles on collecting old Australian books in various genres. She'd contracted specialist writers for those; now, she'd decided, she'd write something herself. Already, though, she was beginning to have qualms about her assignment. She had never worked as a journalist, having gained her job on the magazine thanks to several years of editing a list of antiques and art titles for a book publisher. So she had never interviewed anyone before and was worried that she wouldn't ask the right questions, in fact that she'd make a complete mess of it.

She had fixed up a couple of interviews as soon as her bosses had given her the go-ahead to attend the Tales Out of School Conference and to write an article on collecting girls' school stories for a future issue. One of them would be with Valerie Teague, who, she had learnt from the internet, was a book dealer specialising in what many collectors in the genre called 'girls' own' fiction or 'G.O.' for short — school stories, pony stories, adventure stories and family stories aimed at girls. Valerie ran an online shop called Fine Print Books, and Sally had arranged to meet her tonight in the book-sale area.

Her other prospective interviewee, Leonie Carr, was the host of Chalet Girls, an internet forum dedicated to the works of Elinor M. Brent-Dyer, creator of the Chalet School series — they were going to look out for each other at dinner tonight and arrange an interview then. Sally was a regular visitor to Chalet Girls and liked what she'd seen of Leonie online. Valerie Teague, however, never posted on online forums, and Sally wondered what she would be like. She'd been put on to her by Leonie, when she'd told her that she wanted to interview a book dealer for her article, and the email she'd received back from Valerie had been abrasive to say the least. Sally sighed and took a gulp of water. She hoped she'd be able to handle

Valerie okay and glean the information she needed from her to write a good article. Having work agree to her trip had made it much more affordable for Sally, but with the interviews so imminent, she half-wished she was attending the conference as an ordinary delegate and not in a professional capacity.

She took a final long drink of what was by now warm spring water — Britain was enjoying a surprisingly sunny tail-end of summer and the heat felt stifling, even to Sally, who was used to Melbourne's hotter climate — and decided to wander over to the café she'd spotted across the road and buy another bottle for the train journey. You never knew — if the train broke down, the eleven-minute journey could turn into several uncomfortable hours stuck between stations in an oven-like carriage. She shoved the conference programme back into her backpack, and headed out of the station and across the road to the café.

The café was small — six tables made it appear crammed — and arty, with reproduction posters advertising 1940s-era movies, books and records adorning the walls. Sally took her place at the back of a short queue. As she stood, she glanced at the occupant of the table nearest to her. A small, very thin woman in her early twenties with short red hair sat nibbling a sandwich, sipping Diet Coke and reading a paperback copy of *The Unforgettable Fifth at Trebizon* by Anne Digby. Sally wondered whether she was a fellow delegate.

The queue moved quickly; when her turn came, Sally purchased a bottle of water and turned to leave. As she did so, the younger woman put her Trebizon book to one side, looked up and met Sally's eyes. Her face was pale and sprinkled with freckles. Sally noticed that she was wearing a long-sleeved black T-shirt and black jeans, and wondered how she could bear to wear such clothing in this heat. Sally was only wearing a loose-fitting sundress and she was still hot.

"Hello," Sally said, stopping by the table and smiling at the younger woman. "Are you heading for the Tales Out of School conference as well?"

The other woman smiled back. "I am, yes. Are you?"

"Yes," nodded Sally. "I'm Sally Meredith."

"I'm Margaret Wilks," the other woman introduced herself. She pointed to the empty chair at her table. "Would you like to join me? There's still another twenty minutes till the train's due. That's if you *are* waiting for the train?" she added.

Sally nodded as she sat down and twisted the top off the Perrier water. "Yes. I hadn't expected such a long delay. I've been wishing I'd hired a car."

"You're Australian, aren't you?" Margaret asked curiously.

"Sort of. I'm an Australian citizen and I've lived in Melbourne for more than 20 years. I'm from England originally, though — from the Midlands — but I suppose I've picked up an Australian accent by now," Sally explained.

"Have you come over here just for the conference?" Margaret asked, looking impressed.

"Sort of," said Sally again. "I'm editor of a magazine called *Australian Collector*. So I'm going to write an article about old British girls' school stories and their collectability. But I'm combining it with holidays and visiting family and friends. I arrived last Sunday and have spent the last few days staying at my cousin's place near Wolverhampton."

"What a wonderful job. Writing about school stories, I mean," said Margaret. "I'd love a job like that."

"Well, this will be the first time I've written about school stories," Sally admitted. "The magazine covers collecting of all types, from expensive artworks to buttons. And I don't usually write the articles, I edit them. But this is an exception, because of my own interest."

"What do you collect?" Margaret asked, finishing the sandwich.

"The Chalet School. Antonia Forest's Marlow books. Dimsie. Malory Towers and St Clare's. Oh, and Mary Gervaise's Georgia books — they have pony titles, but they're really school stories," Sally replied. "I collect Trebizon as well — in fact," she added, pointing at Margaret's book, "the one you're reading is one of only two I haven't got."

"You can borrow it if you like," offered Margaret, pushing the paperback towards her. "It's so short you'll read it easily before the conference finishes."

"Thanks very much — that's really kind of you," Sally replied, picking up the book. It was, like all the Trebizon books, slender — and yet she knew from searching for it on eBay and abebooks.com that *The Unforgettable Fifth at Trebizon*, as the last and rarest in the series, commanded incredibly high prices even as a paperback. "I'd love to read it. I'll give it back to you over the weekend." She tucked it carefully into her backpack, then asked, "What about you? What do you collect?"

"Trebizon, obviously," Margaret returned, with a grin. "And the Chalet School as well. And I've just started collecting Antonia Forest's Marlow books."

"Oh, they're fantastic," Sally enthused. "The four school stories are among my favourite books."

"And the good thing about them," Margaret said, "is that the paperbacks weren't abridged like the Chalet School ones, so collecting them in paperback is okay — though even that's expensive for some of the titles. Do you have any Chalet School hardbacks?"

"A few," said Sally. "I'd like to have more, but they're so hard to find, and some of them are horribly expensive when you do come across them."

"Tell me about it," said Margaret. "I've only got three. And until I get a job, I don't think I'll be buying any more somehow." She glanced at her watch. "We'd better go. The train's due."

Sally heaved her backpack onto her shoulders and picked up her drink. Margaret picked up her own large backpack, grimacing with the effort of lifting it.

"What have you got in there?" asked Sally amused.

"Oh, the kitchen sink," Margaret joked. "Books mostly," she added with a grin.

They left the café, crossed the surprisingly busy road, and headed for the platform. The electronic sign on the platform told them that the Oxford train, which stopped at Cotterford Dene, was due in five minutes. They moved near the edge of the platform in readiness.

"Are you a student?" Sally asked her companion.

"No — I finished university last year," Margaret answered. "I'm unemployed at the moment. I had a job, but lost it in March in a restructure."

"I'm sorry," said Sally. "What sort of work did you do?"

"Admin for a charity. I'm hoping to get a similar post with another charity, but there doesn't seem to be anything around at the moment," Margaret sighed. "So I'm living off benefits, which isn't much fun."

"I hope you find something soon," said Sally.

The train pulled into the station, and Sally and Margaret clambered into one of the carriages, snagging seats opposite each other. Several other women were seated in the carriage, Sally noticed — a couple reading, one knitting, three sitting together and laughing about something. She wondered whether any of them were headed for the conference too.

"Have you been to one of these conferences before?" she asked Margaret.

"No — this is my first," Margaret answered. "I wanted to go to one of the Elinor Brent-Dyer conferences a couple of years ago, but couldn't afford it." Sally wondered how, given that Margaret was a fairly recent graduate and unemployed to boot, she could afford to attend the Tales Out of School Conference, which wasn't at all cheap. Still, she reasoned, it was likely that Margaret still lived at home, and perhaps her parents had helped her out with the money.

"Have you been to one?" Margaret asked her.

Sally shook her head. "No. There aren't any in Australia." She wished someone would organise one, though. There were plenty of fans there — Sally had met some of them, after forging friendships online. There were fans in New Zealand too, who might fly over for such an event. She thought she might mention it to the Tales Out of School people. Perhaps they didn't realise how big the interest was down under.

The train ran on time; soon it was drawing close to Cotterford Dene. The railway line ran along the River Severn, and Sally could see the ruined castle in the distance. She'd been to Cotterford Dene once before — she and an ex-boyfriend had spent a day there a couple of years before she'd emigrated. She remembered it as a delightfully pretty village, with a main street crammed with interesting shops, a couple of atmospheric pubs, and a pleasant riverside walk that took you to the ruins of Cotterford Castle in one direction and to the restored nineteenth-century Cotterford Manor — venue for the conference — in the other.

The train began to slow down, and Sally and Margaret picked up their luggage and moved to stand beside the carriage door. A few other women, farther down the carriage, stood up too. A tall man who looked to be in his late fifties, with grey hair tied back in a pony tail and wearing an open-neck shirt and long shorts, came to stand beside them at the door. "Are you ladies bound for the Tales Out of School Conference?" he asked.

"We are," Sally nodded.

"I am too," he said. "I'm Richard Fingleton." Sally recognised his name from the conference programme — he was one of Sunday's speakers, on the men behind the stories that appeared in the schoolgirl comics of the 1930s.

Sally and Margaret introduced themselves. "Have either of you been to a conference before?" Richard asked.

They both shook their heads.

"Oh, you'll love it," he assured them. "There's always so much to learn and so many interesting people to meet — not to mention fantastic books to buy. And it's a lovely venue this year — wonderful house and grounds. If this weather holds, we'll be able to explore them properly. Which authors do you collect?"

The train jolted to a halt, and Sally put her hand on the door latch, ready to disembark and to relate her list of favourite authors for what she guessed wouldn't be the last time this weekend.

CHAPTER II.

COTTERFORD MANOR

It was nicer even than they expected — a glorious old place, built partly in Tudor fashion of grey stone, and partly of black and white timbers. There were latticed windows, and a porch ornamented with stone balls, and curious twisted chimneys and picturesque gables at odd angles ...

"It looks as if one might have all kinds of adventures there," said Lindsay Hepburn gleefully.

Angela Brazil, *The Manor House School,* 1911

COTTERFORD Manor was located on the outskirts of Cotterford Dene, about a ten-minute walk from the railway station. Sally, Margaret and Richard walked together, Richard explaining that he had been to Cotterford Manor for another conference the previous year, and that he had been fortunate enough to sleep in the manor house itself. "It can't accommodate everyone, so there's an annexe as well. But the annexe was built in the 1980s rather than the 1880s, so it doesn't begin to have the atmosphere of the manor house," he said.

Margaret frowned. "The programme didn't say there were two lots of accommodation," she said.

"Oh well, never mind," said Sally. "I'll be disappointed if I'm not in the manor house, but I guess we'll only be using our bedrooms for sleeping in, and all the activities will be in the house anyway."

"That's right," Richard nodded.

Margaret lapsed into apparently sulky silence. Sally asked Richard if he had interests in children's books beyond the subject he was speaking about at the conference. "Oh yes," he said. "I collect all the old boys' school stories — you know, Jennings, Rex Milligan, Billy Bunter, *Six Stout Fellows and Me*, that sort of thing. Also some of the authors who wrote for both boys and girls — Malcolm Saville, Geoffrey Trease, Enid Blyton. And all the boys' comics from the early part of the twentieth century, obviously. That's what spawned my interest in the men who wrote the stories in the girls' comics — they were mostly the same men who wrote the serials in the boys' comics. Ah — here's the manor house now."

They walked through the open gates and Cotterford Manor stood before them, at the end of a long, red-gravelled drive, sandwiched by immaculate lawns. Several steps led up to the manor house itself. According to the Tales Out of School programme, a manor house had stood on this site since the sixteenth century, but the original Tudor house had burnt down during the nineteenth century. What stood there now was an imposing Victorian mansion, three storeys high. As she climbed the steps that led up to the house, Sally realised what a perfect place it was for a conference on girls' school stories. The manor looked just like the ones that housed boarding-schools in the books.

The front door was open; Sally, Margaret and Richard entered and found themselves in a large, L-shaped reception area, with high ceilings and oak-panelled walls. An information desk stood in the centre of the L, and to the left of the entrance a special display had been put together: two girl mannequins, each one clad in tunic, blazer and tie, stood in the foreground, satchel over the arm of one, violin case in the hand of the other. Arranged around them was schooldays memorabilia — two crossed hockey sticks, a tennis racquet, and a pile of annuals from the 1950s — *School Friend, Girl, Girls' Crystal*. Behind the display was a poster advertising the conference and some photocopied dust-jackets of classic girls' school stories from the twentieth century: *Monitress Merle, The Girls of the Hamlet Club, The School at the Chalet, Evelyn Finds Herself, Chester House Wins Through, The Twins at St Clare's, First Term at Trebizon*. Someone had gone to a lot of work, but Sally found it all a bit twee. Covers and annuals would have been interesting enough, she thought; you didn't really need mannequins.

A tall, slim, dark-haired woman in her early fifties, smartly dressed in a long cream skirt and matching short-sleeved top and sporting an amber necklace and earrings, was standing admiring the display. She spotted Richard and smiled broadly. "Hi Richard! Good to see you again. How've you been?"

"Harriet!" Richard and Harriet kissed each other on both cheeks, then Richard said, "I'm very well. And yourself?"

"Fine. I was—" Harriet smiled mischievously "—I was sorry to hear about you and Valerie."

Richard gave a melodramatic shudder. "Don't remind me about Valerie! I suppose she's here?"

"Of course. If there's a book sale, you'll find Valerie." Ah, thought Sally, interested; unless there was a second bookseller called Valerie, they were talking about Valerie Teague. "As a matter of fact," continued Harriet, "she's in the room next door to mine, so if you fancy a rapprochement, no doubt I'll hear all about it."

"Forget it, Harriet. Oh, here are two more fans for you to meet. Sally Meredith — from Australia now, but originally a Brit, and a young fan, Margaret Wilks. This is Harriet Lenton, ladies."

"I recognise your name," Sally said. "You're giving the talk tomorrow on 'Bullying in the Girls' School Story'."

"That's right," Harriet said.

"Harry's a good speaker," said Richard, "so it's well worth going along to hear her."

"Sorry," said Sally, regretfully, "but it coincides with the talk on caring for old books, and I really need to attend that one for an article I'm writing."

"You're a journalist?" Richard asked.

Sally nodded and explained about the article for *Australian Collector*. "I think the session on caring for old books would be of more interest to the readers who buy the magazine," she explained. "But I hope your talk goes well, Harriet. It does sound interesting."

"You must do a lot of travelling with your job," Richard said.

"Not really," Sally answered. "This is my first article for *Australian Collector*, actually. I usually edit other people's articles."

"It's a good article to begin with, then!" said Harriet. "Look, you three had better get on with registration before a queue forms."

Sally, Margaret and Richard heeded Harriet's advice and headed over to the information desk. Margaret gave her name first, and one of the women on the desk, a sturdy young woman with a long blonde pigtail and serious expression, and with 'Claire' printed on her name badge, ticked off Margaret's name and handed her a slender package. "You're in the annexe," she said. "Room number 18."

Margaret's face fell. "But I really wanted to be in the house," she protested. "Are you *sure* you can't fit me in here or swap me with someone?"

"No, sorry," said Claire firmly. Margaret scowled and said to Sally and Richard, "I'd better go and unpack. I'll see you later at supper, I guess." And she disappeared through the front entrance, to make her way to where the annexe was located.

Sally exchanged an amused glance with Richard, then told Claire her name.

"Ah yes, you *are* in the house — up in the attics — room number 8," said Claire, passing Sally her slim package, with 'Delegate's Pack' written on it.

"Absolutely gorgeous," said Richard. "I had an attic room when I came for the conference last year. What about me?" he added. "Richard Fingleton."

"Yes, house as well, not in the attics though — bedroom number 20 on the second floor."

Sally looked at the map of the house she'd been given along with her delegate's pack, and together with Richard made her way towards the staircase. It wasn't a grand, sweeping one like the one she'd expected, but a narrow one, round the corner from reception — more like a servants' staircase, she thought. She said goodbye to Richard on the second floor landing and carried on up to the attics. She quickly found number 8. She opened the door and found herself in a cute room with sloping ceiling, polished floorboards and a brightly coloured rug. The window looked out over the croquet lawn and adjacent tennis court. The room held a single bed, a bedside table and lamp, a small wardrobe and a chest of drawers, and a door led to a tiny en-suite. It was, she thought happily, a perfect bedroom for someone attending a conference on girls' school stories. It reminded her of 'Sara Crewe', the name given to the attic bedroom where Nicola, Lawrie and Ginty Marlow had slept during the events of Antonia Forest's fourth, and sadly final school story, *The Attic Term*.

She sat on the bed and opened her delegate's pack. It contained an updated programme detailing the rooms where the various talks, discussion groups and book sale would take place; a name badge that Sally promptly pinned on to her dress; and a couple of postcards of the manor house. Sally then unpacked her backpack: she had brought exactly ten days' clothing with her to Britain, knowing that she could make use of her various hosts' washing machines when she was staying with them; she'd done her laundry the previous day at her cousin's house; and would be able to wash clothes again when she went to stay with her friend Rhian after the conference on Monday. Then she set her books and the conference programme and delegate's pack on the bedside table, put her toiletries and hairbrush in the bathroom, and undressed and had a quick shower. After that it was still only half-past five, and there was nothing scheduled until supper at seven. Sally grabbed her map, camera and handbag and made her way back downstairs; she had ample time to explore the grounds before supper as well as heading for the book sale venue to find and interview Valerie Teague.

The grounds were wonderful. Right behind the house were a croquet lawn, tennis court and cricket pitch; behind these sporting facilities stood the annexe, a red-brick, one-storey building, purpose-built when Cotterford Manor had first become a conference centre. Behind the annexe Sally followed a wide and sloping pathway through woods down to well-maintained gardens — roses and marigolds were in full bloom. As she stood admiring the flowers, a couple of young women in their early twenties, both clad in shorts, T-shirt and walking boots, strolled along the path towards her. They greeted her cheerily.

"Hi," said one, with a dark brown ponytail and a nose ring. "Are you staying here for the conference?"

"Yes." Sally squinted at the names on their badges. The woman with the nose ring was Heidi Fitzsimmons. Her friend, a small, fair-haired woman, was Anna Judd.

"Hello, Sally," said Anna with a grin as she eyed Sally's name badge.

"The gardens are beautiful, aren't they?" said Heidi. "If you keep walking you'll reach a big pond. There are heaps of ducks."

They talked briefly about the conference and about the manor house, after which Sally made her way down to the pond past a bandstand; village entertainment of yesteryear, Sally thought. Or maybe they still had open-air concerts here in summer? As Sally approached the pond, ducks began swimming towards her, hopeful of bread. "Sorry," she told them. She stood watching them for a while, then checked her watch. Time to head back.

When she arrived back at the house, several delegates were gathered in the reception area, some looking at the display, others reading notices on a large noticeboard that had appeared, others queuing for their delegate's packs. Conversation was abuzz.

"Hi Laura! Haven't seen you for ages — not since the Brent-Dyer conference last year. How've you been?"

"Fine thanks! This is a great place for a conference, isn't it?"

"Oh, absolutely perfect! It could almost *be* a boarding-school!"

"That's what I thought when I saw the photos of it on the internet and in the brochure. Mind you, it looks even more fabulous in the flesh, as it were. And the grounds are apparently superb."

"And thank *God* there's internet access in all the rooms! I don't think I could survive without my daily forum fix."

"Me neither. I brought my laptop along and I'll check in every night. Might put some updates on Chalet Girls each night so that people who can't attend know what's happening."

"Hi there, you two — are you in the main house or the annexe?"

"Main house, thank goodness. Where are you?"

"Annexe — it's not so bad. And how much time will we spend in it, anyway? Most of the time I'll be over here."

"And of course, the Annexe is in a fine Chalet School tradition ..." The women laughed, and Sally smiled, wishing she'd thought of that to say to Margaret when she'd been so upset about being placed there. In the early Chalet School books, an Annexe to the main school had been established, higher up the mountains, for those girls who were especially delicate. Sally thought the Annexe might be appropriate in Margaret's case — there was certainly something fragile about her.

Making her way through the throng, she headed towards a room just off reception, where the following day's book sale was being held. According to the information in the programme, when Cotterford Manor had been a family residence, the room had, appropriately, been the library. Sally entered the room and looked around; some ten stalls were in the early stages of being set up.

"Who on *earth* gave me this *awful* space?" The speaker was a tall woman in her fifties with short blonde hair, shaking her head over the stall nearest the door. "I do hate being by the door. Hi — Miriam! Miriam! Who gave me this dreadful space?"

Miriam, a pretty woman in her late forties, with short, shoulder-length dark-brown curls and vivid blue eyes, stopped abruptly in her walk across the room. "Valerie. Hello. What's the problem?" Ah, thought Sally, so *this* was Valerie Teague. And Miriam was, presumably, Miriam Lorrimer, who co-ran Tales Out of School and who had organised the conference.

"*This* is the problem," said Valerie, waving at the stall. "I'm right next to the door. I *loathe* being next to the door. Can't I change with someone?"

"Sorry, Valerie, you were the last to arrive. Everyone else had started setting up before you got here. Anyway, it's a decent enough space. You're very visible."

"Not really. Not when people come in — I'm the wrong side of the door. They see Leah's stall first." She pointed towards the stall directly opposite the door. "Well, no surprises there. She's always favoured." Miriam frowned. "They won't spot me till they're on their way out," Valerie continued. "And by then they'll probably have spent all the money they're going to spend ..."

Miriam sighed. "I think a lot of people look all the way round first, *then* decide what to buy. Look, Valerie, if you find that when the sale opens absolutely nobody comes in the direction of your stall, come and tell me, all right? And I'll see what I can do."

"And I suppose if I make *one* sale tomorrow then you'll say it's okay and I was clearly visible," Valerie retorted. "That's the trouble with you, Miriam — you're totally unreasonable. Jess would have listened and would have moved me somewhere else." She opened one of the boxes and began to take out books.

"Wow," said Miriam, impressed. "You've got some terrific books there, Valerie."

"All first edition Chalets," Valerie smirked. "And this box," she tapped it, "contains all first edition Abbeys. So you can see why I don't want people all spent out when they finally find my stall ..."

"I shouldn't think there's much fear of that, Valerie," said Miriam. "If you've got a box of first edition Chalets and another of first edition Abbeys, word will soon spread. Anyway, I have to move on. See you later."

"Hello," said Sally, a little self-consciously as she approached the simmering Valerie. "I'm Sally Meredith from *Australian Collector*. We talked on email ..."

"Oh yes," said Valerie. "I remember. You wanted to interview me for an article on book collecting."

"Can we do that now?" Sally asked.

"I don't see why not. If you don't mind my arranging the stall as I answer questions."

Valerie started arranging the books and Sally took out her notebook and biro. As Sally was flicking through her notebook for a fresh page, Miriam walked past the stall again. "Looks like someone has found you already and we're not even open, Valerie!" she commented brightly.

Valerie glowered at her. "Bitch," she muttered. Then she caught Sally's eye. "Sorry, but that's what she is."

CHAPTER III.

THE FIRST NIGHT

"Now for a real, proper Feast!" said Carlotta, happily. She and the others set out the goodies they had — the cakes and the buns, the biscuits and the sweets. They opened the tins and emptied the contents on to dishes — sardines, fruit salad, pine-apples, prawns, the most wonderful selection of things imaginable!

Enid Blyton, *Second Form at St Clare's*, 1944

"I SAY, Sally, do you fancy a drink after supper?" Sally, heading downstairs on her way to the conservatory, where all the meals were to be held, swung round to see Richard rushing to catch her up. "A drink?" she queried.

"Yes. We'll all have finished eating by nine-thirty — I thought you might fancy a drink down at the local. I've asked Harriet as well, and Leonie Carr says she'll come along. Hopefully one or two others might join us."

"Excellent." Sally could combine a trip to the pub — both of which she remembered as very cosy, comfortable places to enjoy a drink — with a chat with Leonie; she might well be able to interview her at the same time. Her interview with Valerie had gone, she felt, surprisingly well; Valerie had been more than happy to talk about her books, how she'd got into book dealing, and how at nine she'd developed a lifelong love for school stories in general and in particular those of Elinor M. Brent-Dyer and

Dorita Fairlie Bruce.

"How do you manage to find so many books to sell?" Sally had asked her, curiously. "I used to think I'd like to be a book dealer, but honestly, I rarely come across any bargains in junk shops or garage sales."

"It is harder these days," Valerie had admitted. "Sometimes even the charity shops know the value of the books. And although you still get deceased estates, often people will check the value of the books first and sell them on eBay rather than invite a dealer round to look at them. Still," she had continued with a smile, "we all get by. And if the internet means there are fewer bargains around, it also means there's a larger market for us, and that the books we do sell command higher prices."

Valerie hadn't been joking. She had allowed Sally to examine a couple of her books. Carefully, Sally had taken one of the first editions — *The Chalet School and the Lintons* — out of its protective plastic covering and taken a covetous look at it. The book was in almost perfect condition — intact dust jacket, clean creamy pages, just some biro markings where some previous owner had, for some bizarre reason, counted the number of words in each paragraph on the second page of the story. The price was £150. Gingerly, Sally had put the book back in its covering, laid it back down on Valerie's stall and had picked up another Chalet title, *Redheads at the Chalet School*. That, too, was in immaculate condition and was a little less expensive than *Lintons* at £120. Sally had taken her leave of Valerie wondering whether she could possibly splash out on a beautiful first edition as a memento of her trip.

Now, she and Richard had reached the conservatory, which was located right at the back of the house; as well as being the location for meals, it was to be the venue for the following night's folk dancing. Round tables, each seating four people, were scattered about. Harriet, already seated, waved at Richard and Sally to join her.

"I explored the grounds earlier," Sally told Richard and Harriet, when they were all settled with plates of chicken salad, bread and butter and glasses of wine. "They're wonderful."

"Oh, majestic," Richard agreed. "Ah — look, there's your friend, the little one who's in the annexe." He waved across to Margaret, who joined them, looking grateful to spot familiar faces. "How's the annexe?" he asked her.

Margaret smiled a little self-consciously. "It's okay."

"Not as bad as you were expecting?"

"No. No, it's fine."

"Anything like the Chalet School annexe?" asked Sally.

Margaret smiled again. "Probably."

"Sal's coming to the pub with us later," Richard told Harriet. *"Sal,"* thought Sally, irritated. They'd barely spoken to each other, and here he was talking about her as if she was an old chum.

"Jolly good," returned Harriet. "What about you, Margaret? Would you like to come to the pub after supper?"

"Sorry," said Margaret. "I thought I might get an early night. I've had a pretty long day."

"Heidi and Anna are coming as well," Harriet told Richard, "and Leonie too, of course."

"Is that Leonie Carr?" asked Margaret.

"Yes," answered Harriet. "Do you know her?"

"Yes, but only through Chalet Girls."

"I never go to that forum," Harriet mused. "I only go to the JHS. And then I only lurk there, I don't post."

"I post on Chalet Girls and the JHS," Sally said. "I'm 'sallym' on both of them."

"Oh, actually I've seen your posts a couple of times," said Margaret. "I mainly lurk, but I've posted occasionally under my own name."

"Sorry," said Sally, feeling a little embarrassed; the last thing this unemployed and anxious young woman probably needed was to feel she was insignificant in cyberspace as well. "I don't recall seeing your posts at all."

"No, you wouldn't have," Margaret replied. "I've only posted two or three times in the past couple of years. Mostly I go to fan fiction sites. I write a lot of fan fic."

"Ssh," said Richard, indicating that Miriam, seated at a table near the back of the conservatory, was rising to her feet. "The official bit's about to start."

After a couple of minutes, the room quietened down. Miriam began by welcoming everybody to the conference, and then ran through the notices. Her first announcement was a health report on the woman who ran Tales Out of School with her, Jessica Gibson.

"Unfortunately," she said in a shaky voice, "Jess isn't responding well to the cancer treatment and a couple more tumours have been discovered. Please can those who do pray remember her in their prayers."

"Poor old Jess," said Richard, and there were echoes of sympathy around the room. Sally knew from the forums that Jess was a popular member of the 'girls' own' community, and that she had been battling cancer for two years. As well as her work with Tales Out of School, she had written a book, *Girlz' Zone*, which examined the girls' school story from a feminist perspective; it had been published by a smallpress publisher, Vintage Child, about eighteen months ago. Vintage Child republished out-of-print children's books, together with critical works on the genre. Sally had bought several of their republished novels, but so far hadn't purchased any of their non-fiction. She'd read a criticism as background for her article, but that had been published by someone else.

"Please pass on our love to her next time you speak to her, Miriam," a woman sitting at a table at the back called out, and there was a murmur of agreement.

Miriam said she would pass on any messages and then moved on with the notices, ending with an anouncement that the grand quiz on Sunday night would see people competing in groups of four, so could those who wanted to team up make sure they sat at the same table as each other then.

When she'd finished, Miriam announced that coffee would be served in about ten minutes for those who wanted it, and Richard murmured, "Time to head off." About fifteen minutes later, Sally, Richard, Harriet, Heidi, Anna and Leonie — the latter turning out to be a pretty dark-haired woman in her early thirties — met up at the main gate and headed in the direction of the village. Just outside the village was one of the pubs that Sally recalled from her previous visit — a Tudor-style pub called the Rose and Crown. It was a balmy evening, so when they arrived at the pub they opted for a table in the beer garden. Richard disappeared into the bar to order a round of drinks, and Leonie accompanied him to help carry them.

"What do you all think of the programme?" Harriet asked, when Richard and Leonie had returned with the drinks — half a pint of Summer Lightning ale each for Sally (who had spent the few days she'd been back in Britain happily rediscovering real ale) and Harriet, a dry white wine for Leonie, port and lemons for Heidi and Anna, and a pint of Greene King for Richard.

"It looks pretty good," said Sally. "Lots of variety."

Harriet nodded. "They're good organisers, Tales Out of School, especially Miriam. She's very efficient."

"You've been to their conferences before, then?" Sally asked.

"Yes. I came to the last one, two years ago. It was held in university accommodation — nothing at all like Cotterford Manor! Very basic."

"But it did have a bar," Richard pointed out.

"Yes," said Leonie. "It seems really strange that Cotterford Manor doesn't have a bar. It's a conference centre after all — and at conferences, people drink."

"Probably some ancient by-law or something in the deeds that prevents them from selling liquor on the premises," Richard surmised. "Fortunately, there *are* a couple of good pubs here. I came for another conference last year and we all ended up down one or other of the pubs every night."

"What sort of work do you do, Richard?" Sally asked.

"I teach twentieth-century literature at Birmingham University. Harry's a lecturer too — at Manchester University, but she teaches Victorian literature."

"I studied English at university years ago," said Sally, enthusiastically. "At Aberystwyth."

"When was that?" Richard asked her.

"Early 1980s."

Richard mentioned a lecturer he worked with who had previously worked in the English department at Aberystwyth; Sally remembered the name only vaguely. "He started there in my final year," she recalled. "But I didn't really have anything to do with him. He taught Middle English, and I didn't study that."

"When did you emigrate to Australia?" Harriet asked.

"The year after I finished my degree. My parents had emigrated during my second year. I struggled to get a job after graduation, so after a few months I followed them out."

"Do you have family here still?" Richard asked.

"A couple of cousins and an aunt and uncle, but that's it. I'm an only child. I've got several friends here, though." She turned to the rest of the group. "What about the rest of you? What do you do?"

She learned that Leonie worked as a museum curator and that Anna and Heidi both worked for their local council, but in different departments. Harriet and Richard started discussing departmental politics at their respective universities, while Anna and Heidi went off to the bar to replenish the drinks. Sally asked Leonie if she'd mind being interviewed in the pub, and Leonie happily acquiesced. Sally took out her notebook and chatted to Leonie about how she'd first begun collecting school stories until Anna and Heidi returned with the drinks.

"Are you a journalist, Sally?" Anna asked, plonking down another half-pint of Summer Lightning in front of her.

Sally explained about her article.

"What a fabulous job!" Heidi enthused.

It was too, Sally thought, her enthusiasm fuelled by Summer Lightning, a successful interview with Valerie, and the fact that Leonie was a willing and loquacious interviewee. This interviewing lark, she thought happily, wasn't going to be too bad after all.

"I interviewed Valerie Teague earlier," she told them. "While she was setting up her stall for the book sale."

"Any bargains?" Anna asked.

"I doubt that," Richard commented. "Fine Print books at fine prices. Valerie always has been a rip-off merchant."

"You must excuse Richard," said Harriet. "There was a conference on old comics in London last year, which he, Valerie and I all attended, and he ended up having a fling with her. She gave him the elbow straight after the conference and he's bitter."

"I am *not* bitter," Richard protested. "I'm relieved. I only ended up in bed with her because I was drunk."

"Very commendable," said Harriet, wryly. Then she smiled impishly. "Anyway, Valerie's version is that she only went to bed with you because she was suffering from depression at the time. It was just after her husband died," she explained to the other four.

"I don't see why she'd be suffering from depression because her husband had died," said Richard. "From what I could see, she never had any time for him. The poor old bugger probably died of ear-ache."

"I'm sure you're right," said Harriet, "but she was apparently put on antidepressants."

"Is she still on them?" Leonie asked.

"No idea," returned Harriet.

Sally was becoming bored by this gossip, even if it was about someone she'd just interviewed, and Heidi and Anna must have felt the same way, because they exchanged glances, checked their watches, and Heidi said she thought they would head back now as it would be an early start the next day. Sally looked at her watch — it was already after eleven.

"I might head back too," she said.

"We may as well all walk back together," said Harriet.

"Oh, I wouldn't mind another one," said Richard, looking ruefully at his empty glass.

"Well, I've got a bottle of bourbon in my room," said Harriet. "You can come in and have a nightcap with me."

"Good idea," said Richard, cheering up immediately. "I brought rather a nice malt with me. I'll bring that along too."

They all headed off up the road, Anna and Heidi leading the way, arms entwined. As they arrived, a taxi pulled up outside the manor house. A tall, blonde woman in her late thirties wearing an ankle-length blue dress jumped out. Richard, Harriet and Leonie greeted her ecstatically.

"Bridget! Wonderful to see you!"

"Bridget Whodcoat! I had no idea you were coming!"

"Hello Bridget! Good to see you again."

"This is Bridget," said Leonie to Sally, Heidi and Anna. "She has the *best* collection of 'girls' own' books that I've ever seen — never mind the complete set of Chalets, this girl has a complete set of first edition Chalets! How've you been, Bridge?"

"Oh, fine," said Bridget. "Oh, thanks, Richard," she added, as he lifted her suitcase and set off up the steps to the house.

Sally recognised Bridget Whodcoat's name from the JHS. She was one of the regular posters, with an opinion on anything and everything. Actually, her posts sometimes got up Sally's nose. Bridget had enjoyed a life of privilege — exclusive private school, wealthy husband, an expensive house on Hampstead Heath, a second home in the country and a villa in Portugal — but espoused socialist virtues, sniping at anyone who sent their child to a private school and claiming that state education was best. Sally, who had passed the '11-plus' and gone to grammar school only to see it turned into a comprehensive and rapidly go downhill after her second year, disagreed with Bridget's stance on state education. Though she did accept that eleven had been way too young for streaming; Sally's own children had been fortunate enough to gain places at a state-funded Melbourne selective high school at the far more sensible age of fourteen. And she had absolutely no doubt that a state school on Hampstead Heath would be wonderfully resourced, and nothing at all like the wreckage that had been Pendley Vale Comp. She knew from the reactions of the more vocal people on the JHS that Bridget's opinions annoyed quite a few people, especially those who paid for private school education for their children because of wholly inadequate schools in the areas where they lived. She wondered whether Bridget would prove to be as opinionated and bumptious in real life.

Anna and Heidi disappeared as soon as they stepped inside the manor, and Bridget went over to the information desk to get her delegate's pack. Sally was on her way back to her attic room when Harriet said. "Do come in for a nightcap, Sally. You too, Bridge. If I invite Richard in on his own, he'll try to seduce me."

"You should be so lucky," said Richard.

"I should unpack," said Bridget, "but I will join you. Give me my suitcase, Richard, and I'll just dump it in my room. Which room are you in, Harry?"

Harriet told her. Gallantly, Richard accompanied Bridget to her room, carrying the suitcase.

"Will you join us, Sally?" Harriet pressed.

"Okay," said Sally, slightly reluctantly. "Just for a while." She'd already had enough of Richard and Harriet, but was curious about Bridget, and at the same time wasn't really sleepy — jet lag still, she supposed.

Harriet's room was virtually identical to Sally's in layout, but the colour scheme — mainly greens and yellows — was different. She took a bottle of Jack Daniel's from the top of her chest of drawers. "I've only got a couple of glasses," she said.

"I'll fetch a couple from my room," offered Sally.

When Sally returned, Bridget and Richard had joined Harriet in her room and a bottle of malt whisky was standing next to the bourbon on top of the chest of drawers. Richard was pacing the room, tapping on walls.

"What on earth are you doing?" asked Harriet.

"Looking for secret passages."

The three women laughed.

"An old house like this should be full of them," Richard said.

"If this was a girl's own setting, there'd definitely be one," said Sally. She remembered how, once upon a time, she had gone round tapping on walls of old houses hoping a panel would slide back to reveal a secret passage. She'd only stopped doing that in her early thirties, and it was refreshing to find an older person who still did it and wasn't embarrassed about it.

Harriet asked them whether they wanted bourbon or malt. "Let's start with Uncle Jack," suggested Richard, "and leave the best till last." Harriet poured generous amounts of Jack Daniel's into each glass and, upon request, topped Sally's and Bridget's up with dry ginger, leaving Richard's and her own neat. She handed the glasses around.

"Well, cheers," she said. They all echoed her and

drank.

In the end, Sally stayed for a couple of drinks. Nobody attempted to do any gossiping, and at one point Richard turned the conversation to prices of various editions of various books and both Harriet and Bridget chipped in with information that Sally found useful. Then they started asking her about Australia, questioning her about how easy it was to find 'girls' own' books there, when there was a sharp knock at the door.

"Come in!" called Bridget.

The door opened and Valerie's head poked round. "Could you all be *quiet*?" she demanded. "Some of us are trying to get some sleep. It's an early start tomorrow."

"Not that early it's not," Bridget answered. "Unless of course you normally sleep in till ten."

Valerie glowered across at her. "Oh, *you're* here. I should have known that if there was noise, *you* would be involved."

"And we all know that if there's any complaining to be done, you'd be involved," Bridget snapped back.

The two women glared at each other, then Bridget shrugged her shoulders and took a long slug of her drink.

"I once heard," said Valerie, "that at schools like Upland Park, the girls smuggled alcohol into the dormitories and had midnight drinking sessions rather than midnight feasts. Is that true?"

"Why don't you ask your daughter?" returned Bridget. "You sent her to boarding-school, didn't you?"

"Oh, but not one as grand as Upland Park ..."

"Leave it out, Valerie," said Richard. "Why don't you relax a little and join us for another drink? Sally, will you ... ?"

"No. No thanks," said Sally, checking her watch and seeing it was after midnight. "I'm going off to bed now."

"Me too," said Bridget.

"Delighted to hear it. Perhaps I'll get some peace now," said Valerie, leaving and closing the door.

'What a cow," said Bridget.

Sally rose to her feet. "Well," she said awkwardly. "Good night. Thanks for the bourbon, Harriet."

"A pleasure," said Harriet. "Oh, you're going too, Bridge. Good night, then. Good night, Sally. Oh, Richard, would you mind staying for a few more minutes? I just want you to look over the paper for my talk tomorrow — there's something in it I want you to check ..."

"Good night, you two," said Bridget meaningfully, as she and Sally left the room. She winked at Sally when they got outside. "He has a different woman at every conference. Harry's been after him for ages. I didn't think he'd end up with her, though. Tonight I thought he had an eye for *you*."

Sally laughed. She'd picked up on that herself. "Absolutely definitely not interested," she said. "Good night, Bridget."

"Good night, Sally. Nice to meet you. See you tomorrow."

CHAPTER IV.

VALERIE CREATES A SENSATION

Chair and skirt were stuck together as if they had been glued and, in the end, Margaret had to be helped out of her gym tunic. Then Miss Andrews was able to investigate properly. It took her precisely sixty seconds to solve the problem and it was a very angry Miss Andrews who stood up, faced the highly excited form and demanded in no uncertain tones, "Which of you put cobbler's wax on the seat of Margaret's chair?"

Elinor M. Brent-Dyer, *A Leader in the Chalet School*, 1961

SALLY woke early, partly through jet lag, partly due to the fact her throat was slightly sore as a result of the previous night's alcohol consumption. She glanced at the red numbers glowing from the radio alarm clock: five o'clock. She sighed and sat up, feeling too wide awake to fall asleep again. There was internet access in all of the rooms at Cotterford Manor, and Sally decided to plug in her laptop and check her email account. It had been a few days since she'd last been online.

Instructions on setting up the internet connection were on the top of the bedside table. Sally followed them carefully, and was relieved when ten minutes later she found herself online. She went to her own server's webpage and checked her emails. There was one from her mother and another from a friend in Melbourne; the others were work-related, but not urgent, and could wait.

She fired up MSN's instant messenger service, hoping that either Angus or Eleanor might be knocking around on it; they weren't, but her father was. She spent almost an hour chatting to him about how her trip was going so far, and passing on messages to him and her mother from sundry relatives. She asked him if he'd seen the kids; he told her that her mother had spoken to Eleanor on the phone on Monday night and she'd said that both she and Angus were fine. After Sally and her father had finished chatting, she went to check the postings at the JHS and at Chalet Girls. A couple of women had posted on JHS saying they were at the conference; Sally hadn't met them yet. Leonie, as host of the Chalet Girls forum, had also posted saying she was at the conference with a couple of friends.

She disconnected from the internet and glanced at her computer clock; six-thirty. There was still an hour until breakfast. She thought vaguely about reading *The Unforgettable Fifth at Trebizon*, then decided instead to make the most of a sunny morning and walk off her hangover. She took a quick shower, dressed in shorts and T-shirt and headed off down the stairs. She left the house and set off for a brisk walk to the village.

The village was very pretty — two narrow streets with a butcher, baker and greengrocer wedged in among the more touristy shops — craft shops, an antique shop, an expensive-looking ladies' clothes shop and an antiquarian bookseller. At some time over the weekend she would have to explore the latter, Sally decided — though if it had contained affordable — or even unaffordable — school stories, no doubt one of the other delegates had cleared them out already! She checked her watch, and decided to head back. It would be almost breakfast-time by then.

When she arrived back at the house and headed towards the staircase, she found a very angry Valerie Teague standing in the doorway to the old library, castigating an upset-looking Miriam Lorrimer. "The door couldn't have been locked all night like you said it would be! I'm telling you *eight* first edition Abbeys are missing and *seven* first edition Chalets — they were there on my stall last night! Do you realise how much money I've lost there — about four thousand pounds, probably!"

"The door was definitely locked just after eleven," said Miriam. "I locked it myself, when the last person had finished here — that was you, wasn't it, Leah?"

Leah, a plump, blonde woman in her late thirties, who was standing just behind Valerie, confirmed this. "Yes, you locked it behind us as we left."

"And I only unlocked it when you came along and asked me to, Valerie," Miriam said.

"Well, I'm telling you they are MISSING!" said Valerie. "I want the police called and all the rooms searched! Someone from this conference is obviously a thief."

"Valerie, nobody could have got into the room," argued Miriam. "There are only two keys to the room — I have one and had it with me all night. The other is locked in the safe by the conference centre management. It's impossible for anyone to have taken the books. Are you sure you're not mistaken?"

"I *know* I'm not," returned Valerie, crossly. She spotted Sally and said, "*You* saw my books yesterday, didn't you — *you'll* be able to confirm what stock I had."

"Well, I can't remember all your books, Valerie," said Sally, feeling a little awkward, especially as several other women were starting to gather around them, agog at the exchange. "I had a look at *The Chalet School and the Lintons*, though, and also at *Redheads*, and I remember seeing a copy of *The Abbey Girls*."

"There!" said Valerie, triumphantly. "I told you I had *Lintons* and *The Abbey Girls*. *Now* tell me I'm lying, Miriam!"

"All right, all right, Valerie — I wasn't actually calling you a liar. Is anyone else missing any stock?" Miriam asked.

"Not everyone's checked yet," answered Leah. "But I've checked mine and so have Barbara and Corinne and none of us are missing any books."

"Okay," said Miriam, wearily, "can someone go and find the other stall-holders and get them to check their stock straightaway. And Valerie, please, please could you check your boxes, your car and your bedroom to see if you can locate at least some of the books."

"Well, I will look just to pacify you," returned Valerie, "but if I don't find them — and I know I won't — I'm going to phone the police."

"Very well," sighed Miriam. "But don't dial 999. If you don't find them, come and find me and I'll give you the number for the local police. And do wait until the others have checked their stalls. But I must say it seems very odd that even if someone managed to get through a locked door, they should choose to take only your books and not Leah's, for example. I noticed that her stall has a copy of *The Chalet Girls' Cook Book*, which is very rare. Why wasn't that stolen if there's a thief among us? I'll come into the library and wait for the other booksellers to check their stalls. And can the rest of you," she added, raising her voice at the crowd of interested spectators, "*please* go along to breakfast now?"

The delegates grinned sheepishly at each other and some of them began to make their way towards the conservatory. With a loud sigh, Valerie went back to her stall to check her boxes.

"Poor old thief," commented Richard from behind Sally. "Of all the stalls to pick on. The poor blighter has no idea what they've taken on."

"Valerie's steaming," said Richard later as he joined Sally and Harriet for breakfast at a table near the window. "She's apparently searched her boxes, her car and her bedroom and can't find the missing books. *And* none of the other stall holders can find anything missing. Miriam's heard from all of them now."

"It makes no sense," replied Harriet, buttering her toast. "If one or two were missing, I'd say they'd got left behind at her house by mistake. But all those books — she can't mislay *that* many."

"Well, some of the ones she says are missing were definitely there when I interviewed her," said Sally. "I saw them. But what really puzzles me, is if someone has taken them, then why just pick on Valerie's stall? I had a quick look around the other stalls after I'd finished interviewing Valerie yesterday, and there were some really good books on some of them. And why only take *some* of Valerie's books — why not more of them? She had heaps of first editions."

"Maybe the thief was disturbed before he or she could take more?" suggested Harriet.

"Maybe," said Richard, doubtfully. "But you know, I'm not so sure it is a thief. I'm wondering if someone's playing a practical joke on Valerie. You know how angry she gets. Maybe they'll turn up on someone else's stall later."

"It's possible — practical jokes are in the fine tradition of school stories and I've certainly heard of one or two being played at school-story conferences," said Harriet. "Perhaps tonight some of us will find hairbrushes in our beds or our skirts glued to the seats in the lecture room."

"Has Valerie called the police?" asked Sally.

Richard laughed. "Apparently so. For what good that'll do. As if the police don't have better things to do than come out for a bunch of books that *might* have been stolen. As far as Friday night crimes go, even in the country, a locked room mystery like this isn't exactly number one priority for the rozzers."

Sally spotted Margaret, Heidi and Anna heading towards a nearby table and waved to them. The trio walked over.

"We've just heard about all the excitement," said Heidi. "About some of Valerie Teague's books disappearing."

"Sounds like Valerie was in a real bate," said Anna.

"She was indeed," said Richard, happily. "Not exactly the kind of person who's good at taking a joke, our Valerie."

"Do you think it's a joke, then?" asked Margaret. She was, like the previous day, dressed in jeans and a long-sleeved top. Sally wondered whether her extreme thinness meant she felt the cold more.

"It's not a particularly funny one if it *is* a joke," said Bridget, coming up behind them with Leonie. "If you're talking about those books going missing, that is."

"Oh, it wouldn't be funny if it had been played on anyone else," said Heidi. "It's funny because it was played on Valerie. I wonder who it was? It's got to be someone who knows her, don't you think? I mean, none of the workers here at the house would play a joke at random on somebody they didn't know."

"Oh, I don't know," said Harriet. "They hear that a bunch of school-story-mad women are descending on the place and decide to give us a rare treat by way of the practical joke. They probably imagined we'd all, including Valerie, be hooting with girlish laughter at it ..."

"Including Richard," said Leonie, with a grin.

Richard was about to reply when Sally prodded him and nodded towards the doorway, where she'd spotted Valerie walking in with Miriam. Valerie still looked fuming, and Miriam by now was looking exasperated. As the pair drew closer, Bridget said politely, "Sorry to hear about your books, Valerie."

Valerie rounded on her. "Oh really? I can't imagine you caring all that much, Bridget — especially as I'm pretty sure that you're the person who's taken them!"

"Oh come on, Valerie," said Richard. "Bridget didn't even arrive till — what? Nearly eleven o'clock last night? The room was locked up then by all accounts, and Bridget was with us till twelve. Are you suggesting she then somehow got through the keyhole and took the books?"

"Well, someone took them, that's for sure," said Valerie.

"Well, *I* didn't," Bridget told her, quietly and firmly. "I would never do such a thing. I don't know why you think I'd do it, Valerie."

"*Don't* you?" Valerie snorted.

"Come *on*, Valerie, let's get some breakfast," said Miriam, nudging Valerie away from the table. She cast a sympathetic glance at Bridget as she left.

"Goodness me, you must have upset Valerie with something you've said on the JHS," commented

Richard. "She's really got her knife into you."

Bridget nodded and bit her lip. Sally noticed that she looked as if she were trying not to cry. "Excuse me," said Bridget. "I think I'll skip breakfast after all. I'll go out for a walk or something. I'll see you all later on — good luck with your talk today, Harriet."

"Now, that's not like Bridget," Harriet commented as Bridget left the room. "Just coming over all tearful and sloping off after a confrontation. She's normally like a dog with a bone in a fight — won't let it go. What do you think is wrong with her?"

"Time of the month, perhaps?" Richard suggested.

"Hmm. I'd have thought time of the month would have made Bridget even more combative," said Harriet. "You newbies must think we're all really awful," she said to Sally and Margaret. " 'Girls' own' conferences aren't always like this — I mean, there's usually a bit of conflict, but we've had nothing like this before. Spiteful accusations …" She shook her head. "Almost like those who read girls' school stories are descending to the behaviour of the playground …"

"Ah well," said Richard, "at least it's girls' school stories everyone reads here, not the boys' equivalent. So we're not likely to see anybody roasted over an open fire — well, not unless Valerie gets hold of the culprit, anyway."

CHAPTER V.

A BUSY DAY

Still, even Olive Charing could not take all the fun out of their strange, new and amazingly busy life. There were clubs to join, charities to support — everyone was expected to do this — there were games, the choir, country dancing on certain nights. Jenny and Ariel gave the matter of choosing a charity some serious thought, and plumped for Help the Aged. Joining it meant a weekly jaunt to Shenley, and Ariel liked the idea of getting outside the prison walls. Jenny joined because she enjoyed Ariel's company.

Harriet Martyn, *Jenny and the Syndicate*, 1982

THE morning programme was very busy, and Sally found herself absorbed in it and forgetting about the unpleasant episodes involving Valerie Teague. The first session was an overview of the girls' school story, held in the main conference room, where most of the larger sessions were scheduled to be held. It had once been two rooms, a drawing room and a morning room, but when the house had been turned into a conference centre, renovation work had been done to create one large room. The renovations had, however, kept perfectly in period with the rest of the house — high ceilings, oak-panelled walls, window seats. As Sally entered, she saw that the room had been well set up for the Tales Out of School conference — some 100 chairs had been placed in rows of ten; at the front of the room was a table with two chairs behind it and a jug and two glasses of water atop it. Behind the table was a projected backdrop depicting covers from girls' school stories. Many of the delegates were already seated, some with pens and notepads in hand. Sally recognised Miriam seated at the main table, and guessed that the woman seated beside her — who looked to be in her late forties with greying brown hair — must be the speaker for this session, Rosalind Holmes. Sally glanced around the room, spotted Leonie Carr and settled down beside her.

When everyone had arrived and Miriam had eventually managed to obtain silence, she introduced Rosalind. Rosalind stood up and began to talk about the history of the girls' school story, from its origins in the late nineteenth century through to its more recent incarnations. Sally listened, fascinated. She'd read a great deal on the topic, especially in the past five years when she'd begun to take her hobby more seriously, but Rosalind still had plenty of information that Sally had never come across before.

After Rosalind's talk came a coffee break — or *Kaffee und Kuchen* as it was called in the conference programme, after the Austrian name for 'coffee and cakes' used throughout Elinor M. Brent-Dyer's Chalet School series — in the conservatory, where Sally managed to chat briefly to Leah Brindsley, a bookseller in her early thirties, who — like Harriet — was giving one of the talks that followed the break. After *Kaffee*, Sally — who found Leah much more personable and interesting than Valerie and was debating whether to drop Valerie from her article in favour of Leah — attended Leah's talk, which included many helpful hints such as burning tea-tree oil in a burner in the room where the books were kept to get rid of musty smells, and quarantining all 'new' secondhand books so that any spores might not make their way to all your other books.

Afterwards there was another choice of sessions — one in the main room on visiting Chalet School locations, and another in a smaller room on school stories in the pony genre. Sally had opted for the latter, but found it less interesting than she'd expected — the only school-cum-pony books she had read were a handful by Mary Gervaise, and she hadn't even heard of some of the other authors mentioned. Still, she dutifully took notes — there might well be a future article on pony books for *Australian Collector*.

Lunchtime followed, and Sally found herself at a table with Leonie, Bridget and Margaret. This time all the talk was of the morning sessions, what bargains might be found at the afternoon book sale, and what people thought of the latest Chalet School fill-in novel which had been published a month or so ago. Of Valerie Teague's missing books, not one word was said.

The book sale was definitely the highlight of the programme. Sally, squeezed in with all the other excited delegates at the back of the former library, listened impatiently while Miriam Lorrimer talked about the stall holders and the delights they had on offer. Four of the stall holders, Miriam explained, were professional booksellers; the other six sold books in their spare time to support their collecting interests. "And there are some marvellous books to be bought and bargains to be found this afternoon," she continued.

"Then let's just *see* them," Richard implored

loudly. Sally, who thought there was far too much unnecessary waffle holding up proceedings, nodded in heartfelt agreement.

Finally, Miriam declared the book sale open and, in a scene somewhat resembling the start of the London marathon, Sally and the other eager would-be buyers sprinted across to the stalls. Sally had already decided that Valerie's first editions were beyond what she really wanted to spend, so headed for Leah's stall first. Jostling with other delegates, Sally looked at a couple of Chalet School titles from the Tyrol years — *The School at the Chalet*, *The Chalet School and Jo*, her all-time favourite *Eustacia Goes to the Chalet School* — then spotted some Dimsies by Dorita Fairlie Bruce. Sally already owned most of the Dimsie books, but some of them were the 1980s John Goodchild editions which had been updated for a modern audience — electric lights, central heating and 'A' levels had replaced the original gaslight, open fires and somewhat obscure examinations. She wondered if she should buy one of the originals and picked up *Dimsie Goes Back*, which she didn't own at all. It was very reasonably priced, so she bought it, along with a very nice copy of *Dimsie — Head Girl*. She also bought *Eustacia*; if she read her well-loved paperback one more time, she told herself, it would probably fall apart — it was worth spending the money for an upgrade.

The other stalls were tempting too and in the end Sally found herself the proud owner of several titles, including a couple of Chalet School fill-ins which she'd never been tempted to buy in the past, but which she'd been persuaded to try after hearing glowing comments about them by Leonie, Bridget and Margaret at lunchtime.

"I see we talked you into the fillers then," said

Leonie Carr, when the book sale had ended and the delegates, most of them laden with books, had started filing out.

"Yes indeed," Sally said. "As I said earlier, they've never really appealed to me because they're not by Elinor Brent-Dyer, but you were all so complimentary, I thought I'd give them a go." She looked at Leonie, struggling with a high pile of books and laughed. "You've bought *heaps*."

"I always live beyond my means at book sales!" grinned Leonie. "I even bought something from that rip-off merchant Valerie Teague."

Kaffee und Kuchen followed the book sale, but Sally made her way upstairs and examined her new purchases rather than heading straight for the conservatory. When she'd finished looking at them, she decided to padlock the books into her backpack, then keep the key with her in her handbag. You never knew, she thought — Valerie might just be right and there could be a dishonest delegate at the conference.

———

There was a choice of sessions after the break — 'Lesbian Relationships in the Girls' School Story' and 'School Stories and Craft'. Neither was particularly relevant to Sally's article, so, given that she had neither skill nor interest in craft, Sally opted for the former. It was, in the end, a memorable session — memorable for having a dissenter. Valerie, who was seated towards the back of the room, persistently exclaimed "Nonsense!" when the speaker, Sue Parkinson, discussed the fact that a number of relationships in girls' school stories — including that of mistresses Nancy Wilmot and Kathie Ferrars at the Chalet School and Roddy Blake and

Franny Warner at Melling — seemed more than just platonic.

When, at the end of her talk, Sue asked if anyone had any questions, Valerie said, "Yes, I do have a question, but I suppose it's more for Miriam Lorrimer, our esteemed conference organiser, than it is for you. Why are you paid to be here in front of us spouting stuff that's been said a hundred times before? Especially when it was nonsense when it was said the first time. Just because a woman isn't married and has a close friendship with another woman, doesn't mean she's a lesbian."

"But Sue hasn't said anything like that, Valerie," Heidi objected. "She's quoting just a handful of specific examples from the whole spectrum of school stories, all of which contain close female friendships."

"Well, her examples are stupid," Valerie said firmly.

"Valerie," said Sue, "if you don't believe there are *any* lesbian relationships in school stories, why did you attend this session?"

"Just to heckle, probably," said Heidi.

"Sue Parkinson is just trying to make a name for herself in the 'girls' own' world," said Valerie. "But she hasn't come up with anything remotely original in the entire seminar. The Roddy/Franny theory is in Jessica Gibson's esteemed book, and the nonsense about Kathie and Nancy has been discussed for years on internet forums. People write fan fiction about it, so I'm told. So why is Sue being paid for not having one original thought to share with us? Still," Valerie went on, with an exaggerated sigh, "why am I surprised? I can think of at least one other well-known speaker on girls' school stories who's never made an original comment in her life and is far too highly thought of."

"If you dislike being in here and listening to me so much, why don't you leave?" demanded Sue, in a trembling voice.

"With pleasure!" Valerie returned and stalked out.

"What's wrong with *her*?" demanded Anna.

"Who knows?" said Harriet. "She always has her knife into half the people who attend these conferences. Don't worry about it, Sue. Your talk was great."

There was free time after the session, and most of the delegates hung around the main conference room, showing off their purchases from the book sale and discussing Valerie's behaviour during Sue's seminar. Sue was still annoyed, and commented to Richard that she'd always suspected Valerie was homophobic, and that her behaviour in the seminar had confirmed it.

"You're probably right," said Richard.

"I think Valerie's just one of those people who don't like to read old books with a modern eye," said Leonie. "I had a conversation with her at another conference about the way current editions of Enid Blyton's books have been made politically correct — you know, how Dame Slap from the Faraway Tree series has been renamed Dame Snap, and Darrell no longer slaps Gwendoline in *First Term at Malory Towers* — and she really loathes that, thinks it's totally wrong. She thinks all old books should reflect the times they were written in and be judged by those times."

"Well, I agree with her on that," said Sue, "but I think there are definitely overtones of lesbian relationships in some of the books, whether or not their authors intended them that way. And we all know there were closet lesbians at the time the books were written — it's not as if being a lesbian was invented in the 1990s."

"True," said Harriet.

'What are we all doing tonight?" asked Richard, refilling his coffee cup. "Going to the folk dancing?"

"Not me," said Harriet. "God, I loathe folk dancing. Why is it Miriam and Jessica always assume that if you like Elinor M. Brent-Dyer and Elsie J. Oxenham, you must *love* folk dancing? Every wretched Tales Out of School conference I've attended has devoted Saturday night to folk dancing."

"Will you go, Richard?" asked Sue.

"Bags not," replied Richard. "The problem with these conferences is that I'm usually the only man, and if I attend the folk dancing, I'm expected to join in and cheerfully dance with everybody. So I shan't go near the conservatory tonight. I'm going to have a pie and a few pints at one of the local pubs and then come back rather sloshed."

"I'll join you," said Harriet. "What about you, Sue?"

"Oh, I'll go to the folk dancing," grinned Sue. "I actually quite enjoy it once I get into it."

"Sally?" queried Richard.

Sally had planned to avoid the folk dancing — it wasn't her thing and probably wouldn't lend itself to much conversation or interviewing — but she wasn't really sure that she relished another evening in the company of Harriet and Richard. She felt that she had seen rather a lot of them already at the conference, and it would be good to get to know some of the other delegates better. "Oh, I'll give it a whirl," she said cautiously. "And if I don't like it, I can always find something else to do."

"Well, Harry and I will be in the Rose and Crown if you find the dancing isn't to your taste," said Richard.

Sally glanced at her watch; it was six o'clock,

more than an hour before the folk dancing was scheduled to begin. She had, she realised, done the bulk of her interviewing for her article — all she needed really was to speak to a couple more dedicated fans about their passion for girls' school stories and she was done. She might be able to do that tonight, and if that didn't work out, there was plenty of time scheduled tomorrow morning for those who didn't want to attend the Sunday morning service. Pleased with the way her work had gone, Sally decided to go up to her room, have a quick shower, and start reading *The Unforgettable Fifth at Trebizon*. She needed to return it tomorrow night, after all.

CHAPTER VI.

THE FOLK DANCE

"Girls!" — and Cicely slipped the elastic of her big hat under her curls, pushed the hat back comfortably, and faced them with glowing eyes — "I've had an idea! I had it while we were dancing. We'll make the Hamlet Club a dancing club, and learn morris and country dancing. It's easy to learn — I think I could teach it — it's jolly good exercise, and it's jolly good fun. We used to love it at school. It costs nothing to speak of. I can easily get sticks and bells and handkerchiefs from town—" ...

"It's a ripping idea!" Dorothy said enthusiastically. "I'm on!"

Elsie J. Oxenham, *Girls of the Hamlet Club*, 1914

As Sally made her way downstairs, she could hear jolly music coming from the conservatory. When she entered, she noticed that it was already filling up with delegates — and, to her surprise, realised that Richard wouldn't have been the token man after all. There were about five men in the conservatory, chatting with some of the delegates and with Miriam Lorrimer.

"Hi," said Leonie, coming over to her. She was looking pretty in a knee-length dark blue dress with large white spots, and blue shoes with a small heel. "Welcome to the madness that is the traditional Tales Out of School conference folk dancing."

Sally looked around. The conservatory had been decked out for the occasion; the tables they usually ate at had disappeared and balloons with streamers had been attached to the ceiling. Three long trestle tables were at one end of the room, one laden with jugs of wine, water, orange juice and beer, the other two shrouded by tablecloths that presumably hid the food. Down at the other end stood the five-piece folk band. Already a handful of dancers were bounding around the room performing to the music. They were the ones who folk danced regularly and really knew their stuff, Sally guessed.

"Who are all the men?" Sally asked. "I thought Richard was the only male here at the conference."

"He is. But a few of the women don't live all that far from here, and their husbands or boyfriends are joining them for the evening. The ginger-haired chap, fr'ex — he's Miriam Lorrimer's husband."

"I see," said Sally. The band struck up a new tune — the Gay Gordons, which she remembered vaguely from childhood. Her grandmother had taught her how to do it, but she couldn't remember the steps now. "Is the Gay Gordons folk dancing, then?" she asked, surprised.

"Hmm. It's really an Old Time Dance," Leonie replied. "Want to have a go? I'll dance with you if you like."

"I don't really know how to—."

"Don't worry — I'm no expert either. I usually have a couple of dances, then head over to the wine table — or out to the pub."

Reluctantly, Sally followed Leonie to the dance floor. To her surprise, Leonie danced wildly and dragged her along to the music, calling out instructions to her as they went. By the time the dance had finished, Sally was breathless.

"Try another?" Leonie asked, as the music struck up again and, without waiting for an answer, dragged Sally back on to the dance floor. This was a circular dance, involving changing your partner frequently, and more people were joining in. Sally found herself dancing with delegates she either half-recognised or hadn't seen before, but at least the steps to this one were fairly easy to memorise. At one point she found herself dancing with Margaret, clad in a long black skirt and black cardigan. Margaret was sweating slightly already from her exertions; Sally wondered why she didn't take the cardigan off. A couple of minutes later she found herself dancing with Valerie Teague. Valerie looked to be enjoying herself; she smiled at Sally, and danced energetically. Perhaps, thought Sally, she was over her bad mood? Or perhaps the missing books had turned up?

Once the dance was over, Sally headed over to the drinks table and downed a glass of water. Valerie came over too and poured herself a glass of wine. Sally stood near the table, sipping more water and looking round at the crowd. Virtually all the delegates were here now — apart, obviously, from Harriet and Richard, who weren't coming. Other than them, the only person who appeared to be missing was Bridget Whodcoat; perhaps she too had decided to give it a miss. But no — here she was arriving now, clad in a pretty, full skirt with white polka dots. Bridget stood and watched the dancers for a while, then she too came over to the drinks table. Ignoring Valerie, she poured herself an orange juice and came to stand beside Sally.

"Have you done much folk dancing?" she asked.

"Not before tonight."

"It's good exercise if you do it regularly. Beats going to the gym."

"Sounds like you do it regularly."

"I do. I'm a member of an Abbey fan club that also organises regular folk dances. And I go along to dances in Cecil Sharp House in London."

Sally remembered the name Cecil Sharp House from her student days. "That's the headquarters for English folk dancing, isn't it?"

"It is. Is that information gleaned from the Abbey books, or did you know it anyway?"

"I know about it from when I lived in England. I've only read one of the Abbeys."

"And that was?"

"*Selma.*"

"Oh *no!*" Bridget groaned. "Don't tell me — you tried to read it, discovered that it was awful, and have never been tempted to read another Abbey since."

"Correct," Sally grinned.

Bridget sighed. "That happens to so many people. The problem is that *Selma* is one of the retrospectives—."

"Retrospectives?"

"Yes. She wrote *Selma, Schooldays at the Abbey, Secrets of the Abbey, Stowaways at the Abbey, Schoolgirl Jen at the Abbey, Strangers at the Abbey* and *Tomboys at the Abbey* later than her other Abbey books, and wrote them to fill in the earlier gaps. Even a lot of committed Abbey fans don't like them," Bridget continued, "because of course they feature characters like Selma who are never mentioned in the other titles, and they're very formulaic. *Especially* the retrospectives that were written later — *Selma* and *Tomboys.*"

"So I definitely picked the wrong one to start off with, then?" Sally responded with a grin.

"Absolutely. You really shouldn't start with *Selma.* You should start with *Girls of the Hamlet Club.*"

"So I've heard. And I looked for it on eBay and Abebooks and it sells for over £1000."

"I'll give you the URL of a website where you can

find a transcript. At least then you'll know whether you like it or not so you can decide if it's worth shelling out for others in the series. Remind me tomorrow."

"Thanks. I will." Bridget was nicer in person than she was in the forums, Sally decided. She quite liked her.

"Who do you collect then?" Bridget asked.

Sally told her, then asked about Bridget's own collecting interests.

"Oh, the usual — Elinor M. Brent-Dyer, Elsie J. Oxenham, Dorita Fairlie Bruce, Antonia Forest, Angela Brazil. I collect pony books as well — Monica Edwards, the Pullein-Thompson sisters, Ruby Ferguson."

"Your collection sounds brilliant."

"I suppose it is," said Bridget. An unfathomable expression crossed her face, then she said, "What's happened to Richard and Harry tonight, do you know?"

"They've gone to the Rose and Crown."

"I suppose there was no reason for Richard to come given he's already paired with Harry," Bridget mused. "Usually he uses these folk dances to get off with someone."

"Have you ever ... ?" Sally asked curiously.

"Good God, no."

When the current dance had finished, there was a brief pause in the music and Miriam announced that the food would be ready in five minutes. Two of the conference hall staff removed the table coverings to reveal a buffet of sandwiches, party pies, vol-au-vents, sausage rolls, spinach rolls, pizza slices, crisps, nuts and cheese and crackers.

"I'm absolutely starving," Bridget said. "I'm going to dig in first." She walked over to the table and helped herself liberally to the food. Sally recalled that Bridget had missed breakfast; she was obviously making up for lost time. When the music stopped, everyone fell on the buffet. Sally found herself waiting behind Valerie, who piled her plate high before placing it on the nearest table, quickly scoffing a sausage roll, and then returning to the dance floor. Sally helped herself to a more modest amount of food, then walked over to the window where she joined Leonie. They talked for a while about the various forums they visited, then the music began again. Some delegates put down their plates to dance again, while others watched.

"Did Valerie's books turn up?" Sally asked, watching Valerie whizzing around the dance floor with Miriam Lorrimer's husband.

"Not that I know of," said Leonie. "Why?"

"It's just she seems much happier tonight."

"She's had a couple of drinks, that's why," grinned Leonie. "And she thinks she might get off with one of the blokes here."

Valerie danced a couple more dances then went for a re-fill of wine and returned to her food. "She's a greedy cow," said Leonie. "Always eats and drinks more than everybody else at the conference — getting her money's worth is how she looks at it. Do you want to dance again, Sally?"

"No," said Sally. "I've had enough of dancing, really."

"So have I. What about a walk down to the village? We could drop in on the Rose and Crown, if you like."

"Not sure about the pub, but I wouldn't mind a walk." Sally had begun to tire of the noise from the music and dancing; she also felt the need for some fresh air.

"Let's go then," Leonie said.

The two women left the conservatory and made

their way out of the house. It wasn't yet completely dark, and Leonie suggested that if Sally didn't fancy the pub, then they might as well take a walk around the grounds rather than down into the village. Sally agreed, but said she'd nip back to her room for her torch as it was bound to get dark soon. She hurried up to her room to fetch it, while Leonie waited for her just outside the main entrance.

Soon they were walking around to the back of the house, listening to the music and laughter coming from the conservatory. They walked along the path that led past the croquet lawn and the annexe and made their way through the woods, and then down to the flower gardens and duckpond.

"Look — a fire behind the bandstand," said Sally surprised.

They walked towards it. It was a small pyre, and both women gasped as they realised that it consisted of books, several of which had caught fire. Leonie ran towards it and stamped hard on the books, putting out the fire. "Not G.O. books hopefully," said Leonie, picking one up. "No," she said, relieved. "They're old books all right — hardcovers, but not school stories, and not in great condition to begin with. For an awful moment, you know, I thought they might be Valerie's books."

"So did I," Sally admitted. "It's odd, though. Why would you bring books here and burn them?"

"They might belong to someone here, I suppose," said Leonie doubtfully. "People here don't only read school stories. Let's gather them up, Sally, and take them back to the house and ask if they belong to anybody. I just wonder whether it's someone's idea of a joke."

"It's in very bad taste, if so," said Sally, gathering up some of the books. She glanced at the titles — *Shadow of the Lynx* by Victoria Holt, *Death in the*

Stocks by Georgette Heyer, *Hardship our Garment* by Leslie Wood. Together, they made their way back along the pathway. As they came to the flower garden, they heard movement up in the woods. The light was failing, and they couldn't see anyone. Sally wanted to flash her torch, but with her arms full of books, she couldn't get into her bag in time.

"Seems like someone else is hanging around," Leonie murmured.

"The person who set fire to the books, perhaps," Sally whispered back.

A little anxious about who might be lurking, they made their way through the woods and then hurried back past the annexe and sports facilities to the main house. The music had stopped, though the lights were still on in the conservatory; the folk dancing must have come to an end. They walked around the side of the house and turned into the driveway, hoping that enough people would still be milling around to show them the books. But then all thoughts of the books went out of their minds.

For there on the driveway stood an ambulance, and two ambulancemen were making their way carefully down the steps carrying a stretcher. Miriam Lorrimer was walking down the steps beside them, looking anxious. Several delegates stood on top of the steps watching the proceedings. Sally and Leonie stayed where they were rather than climbing the steps to join the others. When the ambulancemen reached the ground, they both took a look at the stretcher. Laying on it, wearing an oxygen mask, was Valerie Teague. Within seconds, the ambulance was on its way to hospital, siren shrieking, and Miriam Lorrimer, upset and anxious, was explaining to Sally and Leonie that Valerie had collapsed in the middle of the dance floor, convulsing and unable to breathe.

CHAPTER VII.

A SHOCK FOR THE CONFERENCE

Fortunately, by the time she returned, Lower IV.A. knew also and were standing around in subdued groups in the garden, trying to come to terms with this chilling, incredible happening. Had it simply been that Marie had left, there wasn't one of them who wouldn't have said, "Oh, *good!*" and forgotten her. Now, however, they felt required to be sorry and speak well of the girl: two things not honestly possible.

Antonia Forest, *The Cricket Term*, 1974

WHEN the ambulance, siren blaring, had sped Valerie Teague away from Cotterford Manor, the conference delegates began to make their way indoors, discussing what had happened and speculating as to what might be wrong. Sally found herself accompanying Sue Parkinson and Heidi and Anna to a small room next to the library, where they found a couple of the house staff organising coffee.

"She was dancing with Miriam's husband, then just collapsed gasping for breath. Like she was having an asthma attack or something," Heidi said.

"*Is* she asthmatic?" Sally asked.

"I doubt it," said Sue. "We'd all know if she was — she'd have told us *ad nauseam*. She's never been one to suffer ailments in silence. Not like poor old Jess."

"Jess?" said Heidi. "Oh, of course, you mean Jess Gibson. It doesn't sound so good for her, does it, from what Miriam said last night."

"That's right," said Sue. "I do feel sorry for Miriam, too, having to organise the conference on her own this time. It can't be easy organising a four-day conference with no help whatsoever. She and Jess used to share the workload before Jess got ill," she explained to Sally.

Sally wondered why, when Valerie had just been whisked off in an ambulance after collapsing in the conservatory, Heidi and Sue were instead discussing the absent Jessica Gibson. Even if Jessica was popular and Valerie wasn't, it did seem a little unfair not to be concerned for Valerie's welfare right now, she thought.

"What are those books you're holding, Sally?" Anna queried suddenly, breaking into her thoughts.

In all the excitement and speculation, Sally had forgotten that she was carrying a pile of badly charred books. "I was out for a walk with Leonie," she explained, "and we came across these books — someone had set fire to them. We put the fire out and rescued them — we both thought they might be the ones missing from Valerie's collection. Leonie has some too." She looked around for Leonie and spotted her in the far corner of the room, talking to a shaken-looking Miriam Lorrimer.

"How bizarre," said Sue. "May I?" she asked, indicating the books.

"Be my guest." Sally handed them over to her.

Sue examined them. "Georgette Heyer. Victoria Holt. Leslie Wood — *Hardship Our Garment*. Sounds a right barrel of laughs, doesn't it? Oh, a Barbara Cartland. Blimey, I know Barbara Cartland wrote utter crap but I still wouldn't *burn* it. Where did you find them, Sally?"

"In the grounds, near the bandstand," Sally answered.

"Weird," said Anna. "I can't imagine anyone from

here burning books. I suppose they could belong to someone from the village and they're using the grounds as a dumping ground."

"What's all this about Valerie?" came Richard's voice, and Sally looked across to see him and Harriet approaching Miriam and Leonie. "We just got back from the pub — someone said she collapsed and has been taken off to hospital."

Sally watched as Miriam outlined what had occurred to Richard and Harriet; they both looked suitably shocked and concerned. While Miriam was talking, Claire, the woman who'd been on reception when they arrived, interrupted her. Miriam followed her out of the room.

"Poor Valerie," said Richard, wandering across to join Sally, Anna, Heidi and Sue while Harriet remained chatting with Leonie. "She didn't seem to be ill at all earlier, did she?"

"She didn't seem ill during the dancing till she collapsed," Sue mused. "She was eating like a horse. And knocking back the wine like there was a shortage of it."

"Perhaps that's the problem," said Richard sagely. "Too much to eat and drink. Happened at all the best midnight feasts — bilious attacks and so forth, being dosed by Matron. Gracious, Sue, what *are* you doing with a Barbara Cartland novel? I'd never have taken you for a slushy romance fan."

Sally explained about the fire, but again didn't mention the figure she and Leonie had seen in the woods. Someone from the conference, perhaps right here in this room listening to her now, might have been responsible for the book-burning, she thought, and it was perhaps best that they didn't know they'd been seen. If Leonie chose to mention it, well, she couldn't help that. But for the moment Sally intended to keep quiet about it.

"Perhaps put a notice on the notice board saying they've been found," Richard suggested. "Or ask Miriam to read it out at Assembly tomorrow morning."

"Anna thinks they might have been dumped by someone from the village," said Sally.

"Dumped, then some local yobbo set fire to them? Could be," Richard agreed.

There was a sudden shushing around the room, and Sally and the others followed people's eyes towards the doorway, where Miriam stood, looking more shaken than ever. In a trembling voice, she informed them all that she'd just received a phone call saying that Valerie had died on her way to the hospital.

At around three o'clock in the morning, Sally gave up on trying to sleep and decided to go online. It had been after one o'clock when she'd come to bed — everyone at the conference had stayed up, gathered in groups, talking about the death of Valerie Teague. Mostly they discussed the manner of her death: whirling around the dance floor one minute, collapsing on the floor in a heap and in apparent agony the next. There was speculation that she'd suffered a stroke or an epileptic fit; some thought she'd had a heart attack or gone into a diabetic coma.

No-one actually spoke well of Valerie, Sally noticed, which was unusual in the wake of someone's death. People commented on the quality of the books she'd sold, but other than that had nothing positive to say about her. Sally learned for the first time that Valerie had two grown-up children, Mark and Veronica, who apparently had long been estranged from her. Harriet wondered aloud what Mark and Veronica would do with their inherited book-dealing business, and whether they would sell Valerie's stock off cheaply. Leonie said that if they did, she hoped that they'd give Valerie's former clients the chance of a few bargains. Sally felt rather sorry for Valerie; she may not have been the nicest person, but it seemed sad that people seemed to care more about what would happen to her stock than they did about what had happened to her.

Eventually, everyone had wandered off to their own rooms. Sally had taken the books she'd found in the grounds up to her own room, having agreed with Leonie that they'd put a notice on the notice board about them next morning rather than bother Miriam Lorrimer with it.

Now, when Sally hooked up to the internet and visited the forums — despite the fact it was daytime in Australia, none of her family were signed into MSN, and she'd received no new emails other than spam — she discovered that some of the other delegates had also retreated online in an effort to cope with sleeplessness. Miriam Lorrimer had posted on the JHS:

> Those of you who knew Valerie Teague of Fine Print books will, I am sure, be saddened to know that she died tonight during the Tales Out of School Conference at Cotterford Manor. We don't know yet what happened, but she collapsed during the evening folk dancing and died on her way to hospital. Our thoughts and prayers are with her children, Mark and Veronica.

A few polite messages appeared underneath with people saying how sorry they were to hear the news, reminiscing about books they had bought from Valerie, and offering their good wishes to her surviving relatives. Sally read some of the other messages on the forum, then visited Chalet Girls. Leonie Carr had posted a message there similar to the one on the JHS; again, one or two messages of sympathy and condolence appeared underneath. Among the other threads, there was a continued discussion of working-class girls in Elinor M. Brent-Dyer's books. Sally read the new posts avidly, then, hopeful of a mindless distraction, went into the Games folder.

Margaret Wilks had been online earlier in the day, it appeared, for she had started a new Twenty Questions game. Sally read the thread; she was usually good at guessing these.

> From: margaretwilks
> To: All
> Thinking of someone ...
>
> From: JR15
> To: margaretwilks
> Is it a pupil?
>
> From: margaretwilks
> To: JR15
> Yes, a pupil
>
> From: Leonie Carr
> To: margaretwilks
> A pupil in Tyrol?
>
> From: margaretwilks
> To: Leonie Carr
> Yes, in Tyrol

A SHOCK FOR THE CONFERENCE 65

From: kiwichaletian
To: margaretwilks
Is she one of the first pupils?

From: margaretwilks
To: kiwichaletian
No

From: emer1984
To: margaretwilks
Is she ever a prefect?

From: margaretwilks
To: emer1984
Yes, a prefect

From: emer1984
To: margaretwilks
Is she English?

From: margaretwilks
To: emer1984
Yes, she's English

From: Jack Maynard's Mistress
To: margaretwilks
Does she have a relative in the San?

From: margaretwilks
To: Jack Maynard's Mistress
Yes, she does

From: Jack Maynard's Mistress
To: margaretwilks
Does she have a sister in the school?

From: margaretwilks
To: Jack Maynard's Mistress
No she doesn't

From: lenconmargot
To: margaretwilks
Does she finish school after Joey?

From: margaretwilks
To: lenconmargot
Yes

From: kiwichaletian
To: margaretwilks
Is she among the St Scholastika's girls?

From: margaretwilks
To: kiwichaletian
No, she isn't

From: Leonie Carr
To: margaretwilks
Is she a close friend of Joey's?

From: margaretwilks
To: Leonie Carr
No, not a close friend of Joey's

This must be Anne Seymour, thought Sally, the sub-prefect who had had the temerity to tell Chalet School series heroine Jo Bettany to put her head in a bag when she'd been disturbing her friends' revision prior to their end-of-term exams. While every right-thinking reader would concede that Anne had a point, Joey and her friends had seen Anne's response as inappropriate from a sub-prefect to the headgirl. Subsequently Anne had proved herself to be too heedless a girl to be trusted with headgirlship — first by wandering off on a walk and slipping and needing to be rescued by Joey, and later almost burning down the school *and* Joey's first published book by forgetting to switch off the iron. Sally tapped in, "Is she Anne Seymour? BTW, hi Margaret, from another delegate unable to sleep tonight," and posted the message, wondering whether Margaret was still up and able to reply.

She left the games and went back to the discussion threads, where she found a brief discussion on sport at the Chalet School. Then, still wide awake, she went back to bed and reached over for the book that had lain on her bedside table since she'd arrived here. It was time, she decided, to finish reading *The Unforgettable Fifth at Trebizon*. Despite a slight twinge of guilt that Valerie's death could be so easily forgotten by reading a school story, she was soon immersed in the final adventures of Rebecca Mason and her friends.

Breakfast was a subdued affair. Around the hall, people were talking quietly, some of them about Valerie's death, others about the programme. Miriam addressed them all in the dining room at eight o'clock, while they were still eating.

"I think you're all here now," she said, looking around. "I just have a couple of things to say to you. I spoke to Veronica Morgan, Valerie's daughter, about an hour ago and she said that it seems her mother died as a result of something she ate and drank having an allergic reaction with some tablets that she was taking. I passed on the condolences of all of us at the conference, and she says that she will send us details of the funeral after the post mortem.

Anyone who wants to attend the funeral will be welcome. She also said that we should carry on with our programme as normal — she said it's what her mother would have wanted. She will try to come up tomorrow to pick up her mother's belongings and take whatever books she hadn't sold in the book sale." Or had had nicked prior to it, Sally thought wryly. She focused her attention back on what Miriam was saying. "So we will be carrying on our programme as normal today. Maria" — she smiled across at the Rev. Maria Laker, a delegate at the conference who was also a Methodist minister — "will say some special prayers for Valerie during the service she'll be holding in the chapel. For those of you who don't want to attend the service, there will be free time. Then our programme will resume with lunch at twelve-thirty."

Normally, Sally wouldn't have attended the church service, but she decided that she would today. She was surprised to see that most of the other delegates also made their way into the small chapel that was attached to the hall. Maria Laker, a tall, slim woman in her fifties, also looked surprised, though pleased, by the attendance. The delegates were no doubt paying their respects to Valerie; it was unlikely that many of them would have actually known her well enough to attend her funeral.

Sally found herself seated next to Margaret in the pew. She was surprised to see that Margaret looked quite pale and unhappy; she hadn't known Valerie, so she wondered if anything else was wrong. As usual, Margaret was clad in jeans and a long cardigan; at least that suited today's conditions, for it was much cooler than it had been yesterday and on Friday.

Maria spoke kindly of Valerie Teague — if she hadn't known her, then she must have spent a bit of time this morning finding out what she could about her, Sally thought. Maria spoke of Valerie's passion for old girls' books, about her bookselling activities, and how the love of boarding-school stories she'd read in childhood had led her to send her own children to boarding-school later on. She talked of how Valerie's books always seemed expensive, but when you looked at them they were real quality — she always sold pristine editions, discarding anything grubby.

She then led some prayers for Valerie's family, and Margaret lent forward to pray. As she did so, her cardigan rode slightly up her arm, and Sally was shocked to see an angry purple gash, with faded red scars criss-crossing it. No wonder Margaret looked pale and miserable — the cut was fresh, done in the last few hours. And the faded scars told of a long history of self-harm, explaining why she always covered her arms — and her legs too, probably. Sally didn't know much about cutting, but she'd read enough to know that it was tied up with lack of self-esteem and deep unhappiness with oneself. She wondered if she ought to speak to Margaret, tackle her about the scars, and plead with her to see a doctor, seek help. Margaret was, after all, not that much older than Sally's Eleanor; she wouldn't have liked to think that if Eleanor had some awful problem and another person noticed it, that person would just ignore it. Sally had finished the Trebizon book earlier that morning — she decided that later she would take it over to Margaret's room in the annexe, and perhaps try to encourage her to open up about the scars.

It was time for another hymn now, 'Love divine, all loves excelling'. Maria had chosen four hymns she thought people would recognise, perhaps from their schooldays if not from church attendance.

After that, Maria gave a sermon, there was a final hymn, and they all prepared to file out. Then Sally noticed Miriam, accompanied by a tall, fair man in a suit, push her way up the nave and to the front of the chapel.

"If I could just have a moment," Miriam said into the microphone, and everyone stopped talking and walking and turned round to stare. "I'm afraid we're actually going to have to have some disruption to our programme after all. This is Detective Sergeant Steve Arrowman. He needs to speak to you all for a moment."

CHAPTER VIII.

THE DELEGATES GET A GRILLING

> Meanwhile, the two Heads, with some help from the staff, questioned the girls as to when they had gone down to the courts, and where they had been just previously. They got through fairly quickly, for most of the girls had been with friends and they had gone down in threes and fours and never been alone all the afternoon. As they were proved blameless, they were sent out until finally only four were left — Mary-Lou Trelawney, Viola Lucy, Jennifer Penrose, and Blossom herself.
>
> Elinor M. Brent-Dyer, *The Wrong Chalet School*, 1952

"SORRY to interrupt you all," said the Detective Sergeant, "but, as you all know, one of your fellow delegates died here last night. Unfortunately, our early enquiries into her death have indicated that it wasn't as straightforward as it originally seemed, and, as a result, we need to conduct brief interviews and take statements from everybody who has been in Mrs Teague's company this weekend. Myself and a couple of other detectives will be taking over some of the rooms here, and we'll see everyone individually. Ms Lorrimer has kindly given us a list of all your names."

"We will try to continue with our programme, but obviously people will need to keep coming and going from this afternoon's sessions," said Miriam. "But we figure it's best to keep going with the programme than to have all of you just milling round the grounds all day, waiting for your turn to be called."

"That's right," said Steve. "We want to cause minimal disruption. Now, we're using the small rooms on the first and ground floors, and we'll start working through the list straightaway. That means — let me see — Karen Appleton and Leonie Carr, would you mind coming with me now, please?"

Having a surname beginning with M had advantages and disadvantages. The main disadvantage was having to wait until the middle of the afternoon to be interviewed by the police. The main advantage was that, by the time Sally's turn came, she had a fairly good idea of what questions she was going to be asked. If keeping the programme going had been an attempt to prevent as much conferring and gossiping among the delegates as was possible, it hadn't worked — especially as a period of free time had been scheduled between the end of the church service and the start of lunch anyway. Rumour and gossip spread quickly.

"They seem to think Valerie committed suicide," Richard said in a stage whisper to Harriet, Bridget and Sally at lunchtime.

"Suicide? *Valerie?*" Bridget laughed.

"Well, it's possible," said Harriet.

"Never in the world," said Bridget. "She was too full of herself ever to be suicidal."

"Well, she *was* prescribed antidepressants," Harriet pointed out. "That's usually an indication that one's mind is disturbed in some way."

"Yes, they were asking me about the antidepressants," said Richard. "Apparently the antidepressants in her system reacted badly with cheese and wine. Both of which she imbibed last night."

"I can't imagine Valerie being so careless," frowned Harriet.

"Which is why they think it might have been deliberate," said Richard.

"I bet Veronica and Mark are uncorking the champagne," commented Bridget.

"Bridget!" reproved Harriet.

Richard laughed. "Oh, she's right, Harry. Let's face it, they haven't spoken to Valerie in — what? — at least ten years. I can't imagine they'll be shattered by her death."

"Why were they estranged?" Sally asked curiously.

"Veronica got pregnant at seventeen and dropped out of school to marry the fellow, despite Mummy's objections," Richard explained. "Valerie had sent them both to expensive boarding-schools and wasn't at all pleased by that particular return on her investment. Veronica had the baby, but split up with the father after a couple of years. She's married to someone else now and has two other children with him. Valerie's husband kept in touch with Veronica, but Valerie refused to acknowledge her from the moment she refused to have an abortion and stay on for 'A' levels. She'd never seen her grandchildren, from what I gather."

Sally, quite taken aback by this tale — she'd known many disappointed grandparents-to-be, but they'd always come around once the baby was born — asked, "What about her son?"

"Oh, he refused to go to university and went off travelling the world instead. He ended up in a kibbutz for a year where he met his wife who, as you've probably guessed, Valerie never approved of," Richard responded.

"Will you go to Valerie's funeral?" Harriet asked

Richard.

"Yes. I think so. Well, I knew her after all, and for a good many years at that. Will you?"

"Yes," said Harriet. "I can't say we always got along, but I'm sorry she's dead. What about you, Bridget?"

"What? Attend her funeral?" Bridget shook her head. "No, absolutely not. I didn't like her, she didn't like me. I'd be a hypocrite if I did go."

One of the delegates, whose face Sally recognised but whose name she didn't know, interrupted them to say that the detective sergeant was ready to talk to Harriet now. Harriet grimaced and left.

"You'll be after Harry," Richard told Sally cheerfully. "At a guess you'll have time for a quick coffee, so shall we all adjourn to the urn?"

The room that Detective Sergeant Arrowman was using for interviews hadn't been used for any part of the conference programme — it was downstairs, along the passage that led from the staircase to the conservatory, and was around the same size as Sally's attic bedroom. It contained a small table surrounded by four chairs, and another, even smaller table in the far corner. Several atmospheric old black-and-white photographs of Cotterford Dene — the village under heavy snow; dancing around the maypole on a now long-vanished village green; the castle ruins shrouded by fog — enlivened the walls. The room — along with two others on the first floor — was, Sally knew from the Cotterford Manor literature she'd been sent upon enrolling for the Tales Out of School weekend, designed for small-group work at business conferences. When Sally entered, Detective Sergeant Arrowman was seated on the window side of the table, with another, younger, female detective to his side, taking notes. Sally sat down across the table from the detective sergeant and looked across at him expectantly, feeling as if she had walked into an episode of *The Bill*.

"Right," said Arrowman. "So you're—." He looked down at the list. "Sally Meredith of 23 Ferndale Road, Warrandyte, Victoria, Australia." He looked up, smirked and added, "You've come a long way for this jolly hockey sticks conference."

Sally instantly disliked him, but at the same time felt an overwhelming need to distance herself from her hobby. "That's right," she acknowledged. "I'm working. I'm the editor of an Australian magazine called *Australian Collector*, and I'm writing an article on old girls' stories." And all she had to do on the article now was write it, she thought with some relief. She'd gained enough information from Leah Brindsley to be able to drop Valerie easily from the piece given her demise, and she had got the final 'fan' quotes she needed earlier in the day from Harriet and Bridget, as she'd known that neither was upset enough by Valerie's death to be offended by her questions.

Arrowman smirked again. "What a nice freebie. I wish we could get taxpayer-funded trips across the world, don't you, Detective Constable Willoughby?"

The detective constable looked across at him and grinned. "Definitely, Sarge."

"Anyway, enough of all that," said Arrowman, briskly. "How well did you know Mrs Teague?"

"I didn't really know her at all."

"Not even through the internet?" he queried. "Ms Lorrimer tells me that the school-story community is very active online and that Mrs Teague was a well-known book dealer."

"I had spoken to Valerie by email prior to the conference and I interviewed her late on Friday afternoon. But I don't think that a brief interview about her book-dealing business constitutes *knowing* her," Sally returned.

"What sort of things did you ask her about when you interviewed her?"

"Book dealing. Why she specialises in selling girls' school stories. How she became a collector. The first Chalet School book she ever bought." Sally smiled slightly at his obvious irritation. "Things like that."

"How long did you spend with her?"

"Not long. I interviewed her, had a quick look at her books and that was that."

"Did you have anything more to do with her after your interview?"

"No. But I was present when she had conversations with other people."

"And from what you saw of her, what would you say her state of mind was like?"

Sally considered. "Well, she was fine with me when I interviewed her — she was happy to answer my questions. I suppose she looked forward to the increased publicity that the article would give her. But most of the time she seemed angry."

"Angry about what?"

"Well, she was annoyed about the stall space she'd been given in the room where the booksale was held. The second time a few of us were having a drink in another delegate's room, and she came in and complained about the noise."

"Ah yes," He looked at some notes on his desk. "That would be in Mrs Harriet Lenton's room, yes?"

"That's right," Sally agreed, smiling slightly at the realisation that the flirtatious Harriet was a Mrs; she wondered if there was still a Mr Lenton.

"Go on," Arrowman prompted.

"The next time I saw her was yesterday morning when she discovered her books were missing."

"Ah yes," he said again, with a wink in Detective Constable Wiloughby's direction. "The practical joke. Do you have any idea who might have been responsible for that?"

"No," answered Sally.

"Carry on," he said. "Did you see her in a bad temper any more after that incident?"

"Yes. At breakfast, after she found the books were missing, she accused another delegate of having taken them."

"That delegate being ... ?"

Sally felt slightly uncomfortable. Come on, she told herself, firmly, this isn't a school story and you're not the heroine of the fourth form who mustn't sneak. "Bridget Whodcoat," she said.

"Thank you." He looked down at his list. "And were there any further incidents?"

"She had a bit of an altercation in one of the seminars — with the speaker and one of the delegates."

"About what?"

"The seminar was about lesbian characters in school stories. Valerie didn't agree with the speaker's views."

"Who was the speaker?"

"Sue Parkinson."

"And the delegate?"

"A woman called Heidi. I can't remember her surname."

"And why exactly were they arguing?"

"Valerie didn't believe the characters discussed in the talk were lesbians. She thought it was rot. In the end, someone suggested she leave the room, which she did."

Arrowman smiled. "I'd have thought girls'

boarding-school stories were full of lesbians myself, but then I've never read any." *God*, thought Sally, he was unbelievable. When Sally didn't respond aloud, he continued, "Did you know Mrs Teague had been taking antidepressants?"

"Yes. I heard she started taking them after her husband died."

"And did you know if she was still taking them?"

"No. The person who told me didn't know either."

"That person being ... ?"

"Richard Fingleton."

"Ah yes, the token man. And, we understand, one-time lover of the deceased." He smirked again and Detective Sergeant Willoughby smothered a giggle.

"Did anyone mention what kind of antidepressants Mrs Teague was taking?"

"No."

"Did anyone mention that she shouldn't take them with cheese or wine?"

"No."

"And did you see anything of Mrs Teague after the lesbian incident?"

"I saw her at the folk dancing. She seemed a lot happier there — more relaxed."

"She was enjoying herself?"

"Yes."

"And were you present when she collapsed?"

"No. I'd gone for a walk with Leonie Carr. When we returned we saw the ambulance and Valerie being stretchered out."

He flicked through a pile of notes. "Ah yes. Ms Carr commented that you came across some burning books as you walked through the grounds."

"Yes. We thought at first they were the ones that Valerie had had stolen. But they weren't."

"And where are these books now?"

"I've got some of them in my room, Leonie has the

rest in hers. We put a notice on the notice board this morning, saying if they belong to anyone, they should contact one of us. But no-one has so far."

"All most mysterious," Arrowman said, smirking again. "What's your theory about Mrs Teague's missing books, Ms Meredith?"

"Theory?"

"Yes. Do you believe that some books were stolen, or do you think it was a practical joke as Miriam Lorrimer suggests? Or do you think it's possible that she might have mislaid them, or forgotten she never brought them in the first place?"

"I'd seen some of the missing books myself when I interviewed her, so they were definitely there. I honestly don't know whether it was a joke or if they were stolen — or how they disappeared from a locked room."

"How did you feel when you heard that Mrs Teague had died?" he asked her.

"Feel? Well, a bit shocked — I wasn't upset, because I didn't really know her. But I suppose I was stunned that someone who I'd seen only a few hours previously had suddenly died."

"Right," said Arrowman. "There's probably nothing else you can help you with at present. We might need you to give a statement ... How much longer are you in the country?"

"Another three weeks."

"And you're staying where during that time?"

"Well, I'm travelling around quite a bit — visiting relatives here, as well as some old friends and visiting places I've always wanted to see."

"It's just we'll need contact details in case we need to talk to you again."

Sally gave him her mobile phone number. He thanked her for her time, then asked her if she could find Sue Parkinson and send her up.

CHAPTER IX.

QUIZ NIGHT

There followed what to most was the climax of the afternoon, the distribution of prizes and certificates. Sheila, Monica and Hilda were among the lucky ones in IVa, and Winnie, as captain of the junior tennis club, bore off the silver cup that was the trophy to be placed on a bracket in the hall. Each girl in turn mounted the platform, received her prize and shook hands with the chairman, while the school clapped heartily.

Angela Brazil, *Three Terms at Uplands*, 1945

"BRIDGET'S been with the defective sergeant for quite a while now," commented Richard at *Kaffee und Kuchen*. "I'm beginning to think that perhaps the police suspect murder."

"Murder?" said Harriet, filling up her cup from the urn. "Surely not? Who would want to murder Valerie?"

"About three-quarters of the people here at one time or another, I should think," replied Richard.

Harriet laughed, as did Sally, Leonie and Sue and a couple of other people who had heard Richard's comment. "No, but seriously," Harriet persisted, "there's a big difference between *feeling* like murdering someone and actually doing it. After all, if we were all as capable of murdering people as we are of feeling like we'd like to murder them, there'd be very few folk left on earth. If any."

"Well," said Richard, lowering his voice, "I've heard a rumour—." He looked around to see who else was listening, then continued quietly, "I've heard a rumour that Valerie was no longer taking antidepressants, that she'd finished the course some time ago."

"Who did you hear that from?" Sally asked curiously.

"Miriam told me. She's been in touch with Valerie's daughter who's coming to collect her things. Veronica told Miriam that the post mortem results revealed only small traces of this particular antidepressant, indicating that she hadn't been taking it regularly. And apparently Valerie's GP has confirmed that Valerie hasn't been taking the tablets for a while."

"How very cloak and dagger," said Harriet. "If what you say is true then it is looking more like suicide."

"Or murder," said Richard. "Which is why no doubt they're grilling Bridget, since she and Valerie had that long-running feud going."

"Surely, though," said Sally, "even that prat of a detective sergeant can't think that Bridget would murder Valerie because she didn't agree with her views on private education?"

"You're right," said Richard. "Arrowman is a prat."

"I wonder if the missing books and the books *we* found, Sally, have anything to do with it?" mused Leonie. "It's really strange that something like that should be done to Valerie and then — if Richard's right — she's murdered."

"It doesn't make sense, though," said Sue. "How would you get Valerie to take an antidepressant? It would be hard to slip it into her food — she's not a vegetarian or anything, so it's not as though she has separate meals from the rest of us."

"That's true," Richard agreed. "Maybe suicide is the most likely explanation then, even if Valerie didn't seem the suicidal type. I suppose you never can tell. Ah, here comes Bridget. Well grilled, Bridget?"

"Cremated," said Bridget with a grimace. She picked up a cup and poured herself a coffee. "God, where'd they get that awful Arrowman fellow from? He's like something out of *Life On Mars*."

"Richard thinks the police think Valerie was murdered," said Sue.

"I think he's right about that," said Bridget. She took a long gulp of coffee. "That's better. It was a bit hairy in there, but I think Arrowman was finally convinced I'm not headed for a noose." She grinned.

"Well, now that you're here, Bridget," said Richard, "I want to know what you think about being on my team for tonight's quiz. You'd be with me, Harry and Sue. We did ask Sally to join us," he continued, acknowledging Sally, "but she's already teamed up with Leonie, Margaret Wilks and Maria Laker."

"Why not?" said Bridget, draining the rest of her coffee. "I should manage the quiz questions better than I managed Arrowman's anyway."

The rest of the day passed quickly. The police remained on the premises and Steve Arrowman called one or two delegates back to give official statements, but Sally wasn't among them and she was thankful for that — the fifteen minutes or so in his company had been more than enough. Tomorrow, she thought, the conference would finish and she would head off to London for a few days to catch up with a couple of old university friends. She was looking forward to that — they were going to a Shakespeare production at The Globe, which was something she'd never done before. The Globe hadn't been open when she was last in London.

At first, Miriam had been worried that the police wouldn't want anyone using the conservatory, given that it was where Valerie had collapsed, but Arrowman told her that there had been far too many people in the room over the weekend for them to be able to glean anything useful from fingerprints. So the grand dinner took place in the conservatory as planned, and the atmosphere when Sally arrived and took her seat at a table with Leonie, Margaret and Maria was no less festive than it might have been had a death not occurred during the conference.

"I really must assure you, Sally," said Richard, leaning over from the adjacent table, "that this is absolutely not par for the 'girls' own' conference course. Death, police questioning, all that."

"I should hope not," answered Sally. "A murder at every conference and there wouldn't be too many school-story fans left." She remembered that Richard's talk had taken place that afternoon; she'd missed it as a result of her interview with Arrowman. "How did your talk go?"

"Oh, it was okay. It was just very hard to get people's attention when the whole house is buzzing with rumour and counter-rumour," replied Richard.

Dinner was an enjoyable affair, apart from when it was briefly interrupted by Detective Sergeant Arrowman, who addressed everyone to say that the circumstances of Valerie Teague's death were still being investigated and he might well need to speak to some of them again over the next few days — anyone who hadn't yet given the police their personal contact details, he said, should do so now.

Detective Constable Willoughby wandered around the tables, jotting down the contact details of the guilty parties. When the two detectives had left the room, though, everything returned to normal again. The food was good, and the wine flowed freely. After the pudding, coffee was served and then Miriam announced that the quiz would now begin, passing answer sheets around the tables.

"Thank goodness Bridget and Leonie aren't on the same team," commented Sue. "No other team would stand a chance. As it is I think the contest is between these two tables. Both Bridge and Leonie have encyclopaedic knowledge of the books."

"No wonder with the number of books they've got," said Harriet. "You should just *see* Bridget's collection," she told Sally. "More first editions than the British Library."

"Now that's an exaggeration," said Bridget.

"Not much of one."

"I don't even own a single first edition Chalet," sighed Sally.

"When you visit London, you should go and see Bridget's books," said Richard. "She'd be welcome, wouldn't she, Bridget?"

"Yes, of course, though the house is a bit of a mess at the moment," said Bridget. "We're renovating, so a lot of my books have gone into storage. But yes, if you're going to spend some time in London, we should get together, Sally."

"If we can have silence, please," said Miriam, signalling frantically in the direction of Richard's table. "It's time to start. The first round of questions is on book covers. I'm going to display a series of book covers on the overhead projector and you have to guess the title of the book it's from and also give the name of the author."

Maria Laker elected to write for Sally's team, and

the four of them bent their heads closely together as they conferred on the identity of the book covers. Sally was astounded by how quickly Leonie was able to recognise the covers. "How do you *know* all of this stuff?" she marvelled when the first round was over.

"Oh, Leonie's specialist interest is covers and illustrations," Maria informed her. "She was telling me earlier that she's thinking of doing a PhD and writing her thesis on the covers and illustrations in the 'girls' own' genre."

"My excuse for not knowing any of those covers is that I don't have many hardbacks," said Sally.

"Oh, four of them were from paperbacks," said Leonie. "Remember the one with the skater on the front, the one I said was *Amanda's New School* by Angela Brazil? The girls were wearing miniskirts. So I could tell that was done in the 1960s and that's when they started producing these kinds of books in paperback edition."

"Now, in the second round," came Miriam's voice, "I'm going to read out descriptions of ten series heroines. You have to name the girl and the school she attends. The first one is 'Her cropped black hair was so straight as almost to be described as lank, her big black eyes made the intense whiteness of her face even more startling than it need have been, and her cheeks and temples were hollow with continual ill-health.'"

"Joey Bettany — the Chalet School," Sally, Leonie and Margaret all hissed to Maria, conscious of the same answer being whispered all around the room.

"I can hear that you all got that one," commented Miriam with a smile. "You might find the next one a little harder. 'Pauline meanwhile had reached IIIA and located the dark, thin-faced child she had already noticed. [She] was unlike the rest in that she did not have bobbed hair or plaits; her black curls were neatly tied back with two bunches with green [...] ribbons.' "

"It's Merry from Clare Mallory's Merry series, and the school is Tremayne's," Sally said, pleased to be able to answer something before the rest of her team.

"What's the rest of her name?" Maria asked.

"Merry Arundel," Sally told her.

"I've never heard of those books," Maria said.

"They're by Clare Mallory, a New Zealand writer. They're set in New Zealand," Sally told her.

"I've read a couple of the reprints," said Margaret. "I didn't remember the description of Merry, though."

The next set of questions saw ten opening lines from 'girls' own' novels being displayed on the overhead projector. Sally recognised about half of them, Margaret knew eight and Maria four, but again Leonie knew them all.

In the end Leonie's table defeated Richard's by fifty points to forty, and the four team members were called up to the front of the conservatory to receive their prizes — a book token each.

"Just what you need, Leonie — more books," quipped Richard as Leonie passed their table to return to her own seat. "What you really need is to win some bookshelf tokens to help you house them all."

Now that the quiz was over, the delegates stayed up talking for a while, finishing off their wine and coffee. Then they all started to drift off to bed. The conference was due to finish at midday tomorrow, and many of them had trains to catch or long drives and wanted to pack before the morning session. Sally chatted briefly to Leonie, Sue, Maria, Richard, Harriet and Bridget, and then made her excuses and headed back to her room. She started throwing some things into her case, then spotted *The Unforgettable Fifth at Trebizon* on the bedside table and groaned. She'd intended to return it to Margaret earlier, but had forgotten amid all the huha. Margaret had left the conservatory within only about fifteen minutes of the quiz ending, saying she was tired. Sally decided to go over to the annexe and see if Margaret was still up and hand it back to her now, rather than risk forgetting it or missing Margaret tomorrow.

It had begun to rain, so Sally pulled on her raincoat and headed down the steps. As she passed the main conference room she noticed that the light was still on and could hear the swishing of mops and the sound of voices.

"Honestly, Kate," said a woman's voice, "I can't get anyone to take me seriously. Mary said I must have been mistaken about the spinach rolls and that detective sergeant — well, if he and his sidekick had laughed out loud and called me an idiot to myself, they couldn't have made it clearer that they think I'm off my rocker."

"Those cops seem to think everybody here's off their rocker," said another woman, presumably Kate. "Not that I blame them, to be honest. Reading school stories at the age they are. Why, some of them are old enough to be my grandmother."

"They're *all* old enough to be *my* grandmother," returned the first woman.

Sally bristled and wondered briefly whether to show herself and embarrass them. But curiosity overcame indignation when the first woman decided to return to her original topic of conversation; Sally remained still and listened.

"Do you think I did the right thing, Kate, telling the cops that there were a couple of spinach rolls missing when I came to collect the trolley from the kitchen before setting up the buffet?"

"Well," Kate said, hesitantly, "it is a bit of an odd thing to tell them, Jo. After all, anyone could have taken them — one of the delegates feeling a bit peckish. Even Mary herself, come to that. It's not really relevant to this woman's death, is it? I think I'd just have let it go."

Hearing one of them move, Sally scurried towards the door, but didn't make it in time. The woman, who looked to be mid-twenties, sporting a long plait and nose ring and carrying a mop, glared at her. Sally had seen her in the house on a couple of other occasions during the weekend — putting fresh water in the jug on the speakers' table in the conference room; organising the coffee cups in the drawing room. It seemed that the few household staff at Cotterford Manor shared out all the jobs.

"Sorry," Sally apologised. "I thought someone had left the light on by mistake and was going to turn it off when I realised you were in there."

"Well, it wasn't left on by mistake," the woman returned huffily. "Some of us have to work here not spend our time sitting on our bums and listening to lectures on children's books!"

Charming, Sally thought. She headed outside and hurried through the rain to the annexe. She found Margaret's room, but it was in darkness. Sally tapped lightly on the door, not wanting to disturb Margaret if she was already asleep but hoping to raise her if she was still awake. There was no response. Sally sighed and carried the book back to the manor house. She'd have to make sure she gave it back to Margaret in the morning.

CHAPTER X.

RHIAN MAKES A SUGGESTION

Having consoled Lintie, and recalled Jeems ... Dimsie turned at last to the waiting seniors.

"And now," she said gaily, "let's go off into some peaceful corner and talk. It's lovely to be back — lovelier than I thought it was going to be, when I told Miss Yorke I'd come. I want to find all my old friends and hear what they've got to say for themselves. Where are Ruth and Nan?"

Dorita Fairlie Bruce, *Dimsie Goes Back*, 1927

SALLY carried *The Unforgettable Fifth* at Trebizon down to breakfast the next morning, but Margaret wasn't in the conservatory. Heidi and Anna were seated at their usual table, so Sally went across to ask if they knew where Margaret was.

"She's already left," Anna answered. "She said she had a lunch-time appointment, so she got up and caught an early train home."

"Oh, bummer," Sally said. "I never gave her her book back. Do you have her address, by any chance?"

Anna and Heidi shook their heads. "Ask Miriam Lorrimer," Heidi advised. "She'll have it for sure."

Sally thanked them and walked across to join Richard and Harriet for breakfast for the final time. They exchanged addresses and phone numbers, and Richard urged Sally to visit him in Ludlow before she left the UK. Harriet told Sally if she wanted to spend some time in Cheshire over the next few weeks, she was welcome to stay with her and her husband in Hale. "Only you must promise not to tell Charles about what I got up to with Richard this weekend," she added with a mischievous grin. Sally decided that Harriet and Charles would be the last people she would visit — she didn't want to get involved in Harriet's cloak-and-dagger nonsense.

"Where's Bridget this morning?" she asked as she put her address book back into her handbag.

"Oh, still packing probably," said Harriet cheerfully. "I doubt she'll bother with breakfast on the final morning. Did she give you her address? No? Oh well, I can give it to you and you can drop in on her while you're in London. She won't mind at all."

When Sally had finished breakfast, she went in search of Miriam Lorrimer and found her in the entrance hall, already dismantling the display. Sally explained to her that Margaret Wilks had left before she, Sally, could return her book, and asked if she could have Margaret's address. Miriam led Sally to the small room she'd been using as an office and took the delegates' address list from her briefcase. "Here we are," she said, running her finger down the names towards the bottom of the list. "Margaret Wilks, 28 Lonsdale Road, SE22. That's East Dulwich, I believe."

"Oh, excellent," said Sally, scribbling down the address. "I'm off to stay with an old university friend who lives in Forest Hill, so that's not too far to go at all."

"I've only got her mobile phone number," said Miriam, holding it out to show Sally. "It's probably best to ring her first to make sure she's home."

"Thanks, Miriam," said Sally. "And if I don't see you again, thank you for an enjoyable conference. I've found it really interesting."

"Thank you, Sally. It's been a pleasure to meet

you. I hope Valerie's death didn't cast too much of a blight over proceedings."

Sally wasn't sure how to answer this; it seemed to her that Valerie's death hadn't really affected the delegates much at all. "Well," she said at last, "it was a bit hard to concentrate on the talks sometimes with the police around."

"Wasn't it just! Oh well," said Miriam, briskly. "I must get on — lots of clearing up to do."

Sally took the point and made her way to the main room, where Rosalind Holmes was preparing to give an overview of the conference. Most of the seats were already taken and Sally found herself sitting towards the back of the room, well away from Richard and Harriet for a change. In another two hours, she'd have said goodbye to everyone and would be on the London-bound train ready to catch up with old friends. Once she was ensconced at her friend Rhian's, she would telephone Margaret and arrange a time to return her Trebizon book.

It was only then that it struck her. Margaret lived in London. And the London train stopped at Cotterford Dene station — so why had Margaret been waiting for a connection at Clinton Manning station when her train from London would have stopped at Cotterford Dene en route to Clinton Manning in the first place?

"Rhian!"

"Hi, Sal."

Sally and Rhian Jenkins hugged for a long time, then stepped back to survey each other. Sally hadn't seen Rhian for eight years now — Rhian had spent three weeks in Melbourne before going on to New Zealand for the skiing. She hadn't changed much, even since university days, Sally thought. She still had an elfin figure and face, though her grey eyes had lines around them now and the short brown hair was streaked with silver.

"You haven't changed at all," Rhian said.

"I'm a few pounds heavier," Sally said. "And I've got a few lines and grey hairs."

"Not many," Rhian said. "D'you need help with your bag?" She reached for it.

"No, I'm okay. Did you bring your car, or are we taking the tube and train?"

"I drove here. London traffic's bad, but since the last bombings I haven't felt too comfortable on public transport." Rhian led the way out of Paddington station and along the streets to a multi-storey carpark. "By the way," she said, "I've been hard at work today finding out all about someone who attended your school-story conference."

"Oh yes?"

"Oh yes — I've been investigating the death of the book dealer," Rhian grinned. "Did you know the woman who died?"

"Not really," Sally answered. "I interviewed her on Friday—."

"You *interviewed* her?"

"Yes. About her work and books." Sally explained about the article for *Australian Collector*.

"Well, well, well ... Joining the ranks of the press, eh?"

"Hardly," said Sally. "I've written an article on something I already know a bit about — and you'd never believe how nervous I felt before interviewing Valerie Teague. I'd never be game to cover something from scratch and ask the really hard questions the way you do."

"So from that I'm to understand that you didn't ask her about anything other than what made her take up selling children's books?"

"Correct," Sally grinned.

"What about outside the interview, then? Did you talk to her much during the conference?"

"Not really," Sally said again. "She wasn't particularly friendly."

"Wasn't she? That's a shame — I was hoping you'd become best pals with her and would be able to help me with my story." Rhian had located her blue Vauxhall Corser and unlocked the boot. Sally heaved her bag into it, then got into the passenger seat beside Rhian. "She took phenelzine, apparently," Rhian told her.

"I knew she took some kind of antidepressant, but I didn't know what."

"It's an antidepressant that reacts adversely with alcohol and things like cheese, Marmite and broad beans. The *Clarion* have asked me to write a feature on the dangers of the side effects of antidepressants as a result of this woman's death." Rhian worked as health editor of the *Clarion*; she and Sally had both studied English at Aberystwyth University and had stayed in touch despite going their separate ways post graduation. Rhian, Sally thought, had always been the most successful of her old university friends career-wise. After graduating, Rhian had spent three years as a trainee journalist on the *Cambrian Echo*; this had been followed by several years of news reporting on the national dailies before she decided to specialise in health.

Whereas Sally had met and married her husband, Phil, within a year of starting her first job as a book editor with a publishing company in Melbourne, and a couple of years later had given up work to become a full-time mother. When she and Phil had split up, Sally had started editing again, this time in a freelance capacity to fit in with the kids' school hours, and it was then that she'd started editing the antique and art titles which had eventually led to her gaining the editorship of *Australian Collector*.

"Well, Valerie certainly knocked the alcohol back on Saturday night," Sally responded as Rhian began to weave her way out of the car park. "I think she ate cheese too — I can't remember for sure."

"It's strange, because there are clear warnings on the tablets and it sounds as if Valerie Teague obeyed the instructions when she was taking them," Rhian said. "And then, when she'd supposedly stopped taking them, she died from the reactions. I spoke to the police about it and to her doctor — the latter off the record, of course, but he's very puzzled about it," she explained.

"They're thinking murder, then?"

"Murder, suicide, or misadventure — maybe Valerie had a stray tablet in her handbag and took it by mistake, perhaps thinking it was a headache tablet. Detective Sergeant Arrowman said a couple of headache tablets were found in her handbag, so she might have inadvertently taken phenelzine. If it's murder, though, " Rhian continued, "they're going to have a problem proving it. Who's going to have access to phenelzine unless they were taking it themselves? And you have to get it prescribed by a doctor — they don't hand it out willy-nilly. You've really got to be suffering pretty badly from depression for them to prescribe it." She glanced at Sally. "You spent the weekend at the conference. Reckon any of them might have slipped her something?"

"I don't know. She wasn't very popular, but like you say, you'd have to be lucky to be prescribed the exact same medication as Valerie had been." Sally remembered the spinach rolls that Jo from Cotterford Manor had insisted had gone missing prior to the Saturday night festivities, and thought suddenly of Margaret and the gashes on her arm. If Margaret had been depressed enough to harm herself, it was possible that a doctor might have prescribed her a heavy duty antidepressant.

"What are you thinking?" Rhian asked.

Sally told her about the missing rolls and about Margaret, the self-harm, and the fact she had inexplicably caught the train south to Cotterford Dene from Clinton Manning when theoretically she should have been travelling in the opposite direction from London. "She was really upset about not being in the manor house too," she said. "Maybe she didn't want to be in the annexe because she wanted proximity to Valerie."

"You should look into it," Rhian said. "Write a feature for that magazine of yours. 'Murder among the collectors.' It could be fun."

"News reporting's not my thing."

"It's mine, though. I wouldn't mind doing something in addition to the health feature. And you could help and write up something for your mag, depending on what we find. I'm betting that the police won't be able to establish anything. Too many delegates, the strong possibility that Valerie committed suicide ..."

"Did the cops mention Valerie's books at all?" Sally asked. She had forgotten what a bulldozer Rhian could be when she thought she was on to a story, and was starting to feel overwhelmed by the idea of being coerced into helping with an investigation into Valerie's death. It was all right for Rhian, she thought — she found it easy to badger people for information. Sally had no idea how to go about doing that.

"Her books? No. What about them?"

Sally told her about the books that had mysteriously gone missing from a locked room, and about the novels that she and Leonie had found burning in the grounds and the figure they'd seen running away.

"This is amazing!" Rhian laughed. "Pure Agatha Christie!" She glanced at the clock on her dashboard. "I've arranged for Fiona to arrive at my place at five and we'll get pizza and open some wine. Is that all right?"

"Sounds great," Sally said, pleased.

It was nearly five o'clock when they reached Rhian's flat in Forest Hill. Her flat was on the second floor of a converted house in a long street of Victorian terrace houses; she'd lived there for more than ten years now, but Sally had never seen the place. She followed Rhian up the carpeted staircase into a large lounge-cum-dining-room, with sash windows overlooking the street. Sally's eyes were drawn instantly to the built-in bookcases on either side of the ornate fireplace. Of course, she knew Rhian well enough to know that there would be no school stories on the bookshelves. Rhian's tastes had always been more literary; but all the same, it was always interesting to look at other people's reading matter. As she'd expected, the classics stood alongside contemporary literary novelists like Zadie Smith and Joanne Harris. The only children's books on the shelves were young adult titles like *How I Live Now* and *The Curious Incident of the Dog in the Night-time*. Sally picked up *How I Live Now* and started browsing through it.

"I'm just going to open some wine," said Rhian. She pushed open a door on her way to the kitchen. "This is your room, by the way. Drop your bag in there."

Rhian's spare bedroom was small — it just had room for a double bed, chest of drawers and a wardrobe — but she'd decorated it prettily with matching floral curtains and duvet set, and old photographs depicting famous London sights — the Tower of London, Hampton Court, St Paul's Cathedral — on the walls. Sally plonked her backpack on the bed and went to join Rhian in the tiny, but compact kitchen; unpacking could wait till later.

"That'll be Fee," said Rhian as the doorbell rang. "Can you take the wine into the living room, Sal?"

Fiona Geeson had studied English with Sally and Rhian at Aberystwyth, but unlike them she had gone into librarianship rather than journalism and now worked in a university law library. She'd visited Sally in Australia only a couple of years ago, so seemed to have changed even less than Rhian had — she still had long blonde curls and, as in university days, remained the plumpest of the trio.

They all settled around Rhian's dining-table with the bottle of wine, and Rhian telephoned for takeaway pizza. "Well, cheers, Sal," she said, as she put down the phone and lifted her wine glass. "Great to have you back here with us again."

"Yes," echoed Fiona. "It's like old times, isn't it?"

"Yes," agreed Sally, "except Rhian's flat is rather nicer than the student digs we shared at Aber."

"And we can afford decent wine instead of cheap plonk," added Rhian.

"Mind you, Rhian's culinary skills haven't improved since we were at Aber," Fiona said. "She still lives off toast and takeaways."

"Not always," Rhian returned with a grin. "I often eat at restaurants."

"I like cooking," Sally said. "I'll cook for you one night while I'm staying here."

"You never used to like cooking," Rhian said. "Neither did you, Fiona, for that matter. Still, I suppose you've both done the housewifely thing, which I haven't, and that's helped you get used to cooking."

"Garbage," Sally said. "Phil did most of the cooking when we were together. It's only been since he left that I've really learned to cook. And actually, Eleanor does quite a bit of it now."

"How *are* your kids?" Fiona asked her.

"Good. Eleanor's in her first year at uni studying to become a vet. Angus is taking VCE this year — that's our equivalent of 'A' levels," Sally added by way of explanation.

"Eleanor's still at home, then?"

"Yes. She got her licence last year and drives to uni every day. What about Georgia? What's she up to these days?" Georgia was Fiona's daughter; Fiona had revealed she was pregnant on the last New Year's Eve that Sally had spent in Britain prior to deciding to follow her parents out to Australia.

"She's fine," Fiona replied. "She's at Nottingham University now, studying law. Here's a photo of her." She produced a photograph from her bag; Georgia looked very much like Fiona had back in university days, Sally thought, studying the photograph — the only difference was that she was thinner. She slipped into her bedroom to produce photographs of Eleanor and Angus — Eleanor tall and dark, as Phil had been, and Angus on the shorter side, with reddish brown hair, like Sally.

"God, they're growing up fast," marvelled Rhian. "You two will be grandmothers before you know it."

"Thanks for that, Rhian," said Sally, putting the photographs back in her purse. "What are you up to then, outside work? Still seeing that married bloke?"

"Ted? Yep," answered Rhian cheerfully. "We've been together ten years now, so we're obviously doing something right."

"And his wife still doesn't suspect anything?"

Sally asked doubtfully.

"Who knows? Who cares?" said Rhian. "I'm happy with things the way they are — I get wined and dined and the other and I don't have to bother with his dirty laundry. Seems to me like marriage is overrated — look at you two. Married Mr Right only to find yourselves suddenly bringing the kids up on your own."

The pizzas arrived, and when they all started eating, Fiona asked Sally what she planned to do during her week in London.

"Oh, see all the sights," Sally said cheerfully. "All the new places that have sprung up in London since I was last here, as well as the Tower of London and Kew Gardens and Greenwich. And there are some good places to visit around here as well." She had discovered in one of her conversations at the conference that Enid Blyton had been born in nearby East Dulwich, and Sally wanted to see her birthplace as well as visit some of the more well-known Dulwich landmarks detailed in the Lonely Planet guide she'd brought with her — the Dulwich Picture Gallery and the Horniman Museum.

"What was the school-story conference like?" asked Fiona, as if reading her thoughts. Sally told her a little bit about the conference and then about Valerie's death — the latter subject drawing rather more interest from Fiona than the first.

"I've been trying to convince Sal to do a bit of sleuthing and write something about Valerie's mysterious death for her mag now that she's joined the ranks of the press," said Rhian, opening a second bottle of wine and refilling everyone's glasses.

"Yes, you should," agreed Fiona.

"I couldn't," Sally said. "I've no experience with that kind of thing."

"Now's your chance to get some, then," said Rhian. "You've spent too many years of your life putting commas into other people's work while you've been bringing up the kids. Now they're off your hands, it's time to spread your wings a bit — do something different, be you again."

Sally had been thinking along those lines herself; that had been partly why she'd accepted the job at *Australian Collector* — for too long her life had revolved around the school run and ferrying the kids to sporting activities. And while freelance editing from home had fitted in well with the kids, it had meant that her social life had become even more restricted.

"If anything, I could do with a few more hobbies and some good nights out," she said, "Not doing work as a news hound in my spare time."

"Well, you're caught up in this investigation whether you like it or not, you know the school story world well, and I'd appreciate your help. I can help you out with what questions to ask and all that," Rhian told her.

"Try it, Sal," Fiona said. "Rhian'll give you no peace till you agree, and you could look at it as an Enid Blyton adventure come to life, that kind of thing."

"She even has a Number One suspect," said Rhian.

Sally repeated what she had already told Rhian about Margaret Wilks and then the incidents with the books.

"I think I'm going to write something anyway, even if you don't want to help," said Rhian. "You've got contact details for a few of the folk I'd like to talk to."

"I'm going to have to talk to Margaret again anyway," said Sally. "I borrowed a book from her and never got round to giving it back. She only lives in East Dulwich, so I'll phone her tomorrow and see if I can take it round for her."

"That way you can ask her why she was going the wrong way to the conference from London," said Rhian.

Sally shrugged. "I don't know if I'll do that. But I will ask her about the self-harm." And she would try to get some idea, she thought, of whether Margaret might be taking antidepressants.

CHAPTER XI.

SALLY ON THE TRAIL

It was dark in the san, and Tess was not very sure of the lay-out, but she admitted to herself ... that such minor hindrances did not matter to a person with such an unusual detective flair as her own. Now for some data. Gentle breathing told her that Miss Logan was asleep; experience told her that the patient's fruit would be placed within reach of the bed, and a resounding crash told her that she had knocked over a small table laden with china.

Nancy Breary, *So This Is School!*, 1959

SALLY telephoned Margaret the following morning and made arrangements to call round with the book at about eleven o'clock. She caught the No. 185 bus from Forest Hill to East Dulwich and then, consulting Rhian's *A-Z*, walked around to 28 Lonsdale Road. Margaret lived in a two-storey terraced house with a neat front garden. Sally rang the bell and soon heard footsteps clattering downstairs. Then the front door swung open and Margaret stood there smiling, clad as usual in long sleeves and jeans. It was much cooler today, at least, so she didn't look as uncomfortably hot as she had at the conference.

"Thanks so much for returning this," said Margaret when Sally handed over the book.

"That's okay," said Sally. "I'm staying in Forest Hill and I didn't really want to trust a valuable book like that to the post."

"Would you like a coffee?" Margaret asked.

"Yes, that would be lovely. Thank you."

Margaret showed Sally into the hall and then led her upstairs and into a room just along the landing. "We'll have to use my room, I'm afraid. We don't have a communal living-room and the kitchen is a bit of a mess," she said.

"That's fine," said Sally. "I remember my own house-sharing days."

"Make yourself at home," said Margaret. "I'll make a pot of coffee. How d'you take it?"

"If it's real coffee, white, without." Margaret replaced *The Unforgettable Fifth at Trebizon* on her bookshelf, and then disappeared.

The room that Sally found herself alone in was small and square with a single bed against one wall, a big bookcase on another, and a wardrobe and chest of drawers in the corner. A small pine desk stood in the bay window with Margaret's laptop on it. Sally aimed for the bookcase — all six shelves were devoted to children's books, though there were some large gaps between books, as if Margaret had been caught in the act of rearranging the shelves. Margaret owned a complete set of Chalet School paperbacks, plus three hardbacks in dustjackets; a complete set of Trebizon paperbacks; five Antonia Forest paperbacks; plus several Enid Blyton paperbacks, including Malory Towers, St Clare's, and the Naughtiest Girl books (the first three written by Enid Blyton, the later ones by Anne Digby) and J.K. Rowling's Harry Potter books.

There was also a pile of books on the desk — recent fill-ins for the Chalet School series, a couple of Maeve Binchy novels and some Miss Reads. The only sign Margaret ever read anything that wasn't comforting was *Strangers on a Train* by Patricia

Highsmith, which lay at the bottom of the pile.

On the desk beside Margaret's laptop sat a magazine, open at pages 4 and 5. Sally picked it up; it was called *Christians and Wildlife* and was a quarterly magazine put out by a Christian wildlife charity. She was about to put it back down again, open at where Margaret had left it, when her eye was caught by a news item on page 5; the small London office that the charity operated from had been badly vandalised a couple of months ago. The director had commented that the culprits were probably kids, but the police had said that they suspected only one person had been involved and that it appeared to have been an inside job; the security alarm had been turned off and the offender had appeared to know where everything worth trashing was. On the same page was a brief item welcoming a new office worker to the charity, replacing Margaret Wilks who had now left.

Sally frowned; the premises had been vandalised after Margaret had left, and the person had known the layout of the offices and how to turn the alarm off. She couldn't help wondering whether Margaret had been involved in some way. The vandalism somehow reminded her of the disappearance of Valerie's books and the burning books she and Leonie had found. Had Valerie upset Margaret in some way? Did Margaret's way of getting even with people who upset her involve wrecking their things?

Margaret came in, bearing a tray laden with coffee pot and mugs. She placed it on the desk, and invited Sally to sit down on the room's single armchair. She poured coffee, passed a mug to Sally, then perched on the bed.

"I was just looking at that magazine on your desk," said Sally. "I don't know it at all."

"Oh, it's the magazine put out by the charity I

used to work for," said Margaret brightly. "I still support the charity even though I no longer work there."

"When did you say you left?" Sally asked.

"In March. There was a restructure and my job disappeared." That was odd, Sally thought; the magazine article had made out that the new employee was a direct replacement for Margaret. She found herself suddenly interested in delving into Margaret's past a little — it wouldn't be hard to contact the charity, talk to Margaret's old boss, find out what had really happened with regard to Margaret's employment.

"I was looking at the news item about the offices being vandalised," Sally said casually. "That's terrible. It's awful when a charity is attacked like that."

Margaret flushed and hid her face behind her mug of coffee. "Yes," she said carefully, "it was terrible. Apparently it happened a couple of months ago — just before the magazine went to press."

"Do they have any idea who did it?"

"The magazine says kids or maybe an employee."

"Aren't you still in touch with some of the other employees, though? They'd know the inside gossip, surely?" Sally pressed.

"No," Margaret replied, "I don't keep in touch with them. You know how it is — they're all busy and I'm busy too really, what with job hunting and writing."

Sally changed the subject then; she didn't want to arouse Margaret's suspicions. If the opportunity arose, she thought, she'd get Margaret out of the room for a while again and take another look at the magazine — jot down the address and telephone number for the charity's offices. And maybe even poke around the room a bit — look in the wardrobe, in the drawers. It seemed a bit underhand, but Sally was sure that Margaret had something to hide. And maybe, ludicrous as it seemed, all this was somehow connected to Valerie's death.

So she instigated an animated discussion about school stories, and soon they had finished the pot of coffee. Margaret, glad of the company and enjoying the conversation, asked Sally if she had time to share another pot, and Sally happily agreed. Margaret disappeared, and Sally set quickly to work. She made a note of the charity's address — the offices were in Streatham, which was conveniently close to where Sally was staying — and then quietly opened Margaret's wardrobe.

At the bottom of the wardrobe was the backpack Margaret had taken to the conference. Keeping her ears pricked for footsteps, Sally carefully opened the backpack. Inside was a pile of hardback Chalet School and Abbey books, way too expensive to have been bought by an unemployed 22-year-old and, in their pristine condition, bearing a startling similarity to those that had been on Valerie Teague's stall on the opening night of the conference. Sally looked carefully through the titles then gingerly took out the one she was searching for.

Sally opened the first edition copy of *The Chalet School and the Lintons* to the second page of story. And there, just as she'd expected, were the markings she'd spotted when she'd thumbed through Valerie's copy on the opening night. Biro markings where some previous owner had, inexplicably, counted the number of words in each paragraph.

Now that she knew Margaret *had* stolen Valerie's books, Sally wasn't too sure what to do. She carefully placed *Lintons* back where she'd found it, closed the backpack and wardrobe and settled back down in the armchair. She didn't feel comfortable about tackling Margaret about the books — Margaret had stolen from Valerie and had apparently wrecked her former employer's offices. She might well have killed Valerie, for all Sally knew — who knew what she was capable of?

Certainly the whole book thing seemed to have been planned — Sally remembered how heavy Margaret's backpack had been en route to the conference and guessed it'd been full of the novels that Sally and Leonie had later found burning. Their weight in the backpack had been replaced by Valerie's books, but so many questions remained — how had Margaret got into the locked room? Why had she burnt the novels? Probably she needed to go to the police with this, but first, Sally thought, she'd discuss it with Rhian, see if together they could make some sense of it all.

Margaret returned with the fresh pot of coffee, but somehow Sally couldn't bring herself to resume their lighthearted discussion of school stories. Instead, she fingered her mug hesitantly, and finally said, "Margaret, do you mind if I ask you something? It's a bit awkward."

A guarded expression crossed Margaret's face. "Yes?" she asked frostily.

"It's just that I've noticed you always wear long sleeves whatever the weather ... and ... Well, on that day in the chapel, one of the sleeves rolled up and I noticed ..."

Margaret visibly relaxed. "I do cut myself," she admitted, matter-of-factly, "when I'm stressed out. But I'm already getting help for it, if that's what you were going to suggest."

"Well, yes, I was," Sally admitted.

"My GP knows and I'm seeing a counsellor. I'm also attending a self-help group. So I'm doing everything I possibly can to get better."

"Is it helping?"

Margaret sighed. "It's hard to tell, really. I think I am getting better — a bit better — but often after a counselling session when I've been talking about stuff that really bothers me, well, I find sometimes it can make things worse. But that's normal, apparently."

"That makes sense, in a way," Sally said. "What about antidepressants? Did your GP recommend those?"

"No," said Margaret. "Which is good really, I guess, but I sometimes wish he'd give me some. Much easier than having to work your way through things in counselling sessions and self-help groups."

Sally finished her coffee and rose. "I'm really going to have to leave now. I'm meeting a friend in the city this afternoon and I don't want to leave it too late to catch the bus." She pulled on her coat. "I hope you didn't mind my bringing that up, Margaret. It's just that I was worried."

"No," Margaret smiled. "It's OK. I didn't mind at all. I'll see you out."

At the front door, Margaret said, "Thank you for coming. It was lovely to see you again and have a chat about G.O. I've missed that already since the conference!"

"Oh, well, it couldn't have been more convenient for me to call round here," said Sally. "Actually I was really surprised when I discovered you lived here in East Dulwich. When I met you on the station at Clinton Manning I imagined you were travelling south to Cotterford Dene."

"Oh," said Margaret, "I visited my aunt in Nottingham for a couple of days. I bought a return train ticket via Clinton Manning — you can break your return journey."

"Right," said Sally, not really believing her. "Well,

it was nice to see you again, Margaret. Take care of yourself." And she walked out into the street and headed in the direction of the bus stop.

CHAPTER XII.

A DISCOVERY

" ... And when I looked into it closely, I observed that whenever there was a robbery there had been books for sale; sometimes merely as part of a much bigger sale, but sometimes alone. I got firmly fixed in my head, some sort of connexion between the robberies and books. I sort of got a hunch about it.

"So whilst other people were working on all sorts of other theories, I stuck to mine about books and plodded along at that."

A. Stephen Tring, *Penny Dreadful*, 1949

SALLY wasn't meeting anybody in the city; she'd used that as a convenient excuse for getting away from Margaret. Her plan for the day, after dropping the book off at Margaret's, had been to explore the sights of Dulwich. But as she walked to the bus stop, she found her curiosity sufficiently aroused to debate travelling over to Streatham and trying to talk to someone at Wild for God. After looking through the *A-Z* and Lonely Planet guide, though, she reluctantly decided against it. Streatham might be close enough to East Dulwich as the crow flies, but it wasn't on a bus route from there; she'd need to go to a train station and catch one of the irregular trains west. It would be better to go by car, if Rhian would lend her hers or drive her over. And in the interim, she realised, she could at least glean *some* of the information she needed

A DISCOVERY

with a phone call to the Wild for God charity. So she decided to head back to Rhian's.

She had to wait fifteen minutes for a bus and then, as London legend had it, three came along at once. And just another fifteen minutes later, she was ensconced in Rhian's flat, jotting down notes for a cover story she intended to use to speak to Wild for God. The director's name was Robin Horlick, and Sally found herself put through to him straightaway despite the fact it was lunchtime. She introduced herself a little self-consciously — her name was Sally Meredith, she was a human resources officer with a small media agency in south-east London, and they were currently recruiting an administrator. A previous employee of his, Margaret Wilks, had applied for the job, been interviewed, and had given his name as a reference.

"I see," he said, a little heavily, when Sally had finished.

"Is providing a reference a problem?" Sally asked.

"I'm not sure," he said. "I'm just very surprised that she's given my name as a referee, that's all."

"But you are her last employer, and on our application form we specifically asked for a reference from the candidates' last employer," Sally said, beginning to warm to her cover story.

"Right. I see." He paused. "What exactly has Margaret told you about her employment here?"

"Well, simply that she was employed in an administrative position, and the tasks she carried out in that position are comparable with those we would expect her to carry out," said Sally. "She also told us she left you in a company restructure."

"A restructure? No, that's not quite accurate," said Robin Horlick.

"No? Why did she leave, then?" Sally asked.

"Well ... we sacked her," Robin said. "She had

some — let's just say — emotional problems and this led to a great deal of absenteeism. In fact, she called in sick on average twice a fortnight. Then sometimes she would be ill and need to go home mid-afternoon. Her absenteeism affected her ability to do her job and affected our productivity badly. We tried to help her — even encouraged her to see a doctor or seek counselling — but in the end, it became too difficult to work with her, and we asked her to leave."

"These problems," said Sally. "Would they be to do with the self-harm?"

"She told you about that?" Robin Horlick asked, surprised.

"She did," said Sally, realising that this was the only honest comment she'd made in their entire conversation. How easy it was, she thought exultantly, to get information by pretending to be someone you weren't — perhaps Rhian was right and she would enjoy this investigating lark after all.

"Then maybe she's tackling her problems head on; that's a good sign," he said.

"If you leave the self-harm and the absenteeism out of the equation," said Sally, "would you say that Margaret would make a good employee?"

"Being honest with you, no I wouldn't," he replied. "She seemed enthusiastic about the job to begin with, but after a while, when she came in at all, she tended not to be particularly conscientious. She'd spend a lot of time online, for example, and she also used to spend time writing stories when she should have been working. Certainly if she'd been diligent at work, then we might not have sacked her in relation to the absenteeism, given that we were aware of the emotional problems she was having."

Sally wondered whether it was worth asking him about the vandalism and whether he suspected

Margaret of playing any part in it. It was possible he might become suspicious, start to doubt her cover story. But then, she told herself, perhaps that didn't matter — she'd already gleaned more information from him than she'd expected.

"When Margaret applied for the position with us," she said, "we got hold of a copy of your magazine to see what sort of company she'd worked for before. I read about the vandalism at your office — that sounded very unpleasant."

"It was," he replied. "It's not very nice to come into work in the morning and find everything wrecked — all our files had been destroyed and paint had been thrown over all the walls. Even a couple of computer monitors had been smashed. Why are you asking about this?" he added, suddenly suspicious.

"Oh, it's just that the article said it appeared to be an inside job — and, well, after what you were saying about Margaret, I wondered—."

"Wondered if she might be responsible? Well, so did we for a while, because when the police asked if anyone might have any grudges against us, she was the one who sprang to mind. She'd been sacked and was angry about it. And we hadn't changed the security combination after she'd left. The police looked into it, and she had a solid alibi for the night in question — she was away in Scotland with her church, with about forty people all vouching for her. So whatever else she was, she wasn't our vandal."

―――

"All very interesting," said Rhian that evening. They'd gone out for dinner, to a small Italian restaurant around the corner from Rhian's flat. At weekends you had to book well in advance given that it only had ten tables. On a Tuesday night, though, it was much quieter, and Rhian had booked it only that morning. It was a quiet, intimate restaurant, with lacy tablecloths and flickering candles on each table. All the other diners appeared to be couples.

"I was hoping that Margaret was responsible for the vandalism," Sally sighed. "If there'd been proof of that, I felt I could go to the police at Cotterford with that information as well as the stuff about the books. If I just tell them about finding the books in the backpack, Arrowman will laugh at me."

"He shouldn't — they're books of Valerie's that were stolen and have turned up in a delegate's bag." A waiter arrived with a large plate of antipasto and a bottle of white wine for them to share.

Sally waited until the waiter had left their table before responding. "Even if Valerie was murdered, the two things might not be connected." She sipped her wine.

"They must be, surely? It would be odd if they weren't."

"You know what *is* odd? The whole book thing. I know that Margaret stole the books. Now, if you take away the fact that she somehow got them out of a locked room, stealing the books is a reasonable thing to do—."

"Oh, yeah?"

"I don't really mean reasonable," Sally corrected herself. "Maybe excusable, if you're in your early twenties, broke, love the books and can't afford them. She wouldn't be the only person in the world to steal something that she couldn't afford to buy. *But* why go to the trouble of burning the novels? I'm guessing that she took them with her, because her backpack was heavy on the day we travelled to the conference — she couldn't have fitted any more in."

"She could have had a second bag," Rhian

suggested. "You didn't see her leave."

"True," Sally acknowledged. "But if she didn't burn the novels, who did? There has to be a connection — there are far too many weird things going on for there not to be."

"Do you know for sure it was her? Did you see her at the folk dancing thing you were doing when Valerie collapsed?"

Sally tucked into the antipasto while she cast her mind back to the Saturday night folk dancing. "Yes, she was there for a while at least. I remember noticing how hot she was getting because she was wearing a long black skirt and a black cardigan. I only noticed her once, though — I don't recall seeing her when the food came out."

"And in black clothes she could sneak around the grounds unseen." Rhian finished her glass of wine, poured herself another, then topped up Sally's glass. "Did you see her again that night?"

"No, but—." Sally remembered the Twenty Questions thread that Margaret had started on the Chalet Girls forum on Saturday; it hadn't struck her before but the character Margaret had been thinking of was Anne Seymour, who had *almost burnt Joey's first published book*.

"Go on," urged Rhian.

A disbelieving grin spread over Rhian's face as Sally explained about the Twenty Questions thread. "Do you really play these games, Sal? At your age?"

"So what?" Sally returned, a little defensively. "Everyone needs *some* relaxation."

"What do your kids think about their mum still reading school stories in her forties?"

"They're so busy I doubt they even notice. Anyway, it could be worse — I could still be playing Bay City Rollers records at full bore."

Rhian changed the subject. "So why do you think

Margaret posted that thing on the forum? Was it her way of making a confession?"

Sally shrugged. "I don't know. But, if you don't mind, when I get back to your place, I wouldn't mind checking out some old threads on the forum."

"Why?"

"Just to see whether, on the day the Wild for God offices were vandalised, she posted something alluding to vandalism."

Rhian had broadband, so Sally was able to access the internet on her laptop. She first Googled on Wild for God and found a news report that included the date the offices had been vandalised — the early hours of 3 June. She then clicked on her bookmarked Chalet Girls website — it had been active post-conference, with several threads on some of the seminars that had taken place. Sally clicked on the Games folder; only one Twenty Questions had been started on 3 June and not by Margaret. Even so, Sally trawled quickly through the thread.

From: JR15
To: All
Thinking of someone …

From: Leonie Carr
To: JR15
A pupil?

From: JR15
To: Leonie Carr
Yes, a pupil

From: margaretwilks

A DISCOVERY 117

To: JR15
A pupil in the Tyrol years?

From: JR15
To: margaretwilks
No, not in Tyrol years

From: Jack Maynard's Mistress
To: JR15
In the Swiss years?

From: JR15
To: Jack Maynard's Mistress
No, not the Swiss years!

From: Jack Maynard's Mistress
To: JR15
The island years, then!

From: JR15
To: Jack Maynard's Mistress
Yes, a pupil on St Briavel's

From: emer1984
To: JR15
A prefect?

From: JR15
To: emer1984
No, not a prefect

From: Jack Maynard's Mistress
To: JR15
A prefect later on, then — not just on St Briavel's

From: JR15
To: Jack Maynard's Mistress

No, never a prefect

From: kiwichaletfan
To: JR15
Does she attend the CS at Plas Howell or in Switzerland as well as on St Briavel's?

From: JR15
To: kiwichaletfan
No she doesn't

From: Leonie Carr
To: JR15
Is she the same age as Mary-Lou Trelawney?

From: JR15
To: Leonie Carr
No

From: Leonie Carr
To: JR15
Did she attend the *other* Chalet School before coming to the CS?

From: JR15
To: Leonie Carr
Yes, she did!

From: Leonie Carr
To: JR15
Is it Diana Skelton?

And, JR15's response confirmed, the person she was thinking of in the hours following the vandalism at Wild for God was indeed Diana Skelton. The girl who, in *Bride Leads the Chalet School*, had completely trashed the headgirl's study.

CHAPTER XIII.

A STRANGE ALLIANCE

"We've got to know a bit more about it first," said Tish stubbornly. "There was something creepy about Miss Angel. You felt it too, didn't you, Rebeck — ?"

Rebecca nodded.

"And why did they pick on *Trebizon* to pull to pieces?" persisted Tish. "And assuming they knew about Mulberry Island, how did they know? And how did they know to interview Mrs Tarkas and that she's a gas-bag and scandal-monger?"

Anne Digby, *Fourth Year Triumphs at Trebizon*, 1985

"JR15," said Rhian, after Sally had shown her the message thread and had explained the significance behind it. "Do you know who she is?"

Sally shook her head. They were both seated at Rhian's dining table, coffee in hand, the laptop in front of them. Sally placed her mug on the nearest coaster and clicked on JR15's profile.

"The only significant information here," she said, "is that JR15 has only made 12 posts in the six months she's been a member, and most of them are in that particular thread. And we know that information is accurate, because her posts have been counted by the website software. The rest of the information in her profile — that she's from the north of England and that she's in her twenties — doesn't have to be correct." Sally clicked on a link that said 'view all posts by this user'. The only thread JR15 had posted in other than her own one on Twenty Questions was the Twenty Questions Margaret had posted on Saturday.

"Could she be Margaret posting under another name?" suggested Rhian.

"She *could* be. She could be *any* of the forum regulars posting under another name. Cyberspace is full of weirdos, and book forums, including those devoted to school stories, are no exception in attracting them."

"What about the initials JR? Did anyone at the conference have them?" Rhian queried.

Sally shook her head. "I don't know. I didn't meet everybody. I suppose I could ask Miriam Lorrimer for a list of delegates."

"That's a good idea. And what about the forum host for this site — wouldn't she have access to more information about JR15? Like an email address she signed up with, something like that?"

"Perhaps," said Sally. "Leonie Carr's the forum host. I got on quite well with her at the conference. It was Leonie who was with me when I found the burning books."

"Okay, then," said Rhian. "It's getting too late to bother people now, but tomorrow you phone Leonie Carr and see what she can tell you about JR15, and I'll get on to Miriam Lorrimer and ask for a list of delegates. I'll also get on to the police and see what stage they're at with the investigation. There must be an inquest coming up soon, I'd have thought."

Sally telephoned Leonie Carr early the next morning and caught her before she left for work. She and Rhian had discussed whether or not to tell

Leonie what they had discovered, and had decided there was probably no harm in enlightening her. Leonie had, after all, been with Sally when the burning books were discovered, and wasn't a friend of Margaret's. It was possible, of course, that she was a friend of JR15's, but Sally and Rhian decided they'd have to risk that. Leonie was unlikely to give out private details about a forum member to Sally without explanation.

The only thing Sally omitted to tell Leonie was about her discovery of Valerie's books in Margaret's backpack. If she told Leonie that, she thought, the news could, through the 'girls' own' grapevine, make its way back to Margaret and give her the chance to hide the books before it became a police matter. So she simply told Leonie that Margaret had made a post related to book burning on the day they had found the burning books — and that JR15 had made a post related to vandalism on the day Margaret's previous place of employment had been trashed.

"How peculiar!" said Leonie, enjoying Sally's story immensely. "I love the idea of mysterious messages being left on my forum! Hold on, I'll just check out JR15's email domain for you. But if she's signed up with a Yahoo address or something like that, I won't be much help." She was silent for a while and Sally could only hear the tapping of keys. Then Leonie said, "Here we are — JR15. Now, *that's* interesting."

"What's that?" asked Sally.

"Well her email domain is haweshill.ac.uk, which is Haweshill University."

"Right," said Sally, doubtfully. She had no idea where Haweshill University was — presumably it was one of the old polytechnics that had been upgraded to universities since she left the UK.

"It's just that the only person I know who works at Haweshill University and who has those initials is Jess Gibson's daughter Justine. Her full name's Justine Rose Gibson."

"Jess from Tales Out of School?"

"Yes. I don't know why I never bothered looking up her email address before. I suppose she hasn't posted much and I didn't pay any attention to her. If I'd checked, I'd have realised it was a little odd."

"Why?"

"Because Justine Gibson has no time at all for her mother's interest in school stories. She never has done, and thinks it's a complete waste of time and money. There's no way known she'd be playing around on Chalet Girls."

"I suppose it might not be her," said Sally. "There could be other folk with the initials JR at Haweshill University. Where is Haweshill by the way?"

"Oh, I'm surprised you didn't notice it on a map or a signpost when you were at the conference," said Leonie. "Haweshill's in Warwickshire, just north of Cotterford — not very far away from Clinton Manning."

A search on the Friends Reunited site revealed that Margaret Wilks and Justine Gibson had not attended the same school or university. But if they hadn't met through school, university or the 'girls' own' world, then they had obviously met through some other interest. Margaret's profile on Friends Reunited simply said that she was between jobs after being made redundant in a recent company restructure, and that she spent most of her time writing. Justine who, like Margaret, was in her early twenties, had written in her profile that she was currently working in the Haweshill University library and played golf in her spare time. Did

Margaret play golf, Sally wondered — she couldn't imagine it. For one thing Margaret wouldn't be able to afford to play on her local golf course, Dulwich & Sydnenham — a course that had, according to Rhian, once been favoured by Margaret Thatcher's husband, Denis.

Sally had arranged to meet Fiona for lunch in Covent Garden and decided this was probably good timing — Fiona was a librarian and might well know someone who worked at Haweshill University library. She glanced at Rhian's kitchen clock — it was still a couple of hours before she needed to make the journey by bus and tube to central London. There was nothing more she could do as far as the Margaret/Justine mystery was concerned — at least not till she'd spoken to Fiona, and later to Rhian. Despite her initial misgivings about investigating the case at all, Sally was now becoming intrigued by the mystery surrounding Margaret and Justine, and wondering whether their acts of vandalism and pyromania had anything at all to do with the death of Valerie Teague. She thought that a trip back to Warwickshire to find out a little more about Justine Gibson was definitely on the cards. In the meantime, though, she decided she may as well head into central London early and do a little sightseeing.

It had been a long time since Sally had set foot in London, and while many things had changed, much of it was still comfortingly familiar. She revisited the National Portrait Gallery and enjoyed looking at the portraits of contemporary politicians, royals and celebrities, before hurrying up to Frith Street to find the Greek restaurant where she'd arranged to have lunch with Fiona.

Fiona was smartly dressed in a light suit, momentarily surprising Sally who was used to seeing her in casual clothes. Still, she realised, this was the first time she'd ever met Fiona during working hours and seen her in professional attire. When they had ordered, she brought Fiona up to date with developments on the case, and asked her if she had any contacts at Haweshill University library.

"Not directly, but I do have a friend who has a friend who works there," said Fiona. "I met her once at a party. Her name's Catherine Dallow. I could probably phone her up and ask about Justine — though what is it exactly that you want me to ask about her?"

"I'm not sure," Sally admitted. "I suppose I just want to work out what the connection is between her and Margaret. I know Margaret worked for a Christian charity, so presumably she's a churchgoer. If Justine is a Christian, that could be the connection. They're about the same age, and there are so many inter-church conventions and rallies that they could have met each other that way."

"What about through the charity Margaret worked for?"

"Wild for God? Yes, it's possible — I hadn't thought of that," Sally admitted. "But if you can find out that she's definitely a Christian, that might be a good start."

"I don't know," said Fiona, doubtfully. "Setting fire to things and trashing offices doesn't seem very Christian to me."

"Oh well, often so-called Christians do some very strange things. You only have to read the newspapers to find that out," Sally pointed out.

"True," Fiona nodded. The waiter brought along their mineral water and tsatsiki and bread.

"Have you thought that they might have met online — in a chat room or something?" Fiona asked.

"They could have," Sally agreed, "and given that they could have used any number of pseudonyms, it'll make it really hard to find them in cyberspace."

"Not everyone uses lots of pseudonyms, though," Fiona pointed out. "You said Margaret uses her own name for the school story forums — if she's game to do that, then why wouldn't she use her own name for forums that *aren't* for adult fans of schoolgirl stories?"

Sally made a face at her. "Good point. But where do I begin with anything like that? I can't just go into every forum that exists on the internet and look for posters called margaretwilks and JR15." As she was speaking the thought struck her: she could look for those usernames in livejournal at least, and perhaps in other book forums, and take it from there. Margaret and Justine might both be into cosy fiction of the Miss Read variety. Or perhaps crime fiction — Margaret had, after all, had a copy of *Strangers on a Train* in her room ...

"*Strangers on a Train!*" she exclaimed.

"What?" said Fiona.

"*Strangers on a Train*. You know — the Patricia Highsmith novel where two strangers agree to commit murder for each other. Margaret had a copy in her room — I *thought* it seemed out of place with all the other books she had."

"So?"

"*So*," Sally said excitedly, "I think Margaret and Justine are acting out that scenario — they know each other somehow, through something, but nobody knows that. So they're committing crimes for each other, perhaps for revenge. Margaret has a grudge against the guy who sacked her and his offices are vandalised. So perhaps Justine has a grudge against Valerie Teague and her books are burnt—"

"Except they weren't," Fiona pointed out.

"No — but Margaret tried to convey the impression they had been. I suspect she carried those books with her so that she could burn them, then she smuggled home the books that she'd arrange with Justine that she'd burn." After all, thought Sally, no 'girls' own' devotee could really burn first-edition Chalets or Abbeys.

"It all sounds rather fanciful," Fiona mused. "But you could have a point. After all, they were sending each other messages through the discussion board basically saying 'the deed has been done'."

"Absolutely," said Sally. "So all we need to do is to find out how Margaret and Justine know each other and what exactly Justine had against Valerie Teague to want her books destroyed."

"Not to mention stolen out of a locked room," said Fiona.

"I think Justine may hold — pardon the pun — the key to that," said Sally. "She lives close enough to Cotterford, and may well have attended a conference there and somehow got hold of a key. That's something else you could find out for me, Fiona — whether the library she works in has attended a conference at Cotterford Manor this year."

"Great," said Fiona, grimacing. "And what will you be doing while I'm doing all these jobs?"

Sally grinned. "Getting in touch with some of the delegates and finding out whether they know anything about a link between Justine Gibson and Valerie Teague."

CHAPTER XIV.

A GOSSIP WITH BRIDGET

> "Excuse me," said the man, before Georgie could reply. "I confess to a certain curiosity. Where do you go to school?"
>
> "The Grange!" both girls said together, and Georgie elaborated: "It's a lovely old house at High Lennet — on the borders of Hampshire and Dorset. It's a riding-school really — at least, it was. Last term it opened as a boarding-school as well, though everyone rides — except me!"

Mary Gervaise, *Ponies in Clover*, 1952

BRIDGET Whodcoat was home when Sally rang her on her mobile. She said she had no other plans for the afternoon and would be happy to catch up with Sally. "It would be great to see you again," she told Sally, "and I'd invite you to my place, but with the renovations being done it's not exactly relaxing around here! If you're at Covent Garden, we could meet somewhere, perhaps ... what about Camden? You could walk down to Leicester Square and take the Northern Line north to Camden Town. Or better still, get off at Chalk Farm. There are a few decent cafés along Chalk Farm Road, and if you wanted to wander around Camden Lock Market later, it's not too far to walk."

They agreed to meet at the Bluebell Café on the corner of Regent's Park Road and Chalk Farm Road forty-five minutes later. Sally and Fiona settled the bill and went their separate ways. They were meeting up again that evening, together with Rhian: it was tonight that they were going to see *King Lear* at the Globe Theatre.

Bridget was already seated outside the café when Sally arrived. She was reading a book and sipping latte. Her hair was tied back in a pony-tail and she was wearing a dark green shirt, long khaki-coloured shorts and green shoes. She looked up and smiled when Sally joined her.

"Hi, Sally. Thanks for phoning me. It's good to see you again." She nodded towards the café's open door. "You have to go in and order but they'll bring it out to you. Would you mind ordering another latte for me while you're in there? I've nearly finished this one."

Sally went inside to order the drinks. The café was small, but crammed with people and there was a queue at the counter. It was a sunny day again and the café was hot and stuffy; the whirring fan only blew hot air around. Why was it, Sally wondered, that the British didn't seem to understand that the way to keep your house or premises cool in the heat of the day was *not* to open doors and windows to the elements? Finally, she reached the front of the queue, ordered the coffees and rejoined Bridget outside.

Bridget downed the remainder of her coffee, and put her book to one side.

"What's that you're reading?" Sally asked.

"*Storm Ahead* by Monica Edwards. Brilliant book. Have you read it?" Bridget held the book out for Sally to look at.

Sally took it from her. "No, I've never read Monica Edwards," she said. "I'm not into pony books — the only ones I read are by Mary Gervaise, and that's because they're really school stories despite their titles." She leafed through the book. It was a first edition, in excellent condition.

"I bought it from a bookshop in Charing Cross Road a few weeks ago," said Bridget. "Some of the bookshops have a good range of G.O. titles, but of course they're hideously expensive." She shrugged. "I'm lucky. I can afford to buy them. She's a good writer, Monica Edwards," she added. "You should try her books. I wouldn't really describe them as pony books, though there are ponies in them. But they're not pony books like Ruby Ferguson's Jill books, for example. Mind you, I love the Jills as well."

"Do you ride?" Sally asked her. Sally had never been on a horse in her life and didn't wish to. Anything she knew about horses she'd gleaned from her Mary Gervaises.

"Gosh, yes. I grew up in the country, and in the country, my dear, we learn to ride before we can walk."

Sally smiled. "You seem to have lived the life of a 'girls' own' heroine. I'm quite jealous."

Bridget laughed. "I suppose I have really. Boarding-school from age eleven. A pony of my own and gymkhanas during the holidays. I did everything apart from chase crooks down secret passages *à la* Famous Five. So I still feel I had a deprived childhood!"

"Well, I didn't get to do any of those things, so I'm *definitely* deprived," Sally grinned. "Was boarding-school fun?"

"Lord, no. I hated it. I cried every night during my first year there. I'm sure some boarding-schools are decent places, but not Upland Park, even in the 1980s when I was there. I suppose it's better now, but it was horrendous then. Bullying was rife, they even still used the cane. Awful place. I'd never send either of my boys to boarding-school. They go to the local comp. And a far better education it is too." She chuckled again. "And, of course, what I save on school fees I can spend on first editions of my favourite books."

Not really wanting to get into the politics of state versus private education, Sally decided it was time to begin questioning Bridget about Justine Gibson. On the tube ride to Chalk Farm, she'd worked out a cover story that she thought sounded plausible.

"I'm glad we could meet up, Bridget," she said, "because I wanted your advice on something." Bridget nodded, and she continued, " 'girls' own' is very popular in Australia and I've been wondering whether to approach the Tales Out of School people about running a similar conference out there. Do you think they'd be interested?"

Bridget frowned. "I don't know. It would depend on the expense, I suppose, and whether they'd get enough delegates to make it profitable. Where would you hold it? Sydney?"

"Melbourne. I could probably get the magazine I work for involved in some way — perhaps as sponsors."

"Well, you should ask Miriam Lorrimer about it. The worst she can do is say no."

"What about Jess Gibson? Is she still actively involved?"

"Hmm. Not really. The way her health's been, Miriam hasn't wanted to bother her with trivial stuff — which Tales Out of School is, in the grand scheme of things. That's the other problem, of course — Miriam has to organise everything on her own nowadays, which is a lot of work. I'd be surprised if she'd agree to organising a conference on the other side of the world, to be honest. But you should still ask."

"If anything happens to Jess, will anyone take

over from her?" Sally asked.

"With Tales Out of School? I shouldn't have thought so. Miriam has put out feelers a couple of times, looking for a partner to share the workload, but no-one's really interested. I mean — it's a lot of work with little thanks and a lot of flak. Who needs it?"

A waitress came out with Sally's cappuccino, Bridget's latte and a bottle of water and two glasses. Both Sally and Bridget filled their glasses and drank the water gratefully.

"Jess has a daughter, doesn't she?" asked Sally, casually. "Would she be interested in taking over from her mother with Tales Out of School?"

"Hardly!" Bridget laughed. "I've met Justine a couple of times over at Jess's and she certainly has very little time for her mother's interest. In fact, once poor old Jess dies, her book collection will be up on eBay within hours, I should think, and sold to the highest bidder. I'm sympathetic towards her in a way," she continued. "It must be pretty hard being fifteen years old and having friends or a boyfriend come to your house and find the living room full of school stories and your mother sitting down reading one. I can understand a kid feeling a bit embarrassed by that. Still," she shrugged, "that's easy for me to say. I'm lucky — I've got a separate room where I keep my books. The boys' friends never get to see them, so they don't get teased about their eccentric mama."

"I used to have a separate room for books till my husband left and we had to sell our house and move into a smaller place," said Sally. "Now I keep my school stories in my bedroom and my other books in bookcases in the living room."

"You have kids, don't you?" Bridget asked.

"Yes — a girl and a boy. Eleanor's nineteen and

Angus is nearly eighteen."

"Does Eleanor enjoy the books?"

"No — unfortunately she's never been much of a reader, even as a child. She never liked English at school, always preferred the sciences," Sally sighed. "I was always really disappointed about that — I always wanted my daughter to enjoy the books I read as a child. Well, just to enjoy books, come to that. But if she has her nose in a book, you can bet it's a text book. She's studying to be a vet. Still," she continued more cheerfully, "Angus has always liked reading, and while he's never been tempted by my Chalets, he did at least enjoy a few Enid Blytons and Malcolm Savilles before Harry Potter came along!"

"I think every mother wants her daughter to enjoy what she read as a child," Bridget said. "There are quite a few mothers around who have successfully introduced their daughters to the Chalet School and other school stories."

"But Jessica Gibson clearly wasn't one of them," said Sally, hoping this didn't sound too clumsy a way of getting back on topic. "Did Jess drag her along to all the conferences she organised?" Sally asked.

"No — well, if she did, she didn't take her to any of the ones that I attended, and I've been to most things that Jess has been involved in setting up. I only met her a couple of times — both times at Jess's house. Once when Justine was a teenager and once last year. I'd heard about Jess being ill and went to visit. Justine was there and was very scathing about my being 'one of your Chalet School friends, Mother'. No, I don't think we'll see Justine at the helm of Tales Out of School when Jess dies."

"I should think having a mother really into school stories and having to meet several other somewhat eccentric collectors might put you off for life," Sally said, with a laugh. "Imagine having someone like Valerie Teague come round to your house, for example." Oh, dear, she thought — that really *did* sound clumsy.

But Bridget didn't seem to notice because she was cheerfully agreeing, "Oh yes, that would have been dire. I don't know if Justine would ever have met Valerie, though," she continued. "Valerie's never really made friends on the scene — well, you could see why for yourself. I don't suppose she ever had reason to call round on Jess and so would never have met Justine. So I think Jess did the putting Justine off school-story collectors all by herself! Or maybe I helped, when I called round there," she added, grinning.

That seemed to poke a ruddy great hole in the *Strangers on a Train* theory, thought Sally ruefully. If Justine had never met Valerie, why would she ask Margaret to damage Valerie's books? Unless it was perhaps in revenge for something Valerie had done to upset her mother?

"How did Valerie get on with Jess?" Sally asked. "She seemed to give Miriam a tough time at the conference."

"Oh, Valerie gave everybody a tough time," Bridget replied. "I don't think there was anybody in the world she actually liked. Her dealings with Jess were generally like what you saw with Miriam — complaining about the space she'd been given for her books at book sales, complaining about the content of the conference, complaining that the rest of us were too noisy. I don't recall her having any bust-ups with Jess about anything other than those run-of-the-mill things, and I don't recall her being particularly friendly towards her either. That's one good thing," she added. "If you do get your conference down under off the ground, Sally, then at least you won't have to put up with the book dealer from hell demanding exactly the right stall."

"Oh well," Sally responded, finishing her latte, "if I do get it off the ground, I dare say Australia will have some difficult characters of its own."

After leaving Bridget, Sally decided to go for a walk along the towpath of the Grand Union Canal before exploring Camden Lock Market then making her way back to central London. She felt like she'd spent much of her time in London eating and drinking copious amounts of coffee and wine. She was meeting Rhian and Fiona for dinner at South Bank before going to watch *King Lear*, and couldn't possibly imbibe any more liquid or eat any more food until she'd taken some exercise and blown all the cobwebs away.

What Bridget had said certainly hadn't helped the *Strangers on a Train* theory; all the same, Sally felt sure she was right and that there was some connection between Justine Gibson and Valerie Teague. And it had to be some recent connection for Justine to have reacted as strongly as she did to whatever Valerie had done to upset her. Some put-down by Valerie to the teenaged Justine Gibson would surely not have resulted in the younger woman seeking revenge nearly ten years later. She walked briskly, glad of the exercise. Glancing at her watch, she realised there probably wasn't time to walk all the way to Little Venice and back as well as see something of the market, but given she'd come out this way, she might as well explore as much of the towpath as she could and put the Margaret/Justine mystery out of her mind for a little while.

CHAPTER XV.

FIONA FINDS THE LINK

What more might have been said on the subject was lost, for at that moment the Chorus entered to take up their position, and the Choragus, or Leader of the Chorus, began the intoning with which the play opens. This was followed by a tableau ... A second tableau ... followed, and then there was a rustle as people settled themselves finally. The Play proper now began.

Elinor M. Brent-Dyer, *The Chalet School and Jo*, 1930

RHIAN was already seated at the table she'd booked in a dimly lit, busy and noisy French restaurant near the Globe when Sally arrived. As Sally joined her, Rhian said, "I had a text from Fee a few minutes ago — she was held up at work and will be about ten minutes late. She said to go ahead without her and she'll just have a main course when she gets here."

Sally sat down and perused the menu. "I think I might just have a main course too. My body's getting tired of so much food."

"I ordered some red wine," Rhian said. "I hope you're not getting tired of the old *vino* too?"

"I am, a little," Sally admitted, with a grin. "I don't usually drink as much as I have over the past couple of days."

"You've lost your touch with drinking since you've lived in Australia, you know that?"

"Well, Phil wasn't much of a drinker, so once I was with him I found myself naturally cutting back. We just used to have a glass of wine over dinner, and once he left I didn't bother even with that — the kids weren't old enough to drink and I didn't want them to grow up seeing their mother drinking on her own, even if it was just one glass of wine with a meal."

"Phil wasn't much of a drinker? I thought Aussies were synonymous with alcohol?"

Sally smiled. "For all their reputation, Australians just don't drink as much as the English — or the Welsh," she added in response to Rhian's glare. "Did you find out about Valerie Teague's inquest today?" she asked.

"All of a sudden you really *are* interested in the Valerie Teague case, aren't you?" Rhian teased.

"Well, it's become very intriguing now." She told Rhian what she'd discovered since they'd parted at breakfast time.

"*Very* weird," Rhian said when Sally had finished talking. "How do you think it ties in with Valerie's death, though? Oh, the wine — great."

When the waiter had poured their wine and taken their orders, Sally said, "I don't know how it ties in with Valerie's death — if at all. But it's clear they agreed to commit a crime for each other probably in revenge for something — I'd just like to work out how they actually know each other in the first place. But perhaps Fee will have some answers when she arrives."

"Well, I got a list of delegates faxed through from Miriam Lorrimer," said Rhian. "Very efficient lady. Could do with her in the *Clarion* library. I suppose the list is irrelevant now that you have the identity of JR15, though. There are no JRs on the list, anyway." She passed the list across the table to

Sally. "I also spoke to Arrowman — ah, here's Fee."

"Sorry I'm late," said Fiona, looking pink and out of breath. "I got caught up with something at work just at the last minute. Then, of course, it took ages for the tube to arrive. As ever when you're in a hurry."

"Here, have some wine and relax," said Rhian, pouring Shiraz into Fiona's glass. "Have a look at the menu — when you're ready to order, I'll call the old *garçon*." They all giggled, remembering French lessons from long-ago schooldays when every British child had been told that the way to summon the waiter in France was to click one's fingers and call out, "*Garçon!*" No wonder so many British travellers to France had complained of poor service.

When Fiona had ordered a main course, Rhian resumed what she'd been saying to Sally earlier. "According to Arrowman, an inquest into Valerie's death was opened and adjourned yesterday. There'll be a full inquest in a couple of weeks. He thinks an open verdict will be recorded and, failing that, misadventure. They found some phenelzine in her bathroom cupboard, so it seems she never finished the course. So they're still working on the theory that she had a couple of tablets floating around in her bag and took them by mistake when she was so annoyed on Saturday. In a way, it makes more sense than someone else having given them to her in order to kill her or at least poison her. Even if the person managed somehow to smuggle them into her food — and at a conference with that many delegates," she went on, nodding in the direction of Miriam's list, "you'd run a real risk of someone else inadvertently consuming it — those sort of tablets are impossible to get hold of unless you have a prescription for them yourself. That's why, to me, Margaret still seems a possibility," she said. "I know you said she said she's never taken them, Sal, but we only have her word for that. And I don't know that I'm willing to believe the word of someone who'd have the offices of a charity trashed *and* pretend to burn and then actually steal someone else's valuable books."

"*I've* got some information about Justine Gibson," Fiona cut in.

"Oh great!" said Sally. "You talked to the friend of a friend at Haweshill Uni Library then?"

"Yes. I said I had — wait for it — the 22-year-old daughter of my old university friend Sally Meredith staying with me and that she was trying to trace some people she'd met at an international Christian conference in Australia," said Fiona, grinning at Sally's expression. "I said she'd told me one of them was called Justine Gibson and, given they were about the same age, I'd thought of the Justine from Haweshill."

"And?" prompted Rhian, grinning back at Fiona.

"*And* she said it couldn't possibly be the same Justine Gibson, because this one has never voluntarily set foot in a church in her life. Apparently, her mother brought her up to attend junior church and has very sincere Christian beliefs, which Justine rejected from the minute she could think for herself. She's very scathing about religion in general."

"That's not how she and Margaret met then," said Sally, regretfully.

"Jolly good cover story, though, Fee," said Rhian, approvingly. "You should give up librarianship and become a journalist."

Rhian and Sally's meals had arrived, and Rhian ordered another bottle of Shiraz. "Did you find out whether Justine might have been to a conference at Cotterford Manor?" Sally asked Fiona, picking up her knife and fork to attack her chicken.

"No. After we'd finished talking about Justine, I

made some small talk about current library politics and training courses and so on, and mentioned a couple of conferences I've been to over the past year or so. She said the only conference they'd attended from their library had been one in London earlier this year. She said all the staff had gone to that — presumably including Justine. It was in April, just after Easter, if that's any help," she added.

"Probably not," Sally sighed. "Margaret lives in London but I doubt that's when they met — it's a big city. You don't just start talking to strangers and discover that the person you're talking to is going to be at a conference with the person you hate come September."

"And it's a couple of months too early for the Wild for God office trashing," said Rhian. "You don't know if Justine took holidays in June, do you, Fee?"

"No, sorry, I never thought to ask that," Fiona returned regretfully.

"My fault," said Sally. "I never thought to ask you to ask. Which is why I'll never make it as a news hound."

"Oh, you're not doing so badly at the moment," Rhian said.

"I did find something out that might be significant, though," said Fiona.

"What?" Sally and Rhian asked together.

"After talking about conferences and training and so on, we started discussing library morale and staffing issues," Fiona said. "I was telling her about an ongoing problem I've been having with a staff member and then she started telling me that she's been having one or two problems with Justine. She's been taking quite a bit of sick leave apparently — a day here, a couple of days there — and Christine says she can't prove it but she's fairly certain that Justine is cutting herself."

"Cutting herself!" Sally gasped. "Of course — why didn't I think of it before? Now, there's a definite connection — and thanks to cyberspace, those two don't have to live in the same area to come across each other. Self-help groups for self-harm must be abundant on the internet. If they struck up a friendship online, they might have started emailing each other privately and then made arrangements to commit the crimes for each other. If only I could take a look at Margaret's computer!"

"I know a couple of really good self-help forums," said Rhian. "I spoke to the forum hosts and a couple of their members for an article I wrote last year. I've got the details at work — I'll bring them back home with me tomorrow night or perhaps phone you with the URLs during the day tomorrow, Sal. Of course, there are plenty of other forums around, but these two are known to be really supportive and they're also British-based and run by a couple of very young girls who used to cut themselves. If I were Margaret or Justine's age and doing that kind of thing, I'm sure those would be the forums I'd be visiting."

"I don't think I can wait till tomorrow," said Sally. "When we get home after the theatre, I'm going to go online and Google on self-harm and see what forums I can find — and whether I can find JR15 and margaretwilks in there. Though I shouldn't think Margaret uses her real name in a self-harm forum," she added doubtfully.

"By the way," continued Rhian, "Arrowman also told me that the family has been given the go-ahead for Valerie's funeral to take place. It'll be on Thursday. Do you want to go to it, Sally?"

"Why?" asked Sally. "Are you?"

"If I can wangle it through work, I might. It just struck me," Rhian said, "that if Justine Gibson disliked Valerie enough to have Margaret set fire to her books — and perhaps to murder her, for all we know — then she might well turn up at the funeral. And perhaps we could talk to her and start trying to find out a little more about her. After all, if as Fee says she's into self-harm — well, there's no reason why she mightn't have seen a doctor and been prescribed phenelzine."

"It's no wonder she's depressed," said Sally soberly. "She's only about 22 and her mother's dying. And I think — though I may be wrong — that her father died some years ago. Plus she's never got on with her mother and must feel guilty about it."

Rhian glanced at her watch. "I hope your meal arrives soon, Fee — time's really getting on. Oh," she said spotting the waiter heading towards them, "here it comes at last."

For a few hours at least, Sally forgot all the intrigue surrounding Valerie Teague, Margaret Wilks and Justine Gibson as she drank in the Globe experience. The theatre was a replica of the one where Shakespeare's plays had been performed in the seventeenth century; some wooden seating had been provided, but Sally, Fiona and Rhian, like most of the audience, enjoyed watching *King Lear* Elizabethan-style — standing in front of the stage and moving around for a better or different view of the action. The theatre had no roof and they couldn't have picked a better evening to watch a play in the open air — it had cooled down since lunchtime and the temperature was now in the pleasant low 20s, without a cloud in the sky. Sally was surprised how much of the play she remembered from 'A' level days — even after 26 years she found herself remembering some of the speeches verbatim! And the famous Shakespearean tragedy was not without a touch of unintentional humour — an ambulance passed the theatre, sirens blazing, just at the moment that Gloster's eyes were gouged out.

Rhian had remembered to bring along a flask and, being Rhian, had filled it with mulled wine. By the time the performance had ended and Sally and Rhian had said goodbye to Fiona and made their way back to Forest Hill by bus, Sally was so tired from the fresh air and wine, and her mind so taken over by the play, that she decided against doing internet research that evening. That, she decided, could wait until tomorrow.

CHAPTER XVI.

A SPOT OF DECEPTION

At length, however, with a determined pressure of her lips, she switched on her reading lamp, sat down at the desk and pulled some paper and a pen towards her.

"I simply must find out that girl's secret," she said to herself. "Quite possibly Uncle knows nothing, but, on the other hand, he might. ... I'm sure he wouldn't mind telling me if I make out that we're friends and I want to help her."

Dorothy Dennison, *Rumours in the Fourth Form*, 1925

SALLY had a minor hangover the following morning and got up late. Rhian had already left for work. Sally couldn't face coffee or breakfast, so made herself a mug of black tea and connected to the internet. A Google search on self-harm revealed numerous forums, but most of them were understandably private and you had to sign up for membership. Sally didn't feel like wasting time signing up for numerous forums that Margaret and Justine might not even belong to, so she decided to wait for Rhian's information. Instead she Googled on 'Justine Gibson' and found that she had been well-placed at several amateur women's golf tournaments around the UK.

Justine's name featured in only one non-golf reference: on the list of delegates at the library conference in London earlier in the year that Fiona had mentioned. It had been a two-day conference from Wednesday 18 April to Thursday 19 April, and had been held in a hotel in Russell Square. Sally made a note of the date — you never knew, she thought, Justine and Margaret may have met up at some stage over those two days. Sally then Googled on 'Margaret Wilks': Margaret's name showed up a couple of times in relation to her employment at Wild for God, on a couple of church lists, and on a couple of fan-fiction websites — she seemed, Sally thought, to spend most of her time writing either Chalet School or Trebizon fan fiction. She then tried keying both names into the search engine to see if they showed up on anything together: nothing. She tried the same thing with the names 'Margaret Wilks' and 'Valerie Teague', and 'Justine Gibson' and 'Valerie Teague': again, nothing.

Rhian rang at that point to give Sally the URLs for the two British-based self-harm forums. As she'd expected, Sally had to sign up for them; she received an email back saying that the moderators would give her membership clearance in about twelve hours. You wouldn't want to be feeling desperate to talk to other sufferers, Sally thought, disconnecting. She wondered whether it was worth calling on Margaret and trying to con her into telling her whether she visited a self-harm website and, if so, which one. She could always invent a relative whom she suspected of cutting herself and ask Margaret if she knew of any good online sites that could be of help. Yes, she thought, she'd do that — if Margaret told her which website she frequented, it would cut down on the number of messages Sally would have to trawl through to find a possible link between her and Justine. Only today, Sally thought, slipping her camera into her bag, she wouldn't phone Margaret in advance — she'd just call on her unexpectedly.

This time, a tall young woman of about Margaret's age, with shoulder-length brown hair and glasses, opened the door. "I'm sorry," she said when Sally asked for Margaret, "Margaret's not at home."

"Do you know when she'll be back?" Sally asked.

"Not for hours, I'm afraid," said the woman. "She's gone to visit a friend in north London. Can I take a message for you, or anything?"

Sally thought quickly. She really wanted an opportunity to photograph the books in Margaret's backpack, and wondered if she could somehow convince Margaret's housemate to let her into Margaret's room on her own.

"My daughter is a friend of Margaret's," Sally lied. "Margaret gave her an address for something and she's lost it. It was really important, and as I was passing by, I thought I'd drop in and see if Margaret could give me the address to pass on to her."

"Address for what?" asked the woman.

"Well," said Sally, deliberately awkwardly, "it's personal really."

The woman looked at her sympathetically. "If it's about the cutting, I know about it," she said. "Margaret told me. Is it about that?"

"Yes," said Sally. "Margaret gave Eleanor contact details for the self-help group she attends and, as I say, Eleanor's mislaid it and I think it would be really beneficial if she started attending ..."

"She'll have it in her address book, I'm sure," said Margaret's housemate. "I know where she keeps it. You'd better come in. I'm Mia, by the way," she added as Sally followed her upstairs. Sally hovered in Margaret's doorway as Mia opened the desk drawer. Her eyes fell on Margaret's bookshelves and on the pristine rows of Chalet and Abbey hardbacks that only two days ago had been hidden in the wardrobe — no doubt in anticipation of Sally's visit. "I feel a bit bad doing this," Mia admitted, "but I know Margaret wouldn't mind in an emergency." She took out an address book and flipped through the pages. "Here it is. Got pen and paper?" she asked.

Sally went over to Margaret's desk and took her notebook and pen from her bag. Mia put the address book on the desk and pointed to the relevant address. The group was called 'Cut Quit' — Sally recognised the name, as one of the two forums Rhian had given her was associated with it. The group was based in Euston and met on the third Wednesday of each month. Sally felt a tingle of excitement: April 18 would have been the third Wednesday, and Euston was only a few street blocks from Russell Square ...

"Thanks so much," said Sally. "I'm really grateful." She wondered how she could get Mia out of the room for a moment to give her the opportunity to photograph the books.

"That's okay," said Mia. "I—" The telephone rang at that moment, and Mia said "I'll just get that" and left the room hurriedly.

Delighted by the opportune timing, Sally quickly took advantage of Mia's absence to photograph Margaret's books. She even pulled out *The Chalet School and the Lintons* and took a photograph of the page with the biro markings that had convinced her these were definitely Valerie's books. Then she flipped through the address book to see if she could find contact details for Justine Gibson. There was nothing. Sally slipped the address book back in the drawer and went downstairs. Mia was still on the phone, talking animatedly about something that had happened to a friend of hers the previous night.

Sally smiled and thanked her and let herself out of the house.

When she got back to the flat, Sally caught up with her email. Her mother had emailed a couple of times since Saturday and there was even an email from Angus, and she felt guilty about not having checked into her account for so long. She wrote back to her mother, then emailed Angus with a potted history of what she'd been up to over the past few days, and asked them to pass on her love to, respectively, her father and Eleanor. Sally was also surprised to find an email from Harriet Lenton in her inbox.

Dear Sally,

I'm assuming you're still in the UK for a while, so thought you might be interested to know that Valerie's stock is being auctioned off on Saturday from 2pm onwards. I spoke to her daughter, Veronica, yesterday and she said she and Mark had decided to sell it all off, given they don't want to inherit her book-dealing business. They're holding the auction at Valerie's home near Worthing and have let quite a few people on the G.O. scene know — I said I'd put something on the various forums for them. Anything that's left will go on to eBay. Valerie had some terrific books, as you know, and they were all in brilliant condition — this is a good opportunity to buy for less than the price she'd have set, I should think!

I'll be at Valerie's funeral tomorrow and staying in Worthing until after the auction. Richard is coming down too, and I'm hoping some others who attend the funeral will stay over as well. Perhaps we could all meet up on the Thursday night or the Friday — that's if you're still in London? London isn't far from Worthing by train.

Harriet went on to give Sally Valerie's address and details about the bed and breakfast where she and Richard would be staying until the Saturday evening. Sally wondered whether they'd be staying there together, or if Richard had tired of her now and would be on the prowl for another woman when he went down to Worthing. She was sure, though, that meeting up with Richard, Harriet and whoever else was coming to the funeral and auction would be a good idea. If there was a connection between Justine and Valerie, then one of them might know about it.

So she wrote back to Harriet saying she'd love to meet up with them all, and that she would phone her at the bed and breakfast tomorrow to arrange something. Sally was still unsure about whether she should attend Valerie's funeral. Rhian's comments about Justine Gibson maybe turning up there made her feel as if she'd like to go. However, as she'd said in the immediate wake of Valerie's death, Sally hadn't known Valerie — she thought it might look a little odd if she did turn up. There would, presumably, be people attending who were genuinely grieving for Valerie — Sally felt that if she did go, she'd feel a bit like a *voyeur*. The auction, though — that was a different matter, even if Justine Gibson, with her dislike of all things related to the school-story world, was highly unlikely to come anywhere near it. And, Sally reasoned, even if she didn't come away from the auction with any relevant information, she might at least score a beautiful hardcover Chalet book for a reasonable price.

"I'm not going to the funeral," Rhian announced grumpily when she arrived home that night. "The editor said I've got as many quotes as I need from the family to write a really good article on why phenelzine should be banned. And with an open verdict, or more likely misadventure, being the likely outcome at the inquest, he doesn't want to know about possible murder suspects turning up at the funeral." She glanced across at Sally who was busy chopping vegetables. "What are you doing?"

"Making dinner. I thought it would make a change from eating out."

"That's nice of you. I'll open a bottle." Rhian examined the small wine rack on the kitchen bench, selected a bottle of red, and said, "What did you get up to today?"

Sally brought Rhian up to date with what she'd discovered that day. Rhian grinned. "And there I was expecting a list of all the places you'd visited — what happened to your plans to visit the London Eye and the Tower of London? The way you're going you'll end up as a real journo, not just the editor of a specialist mag."

"I *like* my job," Sally told her, firmly. "This business has just got me curious, that's all." All the same, she thought, chasing up a real story like this did beat sub-editing articles on collecting train sets.

"The woman from Cut Quit is Jenny McIvor," said Rhian thoughtfully, as she poured generous glasses of wine and pushed one across the counter in Sally's direction. "She runs the self-help group in Euston and is the forum host as well. She was really helpful regarding the article. I can have a word with her, see if she'll say anything about Margaret. It'll be difficult, though — confidentiality and all that."

"I was wondering whether Justine might have visited the self-help group on the night she was in London for the conference," said Sally, taking a sip of wine.

"It's possible. They might have met through the forum, emailed each other privately, and when Justine knew she was coming to London she might have either arranged to go to the group meeting or to meet up with Margaret elsewhere."

"Or do both things — attend the self-help group, then go to a pub or for dinner or something," Sally pointed out.

"How many hours do you have to wait now before you're a bona fide member of Cut Quit?"

"I should be a member by nine o'clock tonight," said Sally, glancing at the clock.

"Hmm. Only three hours to go then. And hopefully we can make the connection there, because otherwise, short of getting photos of Margaret and Justine and asking Jenny McIvor if she's seen them in the same meeting together, I don't know how we're going to prove that they know each other. And given we don't have photos of either of them, that's not an option either."

"There are photos, though," said Sally.

"Where?" Rhian demanded.

"On the internet. There's something about Wild for God on one of the websites and there's a picture of Margaret with some other staff there. And there are a couple of photos of Justine on a golf site, after she's been placed in tournaments. We could print the photos out and you could ask Jenny McIvor if she's seen them together."

"Excellent!" beamed Rhian. "I don't know whether she will help, given privacy issues, but I can try, at least. In the meantime, it's forum trawling for us. How long will dinner be, Sal? I'm starving."

CHAPTER XVII.

WHAT SALLY OVERHEARD

"I'm going to find out," said Mabs determinedly. "I shall hide in the gym cupboard — "

A howl of indignation arose from her classmates at this suggestion, for the gym cupboard ... opened off the big classroom.

"Eavesdropper!" cried Dimsie hotly. "And you call yourself an Anti-Soppist!"

Dorita Fairlie Bruce, *Dimsie Moves Up*, 1921

A LENGTHY search through numerous threads on the Cut Quit forum yielded precisely nothing. If they were active members, Margaret and Justine had different usernames to the ones they had on Chalet Girls. If they were lurkers, then there was no hope of finding them. At eleven-thirty, Sally yawned and rubbed her eyes. "I don't think I can handle working my way through countless messages in the other forum," she said to Rhian.

"Me neither. We'll just have to hope Jenny McIvor's willing to breach confidentiality and tell me if Margaret and Justine have ever attended the self-help group together," said Rhian. She had printed the photographs out earlier and put them into her briefcase, hoping to be able to contact Jenny McIvor at some stage the following day. "I do think though, Sal, that you ought to attend the funeral now we know that I can't. I still think there's a good chance that Justine Gibson might turn up at it."

"I don't really want to go. What excuse would I

have for being there? I didn't even know Valerie."

"So what? Lots of people attend funerals for people they didn't know that well," Rhian argued. "And if her kids have been estranged from her for as long as you said they have, they won't know that you weren't her bosom buddy. The other thing is that Margaret as well as Justine might show up, and it could be interesting to watch them together."

So Sally somewhat reluctantly allowed herself to be persuaded, and the following morning saw her rising early, walking up to the railway station and travelling to East Croydon, from where she caught the train to Worthing. The weather was still hot and she had no clothing with her that was suitable for a funeral, so she had had to borrow an outfit — a dark blue skirt and light blue short-sleeved shirt — from Rhian.

Worthing was a large town on the south coast, just over an hour out of London by train. Sally had never been there before, and wasn't overimpressed with either the characterless railway station she alighted at or the streets around it — block after block of cheerless terraced housing. Both Valerie's house and the church where the funeral was to be held were in Tarring, just a couple of miles away, so Sally caught a taxi and was surprised to find herself suddenly in the middle of a pretty, atmospheric village. Tarring gave the appearance of being way out in the countryside, not just round the corner from dull suburban streets. When the taxi pulled up outside a picture-postcard church, Sally noticed several mourners, Richard and Harriet among them, gathered in the grounds, chatting quietly. Harriet spotted her and waved.

"Hello, Sally," she said as Sally joined them. "I didn't realise you were coming today."

"Well," said Sally, feeling slightly ridiculous, "I

thought it seemed wrong to come along for the auction if I didn't come along to pay my last respects."

Richard nodded approvingly. "You're right, of course. Plenty of vultures in the 'girls' own' world. Sally, have you met Veronica? Valerie's daughter?"

"No," said Sally, holding out her hand to Veronica, who was in her late twenties with short dark hair and green eyes. "I'm Sally Meredith," she said. "I met your mother briefly at the conference last weekend."

"It was good of you to come," said Veronica. She looked around at the swelling crowd of mourners. "Good of everybody to come. I wouldn't have believed she had so many friends." She nodded towards someone in a neighbouring group. "I have to go — I think all the family are wanted."

"Hello, Sally!" Sally turned to see Leonie Carr. "How are you? I didn't realise you'd be coming today."

"Well, it was closer for me than for you," Sally replied.

"Yes, but I couldn't miss the book auction so I took some time off work for bereavement — said Valerie was a close friend." Leonie shrugged. "I'll go into London tomorrow — I haven't been there in ages."

"It looks like the coffin's arrived," said Harriet. "We'd all better go inside."

"Hey, Sally," said Leonie quietly, as they all made their way inside the church. "Did you find out any more about what Margaret Wilks and Justine Gibson meant by those messages they placed on Chalet Girls?"

"No, not really," Sally said. "You haven't mentioned them to anyone else have you, Leonie? It's just that I wouldn't like either of them to realise I was suspicious."

"No, I haven't said anything. Jess is here, by the way."

"Jess Gibson?"

"Yes. I saw her with Miriam when I first arrived — she didn't stay outside long, but went straight into the church. I should think she gets tired easily, and it's a hot day. I'm surprised she's here, though, given how ill she is herself. But then, I suppose she's known Valerie for a long time."

"Were they friends?"

"I don't think so. Valerie didn't have any friends, as far as I'm aware."

"You'd never guess it by the number of people here today."

The church seemed to be crammed with people. Sally sat near the back with Leonie, Richard and Harriet. She recognised several other faces from the Tales Out of School conference, including Miriam Lorrimer, Maria Laker and Leah Brindsley. The thin, frail woman wearing a headscarf sitting next to Miriam must be Jess Gibson, Sally realised. But there was no Justine Gibson, and no Margaret Wilks.

The coffin was carried into the church and laid near the front. Veronica and the rest of Valerie's family followed the coffin up the nave and then settled down in the first row of pews. Richard started flipping through his order of service. "Odd choice of hymns for Valerie," he whispered to Harriet. "I'd have expected her to have 'Fight the good fight', wouldn't you?"

"Shh," whispered Harriet, nudging him and giggling. Leonie raised her eyebrows at Sally as if to say "Here we go again". Sally grimaced in return. She shared Leonie's irritation with Richard and Harriet — they were both intelligent people, so why did they constantly feel the need to behave like schoolchildren when together? It seemed stupid to Sally.

The funeral was over quickly. There were just a couple of hymns and prayers, and the vicar spoke briefly about Valerie. Just as Maria had at the Sunday morning service, the vicar concentrated mainly on Valerie the professional bookseller rather than Valerie the person. Sally felt momentarily sorry for Valerie. Usually, when a person died, people had nothing but good things to say about them. Given that she'd apparently inspired no warmth in anyone, Valerie couldn't have had a particularly happy life.

Once the service was over, the coffin was taken to a nearby cemetery. It was within walking distance, so Sally walked there with most of the others. Veronica and the rest of Valerie's family went by car as did, Sally noticed, Jess Gibson. As the mourners gathered around the grave, Sally held back slightly. She watched Mark Teague, Valerie's son, who looked very like Veronica, throw soil on top of the coffin. The mourners formed a line, paying their last respects. Richard, when his turn came, dropped a red rose on to the coffin. Jess Gibson insisted on walking up; Sally noticed her dropping a paperback book into the grave. Curious to see what it was, she joined the line of mourners, picked up a handful of earth and let it fall onto the coffin. The paperback had fallen face-upwards: it was *The Chalet School and Rosalie*.

"A first edition Rosalie," Leonie murmured to Sally as they followed the line of mourners back to the church. "Can you believe anyone would do that? It's a nice tribute to a book dealer, but there are people here today who would rob a grave for that."

Sally was surprised. *The Chalet School and Rosalie* was the only book in Elinor M. Brent-Dyer's

Chalet School series never to have been published in hardback, so if the paperback had, as Leonie said, been a first edition, then it certainly was a valuable book — worth around £250. "Are you sure?" she asked Leonie.

"Of course I am. It had the picture of two girls on the cover, one of them holding a pitchfork," Leonie returned. Sally remembered Leonie's performance during the conference quiz; she certainly knew her covers. If Leonie said it was a first edition *Rosalie*, then no doubt it was.

"You will come back to the house, won't you?" said Veronica, interrupting Sally's thoughts.

"Well, I wasn't going to," said Sally. "I just came out of — out of respect for your mother."

"Oh, please do come. Mark and I would like to meet all her collecting friends," Veronica said.

Valerie's house was within easy walking distance, and Sally joined Leonie and an arm-in-arm Richard and Harriet, who knew the way there. Valerie had lived in a three-storey terrace house that, Tardis-like, was much bigger inside than it looked from the outside. Someone had set up a buffet on the table in the large, country-style kitchen. There was tea and coffee on offer, plus something stronger for those who wanted it. Sally accepted tea, as did Leonie; Harriet helped herself to a gin and tonic, while Richard opened a can of beer. They followed the other mourners into a narrow, neat garden, and stood sipping and chatting on the manicured lawn.

"I see Veronica and Mark have locked up Valerie's office where her books are kept," remarked Richard. "I can't say I blame them. Sad though it is, there are people here today who would nick a first edition Chalet."

"Like who?" Harriet demanded.

"Well, me for one," Leonie grinned. "And I reckon

I deserve a freebie — Valerie certainly ripped me off a few times over the years."

"Speaking of stealing books," said Sally, "do you think anyone's going to dig up Valerie's grave for *The Chalet School and Rosalie*? Leonie here reckons it was a first edition."

"Is *that* what Jess dropped in there?" asked Richard. When Leonie nodded, he gave a low whistle.

"Ah well, Jess is very ill, you have to remember that," said Harriet.

"What's that got to do with it?" he demanded.

"So she's dying. So she's not thinking straight. Why else would anybody put a valuable book in Valerie's grave? It's not even as if Jess and Valerie were close friends."

"They got along all right," said Richard. "Well, as all right as anybody got along with Valerie." He turned to Sally. "Are you hanging around till this evening, Sally? I thought we could all go to the pub."

"I might," said Sally. "I don't want to leave too late, though. I need to get back to south London and I'm not sure how regular the trains are at night."

Mark Teague joined them at that point. He asked them all how they knew his mother and, on hearing that all four of them knew her through the 'girls' own' community, made a few polite remarks about the fine quality of the books up for auction on Saturday and then moved on to the next group.

"Do either of you know where the loo is?" Sally asked Harriet and Richard.

"Go inside and up the stairs and it is, like all good lavatories, the first on the left," Richard told her. Sally headed back into the kitchen, squeezed past a group of people, and made her way upstairs.

The bathroom door was open. Sally was about to go inside when she heard voices from the room across the passage, the door of which was slightly ajar. "Surely not, Jess," came Miriam Lorrimer's voice. "I can't believe Valerie would do something like that."

"Well, she did." Jess Gibson's voice sounded flat and tired. Sally crept closer to the door to hear more clearly. "Please don't tell anyone else, will you, Miriam? You're my oldest friend, and that's why I'm trusting you with this."

"I wish you'd trust me completely, Jess, and tell me what it is she had on you. I might be able to help."

"There's nothing you can do, Miriam. I just wanted you to understand why I'm glad she's dead. She was making my life miserable."

"Oh, Jess. I do wish you'd told me. You had enough on your plate anyway without putting up with being blackmailed—."

Blackmailed? thought Sally, startled. Valerie Teague had been blackmailing Jess Gibson — a dying woman? No wonder Justine Gibson had been angry at Valerie Teague — Jess must have told her about it, and she must have arranged revenge — of a sort — with Margaret Wilks. But what on earth could Jess Gibson have done that made it possible for Valerie to blackmail her — and how had Valerie found out about it in the first place?

But any hope she might hear more details about the blackmail was dashed when Sally heard footsteps on the stairs. She hurried back to the bathroom and locked the door. And when she came out, she found two people waiting for the toilet — Miriam being one of them. The door to the room Jess and Miriam had been ensconced in was now wide open. Their conversation was unfortunately at an end.

CHAPTER XVIII.

MORE PIECES OF THE JIGSAW

"Oh, she's always doing slippery things — ducking games if there's a slack prefect on — Anne or Chris, you know, and Elinor gets a bit up in the clouds occasionally — and slipping down the drive to post letters. She comes up here sometimes at forbidden times, too. That evening I was waiting to be moved to Isolation she dodged someone and came up. Goodness knows what for."

"What evening was this? Do you remember exactly?" Merry's voice quavered with anxiety. Surely this was the clue Claudia had sent her to find?

Clare Mallory, *Merry Marches On*, 1947

THE mourners seemed prepared to settle in and make an afternoon of it. Groups had gathered in the garden and in the kitchen and living room, and were discussing anything other than Valerie. There was almost a party atmosphere, Sally thought, and she realised that Valerie would probably have hated it. Sally was standing with Leonie, Harriet, Richard and Maria Laker, and steeling herself to speak to Jess Gibson. She really wanted to pump Jess for information about Justine, and had thought of a convincing excuse for doing so, but felt bad about lying to a dying woman. Rhian, she knew, would just have done it — even if she had misgivings, Rhian wouldn't let them get in the way of her research. That was why, Sally reflected, she wouldn't have made a news reporter the way Rhian had. She was much too kind-hearted.

"When do you go back to Australia, Sally?" Maria asked her.

"In two weeks' time," Sally said.

"Will you come back in two years' time for the next conference?"

"I shouldn't think so," Sally said. "It's expensive to come over here — this is a one-off trip. Actually," she went on, "I was thinking how great it would be to have a similar conference in Australia. There are plenty of school-story fans out there."

"You should talk to Miriam and Jess about that while they're both here," said Richard.

"Is Jess still involved in Tales Out of School, then?" asked Sally. "I'd have thought she wasn't."

"Well, she's not really," replied Richard, "but I think she'd welcome the opportunity to contribute to a discussion on something like that — you know, having someone treating her as if she's *not* dying."

"She's actually looking quite well today," commented Harriet. "I'm worried that she might be near the end — don't people often seem to get a lot better before really deteriorating?"

Maria nodded. "Yes, that's true. It does seem to happen. Poor Jess. I'm surprised she came, really. I wouldn't think a funeral's the most cheerful thing to go to if you're dying."

"It is if it's Valerie's," grinned Richard.

Harriet slapped his arm. "Richard! Don't say things like that."

"Well, it's true," he protested. "None of us are exactly weeping with sorrow at her demise, are we? You go and talk to them about the down under conference, Sally. I'm sure Miriam would be interested, and Jess is so much perkier today that she'll enjoy discussing it, I'm sure."

So Sally, thus persuaded — it would be easier to strike up a conversation with Jess by suggesting something that she really thought would be a good idea than to plunge right into a lie — went inside in search of Miriam and Jess. She found them sitting together on a white leather sofa in the living room. Mark and Veronica and a couple of other people — presumably family members — were also in there.

"Hello, Sally," said Miriam. "I don't think you've met Jess Gibson, have you? Jess runs Tales Out of School with me."

Sally shook hands with Jess who, she noticed, was looking very weary. "I'm glad to see you both together," she said a little self-consciously. "I wanted to ask you what you thought of the idea of a Tales Out of School conference in Australia."

"It sounds like a super idea to me," said Jess, in bouncy tones that belied her tired appearance. "But Miriam's the one you should really talk to about it. She does all the work these days."

"I'd love to visit Australia and run a conference there," said Miriam, "but I'm not sure about the logistics of it. The thing is, when we run one in the UK, as long as we hold it somewhere fairly central, it's not too difficult for people to attend. But wherever you held it in Australia, it would be difficult for the majority of people, wouldn't it? Sydney would only really be convenient for people who actually lived in Sydney — same for Melbourne or for Perth."

"But if everyone worried about that, there'd never be *any* conferences in Australia on *anything*," Sally pointed out.

"Yes, but business conferences, for example, wouldn't face the exact problems we would," Miriam argued. "Companies wanting to send delegates would pay their air fare and their accommodation costs. With anything like this, people would have to pay for themselves. I'd be really worried about whether we could even break even by the time we've paid for a conference centre, guest speakers ..."

"That's true," Jess nodded. "My daughter's been looking into travelling around Australia for a year and playing on some of the golf courses there, and she was surprised that the internal air fares weren't anywhere near as cheap as we get in Europe. Of course," she added to Sally, "you'd know all about that, given you live there."

"Is Justine still going to Australia?" Miriam asked. "I thought you said she'd given up on the idea with your health the way it is."

"She still wants to go, but I know she won't leave till — well, after I've gone basically," Jess sighed. "It's kind of her, but I feel guilty in a way that I'm making her put her life on hold. She was really looking forward to the trip and then I got worse," she explained to Sally. "She'd even taken on a second job to raise money, because librarianship isn't highly paid."

"That's right — I'd forgotten that," said Miriam. "She took on the cleaning job at Cotterford Manor, didn't she?"

"That's right. And she did some bar work in one of the pubs in Haweshill as well," said Jess. "But she gave all that up when the trip was put on hold."

"When did she work at Cotterford Manor?" asked Sally. "It's a beautiful old house — I was really impressed with it."

"Oh, she worked there for about six months," Jess said. "She only stopped in about June, when my condition really deteriorated."

Now she wouldn't need to lie to Jess, Sally realised, with relief. She'd found out something she hadn't expected to; something that added another piece to the jigsaw. If Justine Gibson had worked as a cleaner at Cotterford Manor *after* she and Margaret had made their plans, then she would have had no trouble having a key cut so that Margaret could steal Valerie's books from a supposedly locked room. Quite how she'd managed to pass that key on to Margaret was something Sally still needed to find out. But given that Margaret had been heading by train to Cotterford in the wrong direction, Sally felt fairly confident that the key had somehow been handed over in Clinton Manning.

Sally had planned to stay in Worthing for part of the evening and spend some time with Harriet, Leonie, Richard and the rest, but now all she wanted to do was to get back to London and tell Rhian what she'd found out at the funeral. So, as the afternoon wore on she made her excuses. Harriet suggested they all met up in a pub in central London the following evening.

"I'll phone Bridget and invite her along as well," she said. "I know she'll be coming to the auction on Saturday, but even so it'll be nice to have an evening out at the pub and perhaps a meal later. Where shall we go? The trains from here go to Victoria, but—."

"We could all meet up in Covent Garden, perhaps, or Leicester Square and take things from there," Richard suggested.

"What about meeting outside St Martin-in-the-Fields?" suggested Harriet. "That's a good central meeting place."

"Okay — six o'clock there," nodded Sally.

It took a long time for Sally to return to Forest Hill. The train from Worthing swept her back to

East Croydon, and from there she planned to catch another train to Forest Hill. But there were delays on the local branch line, and eventually she gave up on the train and got a taxi. When she finally arrived back at Rhian's flat, she found herself thinking how glad she was that she didn't live in a city as crowded as London.

Rhian was home. "Glad you're back," she said. "I was wondering whether to wait for you to arrive so we could eat out, or whether just to order a takeaway for myself."

"Don't you ever cook?" Sally asked.

"Sometimes. But it's such a fag at the end of a day at work — not to mention the drive home in London traffic."

"And you a health writer," Sally said.

"Yes, I know," Rhian grinned. "Terrible, isn't it? So how did things go at the funeral?"

"Very well." Sally told Rhian about the conversation she'd overheard between Jess and Miriam, and about the fact that Justine had worked as a cleaner at Cotterford Manor.

"Excellent!" said Rhian, pleased. "It's all falling into place now, isn't it?"

"Did you manage to speak to Jenny McIvor?"

"I did. And I met up with her, briefly, after work. Of course, I've had to promise her another self-harm story for the *Clarion*, with lots of plugs for Cut Quit, in return for the information she's given me," Rhian sighed. "I don't know how I'm going to justify that to the editor. He'll swear I'm taking bribes."

"Well, you are, aren't you — sort of? An article in exchange for info."

"Yes, but he'll think I'm getting money to plug them twice in a year. Anyway," Rhian shrugged, "you'll be pleased to know that Jenny recognised Margaret's photo straightaway. She attends the monthly meetings and has done for ages. She says she keeps herself to herself, though, and hasn't really made friends among the other people who attend the group. Jenny says she tries to encourage them all to make friends, so that they can support each other. But Margaret told her she finds the meetings useful, but other than that prefers to have support online, where it's more anonymous."

"That sounds fair enough," said Sally.

"Yes. She also told me that Margaret is usually early for the meetings, and sits with her nose in a school story until the meeting is ready to start." Rhian grinned and continued, "Jenny said she feels that Margaret's reading of school stories is perhaps tied up with the problem of self-harm — another expression of not having grown up and not being able to cope with the real world."

"What crap," said Sally, crossly.

"I knew you wouldn't like that! I sat there thinking how funny it would be if I'd taken you along to our meeting and she sat there talking about school stories and arrested development! Anyway," Rhian went on, laughing at Sally's annoyed expression, "I then showed her the photograph of Justine Gibson. And that's where what she had to say got really interesting."

"What was that, then?" Sally asked, trying to calm down and concentrate.

"Well, she didn't know Justine's name, but said that she had attended the group just once — the week after Easter. She said they often get extra people attending meetings just after Christmas or just after Easter, because apparently having to spend more time with family makes people depressed and more likely to self-harm. Which makes perfect sense," said Rhian. "She said that ordinarily she wouldn't have remembered anything about Justine, given she only attended the one meeting. But the thing that struck her is that Justine arrived early and went up to Margaret and started talking. She overheard Justine say something about the book Margaret was reading, and saying her mother still read stories like that.

"And the other thing she remembered was that Margaret and Justine left together after the meeting, apparently to go for a meal. She remembered that because, of course, Margaret's resisted all overtures towards friendship from group members at other meetings. She was surprised that Margaret seemed to make friends with a stranger — but thought it was probably the school-story thing that gave them something in common. I don't think she believed it was Justine's mum who read the school stories, but Justine herself — only Justine wouldn't admit it. Except *we* know, of course, that it *is* her mum who reads school stories," Rhian finished.

"And was being blackmailed," said Sally. "Well, it all fits now, doesn't it? We've made all the connections between them."

"Except we don't know what Jess Gibson was being blackmailed about and whether it was enough to make Justine bump Valerie off via Margaret," said Rhian. "That's a worry for tomorrow. In the meantime, take your choice — restaurant or takeaway?"

CHAPTER XIX.

AN UNEXPECTED DEVELOPMENT

"I can't discuss this with you, it's too absurd. These books belonged to Miss Pickering's father, and I must safeguard them," said Miss Whyte.

"But Miss Pickering always—"

For the third time Miss Whyte interrupted. "I tell you, there's no need to argue. On second thoughts, leave the books, and I'll put them back myself. I should never forgive myself if they came to harm."

Margaret Biggs, *Last Term for Helen*, 1953

RHIAN liked the idea of driving up to Warwickshire and challenging Justine Gibson, but knew she wouldn't be able to do it until the weekend because of work. Sally, keen to attend the auction, ruled out Saturday. Rhian, to Sally's surprise, agreed happily to this, saying that she might well be able to learn something useful from either Jess Gibson or Margaret Wilks at the auction, should they attend.

So Friday found Sally with no investigating to do. In a way, she missed this, because over the past few days she had got used to having things to chase up. On the other hand, it was a beautiful day — sunny and warm but not too hot — just perfect for doing some sightseeing. Sally decided not to go into the city, but to explore some of the more famous local places she'd never seen, such as the Horniman Museum and the Dulwich Picture Gallery. She decided to visit the Picture Gallery on the morning, and quickly discovered that she was still as much of a philistine when it came to art as she had been back in her student days, when, during a weekend in Paris, she'd gone through what she wanted to see in the Louvre in just over an hour. She glanced quickly at the Rembrandts, Lelys and Gainsboroughs that the Picture Gallery had to offer, then departed — it was time she accepted it, she told herself, art really wasn't her thing. She wandered down to Dulwich Village and bought sandwiches and a Coke from a bakery, then carried them back up the road and into Dulwich Park. There, she settled down on a bench by the duck pond to have lunch.

She was just finishing her drink when she spotted a familiar figure in jeans and long-sleeved T-shirt walking past the pond. Margaret Wilks was walking quickly, head bowed, looking at the ground. She was wearing earphones and was carrying an iPod. Sally waved to capture her attention. Margaret spotted her and a look of something — fear? nervousness? — crossed her face. She turned round and scurried off in the opposite direction.

Sally put the top back on her Coke and shoved it into her day pack, then hurried after Margaret. Margaret, who had glanced backwards a couple of times, saw that Sally was following her and broke into a run. She ran past a crowded children's playground and an equally busy kiosk selling drinks, sweets and ice creams in the direction of the East Dulwich side of the park, clearly heading for home. Sally sped after her, thankful that Margaret wasn't the fittest young person on the block. She caught up with Margaret near the park exit.

"What d'you want?" Margaret demanded, panting heavily. She was red in the face and her voice was louder than usual because of the earphones.

"I just wanted to talk to you," said Sally. "Why did you run away?"

Margaret switched off the iPod and took out her earphones. "I've had enough of you," she told Sally, in a shaky voice. "Mia told me about how you came around the other day, pretending you had a daughter with a problem with self-harm, and—"

"Yes, I'm sorry about that," Sally said. "I needed the details for someone else I know, but I thought it might be easier if I just said they were for someone in my family."

"Yeah, right," said Margaret, shoving the iPod in her bag. She looked tearful, Sally noticed, and was trembling slightly. Sally felt suddenly sorry for her; Margaret had known she'd been in her room and that she would have seen the first edition Chalets and Abbeys. It was silly, Sally decided, to carry on lying to her; she might as well let Margaret know that she'd been found out — see how she reacted.

"Look, Margaret," she said, "when I was at your place I couldn't help noticing the books on your shelves. I looked at some of Valerie's books at the conference, you know — before they disappeared. One of them, *Lintons*, was the same copy as the one on your shelf."

Margaret looked away miserably.

"Why don't we sit down?" Sally suggested, waving to a green bench just along the track.

"I don't want to talk about it," Margaret said, her voice still shaking.

"I know that, but you're going to have to at some stage, Margaret. Perhaps I could do the talking first, though — let you know what I've managed to piece together about your arrangement with Justine Gibson?"

Margaret stared at her. "How do you know about that?" she asked fearfully.

"Come and sit down and I'll tell you," said Sally. She was convinced that even if Margaret *had* conspired with Justine to take revenge on both Valerie Teague and her own former employer, there was no way she had murdered Valerie — if Valerie had indeed been murdered. Margaret was too nervous a person for that, Sally thought — she was barely coping with having the theft of the books on her conscience. Now, Margaret numbly followed her to the park bench.

"All right," said Sally. "I've managed to work out that you met Justine Gibson at a meeting of your self-help group and that you made arrangements to take revenge on people for each other. So Justine trashed the Wild for God offices for you and you were supposed to burn Valerie's books — except you didn't. You kept them for yourself and burnt others instead."

"I couldn't burn them," said Margaret. "Even when Justine and I were discussing what we'd do, I knew I wouldn't burn them. I gathered together a bundle of old books to burn instead. That way, Valerie would *think* her valuable books had been burnt. Justine said the only way to hurt Valerie was through her books — thinking that all her profits had disappeared."

"I can understand why you wanted to get your own back on your previous employer," said Sally, "but why did Justine want to hurt Valerie?"

Margaret sighed. "You should really ask Justine about it."

"I will when I see her — if I see her," Sally corrected herself. "But she must have told you why?"

"She'd found out that her mother was being blackmailed by Valerie."

"Blackmailed about what?"

"Look — I don't know exactly. I'm not sure even Justine knows exactly what it was all about and, even if she did know, she didn't tell me. It was something that Jess Gibson was really ashamed of and was embarrassed at Valerie finding out about."

"How did Justine find out about the blackmail, then?" Sally asked. "Is she doing her mother's banking or something, given she's so ill, and noticed money going out of her account?"

"Oh, no," said Margaret. "Jess wasn't paying Valerie any money to keep quiet."

"How was she buying her silence, then?"

"With books, of course," Margaret said.

Justine, Margaret said, had visited her mother on the weekend prior to the library conference she'd attended in London. Her mother was going through a particularly bad phase and had been temporarily hospitalised. Justine had visited her in hospital, and had then returned to her mother's house and decided to do some of her housework, so that if she did come home, then at least the house would be looking nice for her.

Jess Gibson kept most of her school stories in the living room, but also kept some in her spare bedroom, and when Justine had gone in there to dust and vacuum, she had noticed that one of the big bookcases was virtually empty. She had initially thought that her mother, aware she was dying, was selling off her collection, knowing that Justine would have no interest in inheriting it. When she visited her mother again in hospital later, she had mentioned the missing books, asking how much money she'd made for them on eBay. Jess had become upset, saying that she hadn't wanted to get rid of them — even if Justine had no interest in her collection, Jess had hoped that she might at least be able to gain some extra cash through her inheritance. She'd apologised profusely to Justine about it, and in the end the whole story had come tumbling out — that Valerie had somehow discovered something about Jess, and had promised not to mention it to anyone as long as Jess gave her a regular supply of valuable books, which Valerie then sold for considerable sums of money.

Justine had reacted angrily, wanting to challenge Valerie and get the books back — but Jess had persuaded her to say and do nothing, saying that she couldn't cope if Valerie gave away her secret to others. Justine had reluctantly promised not to tackle Valerie. Instead, after leaving her mother and heading down to London, Justine had cut herself in response to the powerlessness that she felt in being unable to protect her dying mother. She had found out about the self-help group that met not far away from the hotel where she was staying, and had decided to attend. She had arrived early, and had spotted Margaret.

"I was reading *A Chalet Girl from Kenya*," Margaret remembered, "and initially Justine was quite hostile towards me — made some disparaging remark about my being 'another of those bloody school-story readers'. Then, during the meeting, I was talking a bit about how I was cutting myself more because I'd been sacked from my job — and part of the reason I'd been sacked was because I'd had to take time off because of the cutting, and what a vicious circle it all was. Then she said she was cutting more because someone was hurting her mother and she couldn't do anything about it. Then after the meeting she asked if I fancied going for a meal and a drink. She asked me if I'd ever read

Strangers on a Train or seen the film. I hadn't then, but she told me the basic plot, and she said wouldn't it be a great idea if she and I could take revenge for each other on the people who had hurt us. That we could harm them and no-one would be able to trace it back to us, because no-one knew that we knew each other. We agreed that we wouldn't contact each other again, just send innocuous-looking messages through the Chalet Girls forum once we'd fulfilled our part of the bargain."

"In the form of Twenty Questions," Sally said. "That's what got me wondering about you in the first place."

Margaret stared unseeingly across the park. "Does anyone else know about it?" she asked.

"Just some friends of mine," Sally said. Leonie Carr also knew that the forum had been used for messages, but Sally couldn't see the point in upsetting Margaret further by letting her know that another collector knew something of what had been done. "Did you agree straightaway on what you'd do?"

"Yes. I knew that Robin Horlick — that was my boss at Wild for God — would be hurt most of all by having his office wrecked. He lives for his work — barely spends any time with his family. When I left, they didn't change the security code on their alarm system, so I just gave that to Justine, and she decided which weekend she'd go to London and trash the place. I made sure I was away that weekend. I knew the police might look at people who had a grudge against either Robin or Wild for God." Margaret smiled slightly.

"And it was Justine's idea to book me into the Tales Out of School conference — she even gave me the money so I could go. That was what made me agree to it, really — I've wanted to go to a conference for ages and I could never afford it. She got a key cut for me, so I could get into the room where they'd hold the book sale — she knew the room would be locked overnight because the books are so valuable. She left it under a particular plant pot in the hothouse in the park at Clinton Manning. I picked it up on the day the conference started, and then just chucked it in the duck pond at Cotterford Manor after I'd finished using it."

She turned to look at Sally, eyeing her apprehensively. "Are you and your friends planning to do anything with this information? Like tell the police?" As Sally tried to think of a suitable response, Margaret continued, "I don't think the police would believe you, you know. It would all be too crazy for them — messages left in internet forums for women who read old girls' school stories. The police who looked into Valerie's death thought we were all crackers — they were laughing at us the whole time."

"I suppose they might consider blackmail to be a reasonable motive for murdering Valerie Teague, though," said Sally, watching Margaret closely for a reaction.

Margaret sighed. "That was the only thing that worried me — Valerie dying like that and the police saying her death was suspicious. That's why I left early — I was worried they'd think that the missing books were tied up with her death in some way, and might search all our luggage and find that I had all those books of Valerie's. But I don't think she was murdered, do you?"

Sally shrugged. "I think they're looking at misadventure — that Valerie inadvertently took an old tablet."

"That's what I think too," said Margaret, looking relieved.

But Sally was now wondering whether Valerie's death had, after all, been murder. Blackmail, as she'd said, was a definite motive — and even though Sally couldn't believe that Margaret might have murdered Valerie, Justine might well have somehow managed to do so. She had, after all, been the brains behind the revenge pact. And, given she cut herself, she might well have had access to phenelzine. Also, as Margaret had been talking, it had struck Sally that Jess Gibson might not be the only blackmail victim. Valerie had been known for always having fine editions of books on sale — who was to say that she hadn't acquired most of them by the same means in which she'd got hold of Jess's books?

CHAPTER XX.

WHO DID IT?

I was crazy about books and could never get enough to read. I had read every Enid Blyton book I could lay my hands on, every Chalet School story, Just William, Biggles, Worrals, L.M. Montgomery, Angela Brazil, Louisa M. Alcott and dozens of others. The first title my eye lit on today was *School Versus Spy* which I seized eagerly, and then I saw *Schoolgirls in Peril*.

Joan Lingard, *The File on Fraulein Berg*, 1980

BACK at Rhian's flat, Sally, with memories of Enid Blyton's Five Find-Outer books, drew up a list of suspects for Valerie's murder. As she'd walked home, she'd re-run in her mind the incidents and conversations at the conference that might have hinted at the possibility of blackmail. She remembered particularly the open antagonism between Valerie and Bridget throughout the conference, and Sally recalled Valerie's angry reaction to Bridget when the latter had sympathised with her over what they had all then thought of as a practical joke.

"Well, someone took them, that's for sure."
"Well, *I* didn't. I would never do such a thing. I don't know why you think I'd do it, Valerie."
"*Don't* you?"

And of course, thought Sally, it would have made

perfect sense to Valerie for Bridget to have taken her own books back — if Valerie had indeed been blackmailing her. She thought of other possible victims of blackmail — Richard? He seemed to have a fling with a different woman at every conference. Was there a Mrs Fingleton at home whom he didn't want to find out about them? And what about Harriet? She was married, and had asked Sally not to mention Richard should she meet her husband. Maybe Valerie had cornered her during the conference and threatened to tell her husband about her fling with Richard? Sally discounted that theory quickly — Rhian had said it wasn't easy to get hold of phenelzine, so Valerie's murder would have had to be planned, and not just a few hours prior to her death.

Then, of course, there were Veronica and Mark, both of whom had long been estranged from Valerie, but who still stood to benefit substantially from her death. Sally logged on to the internet and Googled the names on her list to see if she could find out more about them. She found several references to Richard — he had his own page on the English department staff sites at Birmingham University, and was listed as having given lectures at various conferences and having written and contributed to a number of books and academic articles on boys' fiction as well as on various twentieth-century novelists. A short biography of Richard on one of the conference sites described him as a divorcee. The conference had taken place over a year ago, so presumably there had been no new Mrs Fingleton for Valerie to threaten and bribe him with.

Harriet also merited a number of internet references, including a staff page at Manchester University's English department website. The name Bridget Whodcoat only turned up posts on various internet forums, mainly girls'-own-related, and listed her name as being on the board of governors at a school in Hampstead, presumably her sons' comprehensive. Sally tried Mark Teague next; he lived in Southampton and worked as a solicitor. She couldn't find anything for Veronica Teague and couldn't remember her married name, so left that for another time and decided to Google on some of the other delegates. Sally keyed in Leonie Carr's name next — she showed up as the Chalet Girls forum host, and was also listed as an employee at the museum where she worked. The only reference to Leah Brindsley was to her web page on abebooks.com.

Sally glanced up at the clock — three-thirty. If she was going to make it to St Martin-in-the-Fields by six o'clock, she'd better get moving. Leaving her notebook on the dining table, she went back to her room and started to get ready to go out.

Harriet, Richard and Leonie were already waiting outside the church when Sally arrived.

"Sorry to keep you," she apologised. "Hope you haven't been waiting long."

"Long enough," said Harriet with a grimace. "Now, where on earth is Bridge? Oh, here she comes." She waved as Bridget approached them, laden with shopping bags. Bridget hurried over and gave all of them, including Sally, a hug. "Nice to see you again," she said to Sally. "I enjoyed having coffee the other day. We'll have to do that again before you head back to Melbourne."

"Okay," said Richard. "Where shall we head for?"

"Is anyone else coming?" Sally asked.

"No — honestly, some people are such bores,"

sighed Harriet. "The thought of getting on a train and coming up to London for a night on the tiles is too much for them. They're all staying in Worthing, eating at their guesthouse and going to bed early with their mugs of Horlicks."

"Let's go for a drink first unless anyone's absolutely ravenous," Richard suggested.

They walked in the direction of Covent Garden and Richard spotted an attractive-looking Tudor-style pub at the end of a narrow alleyway. Because it was Friday night it was already brimming with besuited office workers, all celebrating the start of the weekend. As they pushed through the crowd towards the bar, Sally noticed a narrow spiral staircase towards the back of the pub and said, "Perhaps there's some room upstairs? I'll go and check."

Fortunately, there were a couple of vacant tables, and with a ceiling fan running it wasn't too hot. Leonie and Harriet followed Sally upstairs and flopped down at the table nearest the window. Bridget then emerged at the top of the stairs and called over to them, "What do you all want to drink? Richard's getting the first round in. I'll help him carry them." Sally, not wanting to consume too much alcohol that night, ordered a spritzer, while Leonie asked for a bottle of Grolsch and Harriet ordered a gin and tonic. Bridget handed over her shopping bags to Harriet.

"Put them down in a safe place," she said. "I've been to Charing Cross Road and I've got a couple of books there that I don't want beer spilt on!"

"Ooh, can we see?" Harriet called after her, but Bridget had disappeared. Harriet hunted through the bags, discarding a couple containing clothes and then peeking into the third. "Wow," she said, extracting a beautiful, plastic-encased copy of the first edition of *The Chalet School in Exile*. "Goodness, it's the one with the Nazis on the cover. It cost her £1500. Oh, I'm envious. Lucky old Bridge with the wealthy husband."

"What's the other book?" asked Leonie.

"*Rachel in the Abbey*," said Harriet, taking it out. Like the Chalet book, it had been carefully packed in plastic and had the price on the front. "Oh, goodness," she said again. "This one cost £250. Look."

"I thought Bridge already had those two," said Leonie.

"Oh, you know Bridge," said Harriet. "She's probably upgrading because one of the pages of the copy she's got is turned over in one corner or something."

Or was she simply replacing books she's been forced to hand over to Valerie, Sally wondered.

"It's just unfair that Bridget has so much more disposable income than the rest of us," said Leonie. "She'll be able to outbid all of us at the auction tomorrow if there's anything she wants."

"Can I see them?" Sally asked.

"You *can* but you *may* not," Harriet responded teasingly, quoting the Chalet School's long-time headmistress and correct English vigilante, Miss Annersley. Leonie laughed.

"Oh, come on!" Sally protested, irritated with Harriet and annoyed with herself for falling into the trap. "Everyone says 'can' …"

Harriet handed over the books, and Sally examined the cover carefully and enviously, wishing she could afford to buy first editions.

"Richard and Bridge are an age, aren't they?" said Harriet. "I'll go down and see what they're up too." As Harriet headed down the staircase, Leonie chuckled.

"Harry's getting jealous," she commented.

"Jealous?" Sally queried, slipping the books back in their bag and placing them carefully on top of Bridget's other purchases.

"Yes, because Richard's spending too long down there with Bridget — in Harry's opinion. Of course, she'll go down and find they're having a terrible time trying to get served, but she'll stick to them like a limpet, just in case Richard decides to transfer his affections." Leonie shook her head. "As if! Bridget's got a lot more sense than that."

"I don't think I'd risk losing a wealthy husband like Bridget's got just for a fling with Richard," remarked Sally, with a glance in the direction of Bridget's newly acquired books.

Leonie laughed. "Exactly! By the way, Sally," she added. "Any update on those mystery messages on the forum?"

Sally hesitated. She'd have liked to confide in Leonie, but realised that until she knew a bit more about whether Valerie had blackmailed any of the other conference delegates, it was best to keep quiet. After all, she told herself, she didn't really know Leonie at all — Valerie might have been blackmailing *her*, for all Sally knew. "Not really," she said. "Once I have something concrete, I'll let you know, I promise."

Leonie eyed her dubiously, and Sally sensed that the other woman had picked up on the element of mistrust. She felt a pang of regret; she liked Leonie and would have liked to get to know her better, but this would get in the way of any future friendship. Fortunately, Bridget, Harriet and Richard clattered up the stairs at that moment with the drinks, so further, probably awkward, conversation between Sally and Leonie was suspended.

"Boy, do I need this," said Bridget, sitting down

and taking a long gulp of real ale. "It's thirsty work, shopping."

"It must be," said Harriet. "We took a look at your books, by the way, Bridget, and we're all very envious."

"Ooh, books," said Richard. "May I see?"

Bridget produced the books for Richard to examine, then said, "How did dear Valerie's funeral go, by the way?"

"It was pretty good, actually," said Richard. "Quite a party — no-one was exactly mourning, as you can imagine."

"Oh, I *can* imagine," said Bridget, with a grin. She raised her glass. "Here's to her demise, then!"

"Bridget!" Harriet said reprovingly.

"Come on, Harry!" Bridget laughed. "You know there was no love lost! We may as well celebrate the fact that we won't see any more of her."

"These are very nice copies, Bridget," said Richard, changing the subject as he handed them back. "Where did you buy them from?"

"Robert Trussell's shop in Charing Cross Road," Bridget told him.

"Oh, that rip-off merchant," said Richard. "What is it they say about having more money than sense, Bridge?"

Bridget made a face at him.

"I thought you'd already got first editions of those two, Bridge," said Harriet.

Bridget shrugged. "These copies are better. My other copy of *Exile* only had a photocopied dustjacket, and *Rachel* had the imprint page torn out."

"Poor old you," said Leonie. "Some of us only have Chalet paperbacks and horribly mutilated Children's Press editions of the Abbey books!"

"After the auction tomorrow," said Richard, "you

may well be the proud owner of a nice set of hardbacks. You too, Sally."

"I wish," said Sally. "Even if the prices *are* reasonable, I don't suppose they'll sound so great when I convert them back to Australian dollars."

"That reminds me," said Bridget. "I wonder what happened to those books of Valerie's that she said had disappeared?"

"Perhaps one of the other book dealers had anticipated her death and had already swiped them," suggested Leonie, with a grin.

"Perhaps," said Richard. He finished the rest of his beer. "Drink up, you lot. It must be time for another."

Sally arrived back at Rhian's flat at around 11 o'clock. After the second round of drinks, Harriet had suggested they find somewhere to eat, and they'd spent a pleasant couple of hours at an Italian restaurant just off Leicester Square, discussing books and authors. Sally hadn't gleaned any information that was relevant to her investigation, but she'd still enjoyed the evening. Rhian was already home when Sally returned. She waved towards Sally's notebook, still lying on the dining table. "What's that you've been doing?"

Sally showed her the list of suspects and told her what she'd learned from Margaret. "I was thinking that if Jess Gibson was being blackmailed by Valerie, then possibly other people were too — and these are some of the delegates at the conference who I thought *might* have been being blackmailed." Sally outlined her reasons.

"I'll open a bottle," said Rhian. "It helps me to think." She disappeared into the kitchen and returned with a bottle of white wine, two glasses and a corkscrew. "It's a clever idea," she said, as she uncorked the wine. "Demanding books in return for silence. Nothing can be traced to you — not like deposits in the bank." She poured the wine and handed a glass to Sally. Oh, well, thought Sally, she had deliberately kept her alcohol intake low that evening — it wouldn't hurt to have another glass of wine. "And you're probably right — if Valerie's stock was so good and plentiful, the chances are she didn't luck out every weekend at charity shops and car boot sales. So yeah, it's probably worth taking a closer look at the people on that list. Though if anybody did slip Valerie some phenelzine, my money's still on Justine."

"Yes, but how? We know she didn't attend the conference. And I honestly don't think Margaret did it for her. Margaret can barely handle the guilt of having stolen Valerie's books."

"Did you have any complimentary food in your rooms?" Rhian asked.

"No."

Rhian sighed. "A pity. I was thinking it might have been easy enough for Justine to doctor the food in Valerie's room prior to the conference."

"Do you think we should be telling the police any of this?" Sally asked.

"Why? We still don't know that Valerie was murdered, do we?"

"But won't the fact that Valerie was blackmailing people make a difference to the way they look at the case?"

"Well, they can't arrest her for it, can they?" Rhian grinned. "And," she pointed out, "we don't actually know she was blackmailing *people*. We only know that she was blackmailing Jess Gibson — a dying woman. Do you really want Arrowman interrogating Jess Gibson unless it's strictly necessary?"

"No," Sally sighed.

"Look," said Rhian, "if we can find out that Valerie was blackmailing a few people out of books, then I agree that we should tell Arrowman. Because yes, it's possible Valerie was murdered. But I think we should have the chance to dig around first. We're just guessing that Valerie blackmailed other people — we don't know that. After all," she added, with a grin, "just how many dark secrets does the collective 'girls' own' community have, do you think?"

CHAPTER XXI.

A STARTLING REVELATION

...[A]s she read on she recognized it as absolutely identical with the essay on 'A Favourite Hero', which Susie had submitted, and which she had highly commended. Frowning, she rang the bell, and instructed the maid to find Miss Susie Martin ... After about five minutes, her niece appeared.

"Now Susie," began Miss Martin holding out the copy of King William's School Magazine, "will you explain to me how it is that your essay on 'David Livingstone' is word for word the same as this by Gerald Sullivan!"

Angela Brazil, *The School at the Turrets*, 1935

"So," said Rhian, the following morning, "what do you think Jess Gibson was being blackmailed about?"

It was nine-thirty and Sally and Rhian had just got up and were lounging in the living-room in dressing-gowns, eating toast and working their way through a pot of coffee. Sally was lying on the sofa, reading an article of Rhian's in the *Clarion*; Rhian was sprawled across the rug, flicking through a copy of *Time Out*.

"No idea," returned Sally. "I've only met the woman once — at Valerie's funeral."

"What *do* you know about her, then?"

"That she set up and runs Tales Out of School with Miriam Lorrimer. That she's got cancer and doesn't have much longer to live. That she wrote a feminist critique of girls' school stories that was published a couple of years ago."

"A *feminist* critique of girls' school stories?" Rhian said in disbelief.

"Yes. There are quite a few. I haven't really read any, though, including Jess's. But hers is supposed to be one of the best. Vintage Child published it — they're a publishing company that mainly republish kids' books that are out of print. But they publish biographies of old children's authors and criticisms in the genre as well."

"You must know something else about her, surely?"

"Like what? Oh, I know from her biog on the Tales Out of School website that she's a churchgoer and into cross-stitch — and that she was widowed a few years ago. But if she's into kinky sex rituals or has gone off with the church collection on a regular basis, thus giving Valerie a reason to blackmail her, then no, I don't know about it."

"Well, we could try an internet search on her," Rhian suggested. "You never know — if she *has* appeared in court charged with some crime or other, a story might show up."

"If it shows up on the internet, then why allow yourself to be blackmailed about something that anybody can find out about by using Google?" Sally pointed out.

"Good point," Rhian conceded. "Your best bet is to ask at this afternoon's auction — the woman you overheard her talking to at the funeral, for example. She was trying to persuade Jessica to tell her what the blackmail was all about and Jessica might well have done so by now."

"Miriam Lorrimer — yes, they are old friends so Jessica might well have decided to confide in her,"

Sally agreed. "But whether Miriam, if she's at the auction, would divulge her friend's secrets to me is another matter."

"Oh, just challenge her with what you know," said Rhian. "She'll probably tell you stuff then."

She'd probably open up to Rhian, Sally thought, but whether she would open up to *her* was another matter. Still, she reminded herself, Margaret, when challenged, had confided in her, so maybe ...

With the auction beginning at two o'clock in Worthing, Sally had to head off at around eleven-thirty, thus allowing time for possible delays. She had rather hoped that Rhian might accompany her, but Rhian had arranged to meet a friend for lunch. "I'll do some digging around, though," Rhian promised. "I've got that list of delegates from Miriam Lorrimer and I'll see if I can find anything dubious on any of them — especially Bridget Whodcoat, given you seem to think Valerie had something on her. I can pop into the *Clarion* and make use of the cuttings library. There might be stuff on there that never made it on to the internet."

The journey to Worthing went smoothly, and Sally found herself at Valerie's ten minutes before the auction was due to begin. The usual familiar faces were there — Richard, Harriet, Leonie, Miriam, Leah, Bridget and Jess Gibson — as well as one or two others she recognised from the conference but had never actually spoken to. As usual, she found herself captured by Richard and Harriet, and stood talking to them and to Leonie and Bridget before the auction began.

"Some wonderful stock here," Richard remarked. "Just take a look at it all, Sally."

All the books that were being auctioned off were arranged on bookshelves in Valerie's living room. Most, though not all of it, consisted of school stories, and Sally looked longingly at the huge collection of Chalet School hardbacks and wonderful girls' annuals from the 1920s through to the 1980s. She determined that by the end of the auction she would go home with *something*. It wasn't far into the auction, though, when she realised that she would most likely go home empty-handed. The books started attracting bids that were more than she could afford. She watched despondently as the books she'd have particularly liked made their way to other, wealthier bidders.

"Don't worry," Bridget murmured. "They'll be spent out soon, a lot of them. Most people have only so much money they can spend." Bridget was bidding on *School Friend* annuals from the 1950s, as well as on individual *School Friend* comics from the 1920s and 1930s.

"I didn't know you collected annuals and comics, Bridge," Richard commented.

"I do now," Bridget grinned. "I've always had a hankering to follow the fortunes of the Silent Three and the girls of Cliff House School through from beginning to end."

Richard had successfully bid on a couple of Abbey books, while Harriet was bidding on school stories that had been published more recently — Anne Digby's Trebizon series, Harriet Martyn's Balcombe Hall stories, and *Grange Hill* annuals and novels that were spin-offs from the popular television series. Sally, watching the bidding closely, noticed that neither Jess Gibson nor Leah Brindsley tried to buy anything — so what, she wondered, had been their purpose in coming here? Especially, Jess, given her state of health — Leah, as a book dealer, might have hoped for bargains that just hadn't been forthcoming. Eventually Sally made a successful bid on a beautiful edition of *The Vanishing Pony* by Mary

Gervaise, and started to feel that coming to the auction had been worthwhile after all.

"What about a drink afterwards?" Richard suggested as the auction began to draw to a close. "Can you manage it before you go back to London, Sally? What about you, Bridge?"

Sally checked her watch; nearly five o'clock. "Yes, that's fine," she said. "I haven't made any arrangements for tonight."

"I can stay as well," said Bridget. "Though we have some friends coming round tonight at about eight-thirty, so I shouldn't stay too long."

Once the auction had ended, people quickly dispersed. Veronica brewed more coffee for those who wanted to hang around for a while. Harriet, Bridget and Richard loitered, examining their purchases. Jess Gibson sank down on one of the sofas, looking tired and drawn. Miriam Lorrimer went in search of a glass of water for her.

Sally slipped upstairs to the bathroom. It had occurred to her that if Valerie had been blackmailing Jess — or Bridget or anyone else for that matter — then she might have kept something in the house pertaining to the reason for the blackmail. Perhaps a bookmarked internet site, or even something hidden in a drawer. She thought that while the few people left in the house were occupied downstairs, she might take the opportunity to have a quick snoop in Valerie's office. When they'd come for the funeral, it had been locked to protect all the stock. Now, as she'd expected, the door was open. Sally closed the study door carefully behind her and looked around.

The office had certainly had a clear-out. A desk lay under the bay window; there was no computer atop it, and a quick look at the drawers revealed that they were empty. Every wall was obscured by floor-to-ceiling bookcases, which now stood devoid of books. However, someone — presumably Veronica or Mark — had placed two or three piles of paperwork on the shelves. No doubt, Sally thought, as she thumbed through the papers, these had been taken from the desk drawers.

Most of the paperwork was to do with books sold or bought at deceased estate auctions. There were also a couple of print-outs from internet sites covering the G.O. genre — a list of forthcoming titles from Vintage Child, a critique of classic pony books. And there was also, to Sally's surprise, a carbon copy of a typewritten manuscript — she hadn't seen anything typewritten or in carbon in years.

She looked at the title — *Germaine Goes to the Chalet School: A Feminist Perspective on the Girls' School Story*. The author had inserted her name underneath: 'By Mary Walter'. Who was she? Sally wondered; she'd never heard of her. She flipped through the manuscript — Sally hadn't really read very much in the way of school-story criticisms, but she'd read plenty of online discussions about them, and Mary Walter's manuscript didn't seem to contain anything that hadn't already been argued by Jess Gibson, among other people. Perhaps that was why it had remained unpublished. Sally was just wondering whether Mary Walter had been a pseudonym for Valerie Teague, and if her lack of success publishing the book had led to her antagonism towards conference speakers like Sue Parkinson, when the door opened and Jess Gibson walked in and demanded, "Whatever are you doing?"

Sally jumped guiltily. "Sorry," she said. "I got a call on my mobile and came in here to take it — then I got distracted by one of Valerie's old manuscripts." She waved the manuscript towards Jess, then returned it to the shelf. Jess had looked pale to begin with, but Sally, watching her, was sure she turned whiter when she saw the carbon sheets. And what was *Jess* doing in here anyway, Sally thought, suddenly becoming suspicious. She'd been downstairs looking ill only a few minutes ago and presumably, like Sally, had said she was going to the bathroom. Why come into the study? It wasn't as if Sally had left the door ajar or had been making a noise or had left the light on, thus attracting attention. No, she thought, Jess had come in here for the same reason Sally had — to find the evidence for whatever it was that Valerie had been blackmailing her about ...

"Are you feeling better now?" Sally asked. "You weren't feeling too good just after the auction."

"I'm okay." Jess's eyes darted again to the manuscript, and Sally suddenly realised — *that* was what she was looking for.

"You know," said Sally, conversationally, "I think I might ask Veronica if I can have this old manuscript of Valerie's. It looks pretty interesting, and it's of no use to Valerie now. And I shouldn't think Veronica will mind having one less thing to throw out. What do you think?"

Jess swallowed. "I'd quite like to have it," she said. "I have an interest in the feminist perspective on school stories, as you know, and—"

"How do you know that's what it's about?" Sally asked.

"Valerie mentioned it to me at some stage."

Sally picked it up. "Well, I think I'll ask Veronica about it. I shouldn't think you'll find anything in it that you don't already know about, having written a book yourself, and I'd really like to read it."

Jess had closed the study door behind her after entering, and now stood with her back against it. "Please Sally," she said. "I really need to have that manuscript."

"Well," said Sally, "if there's such a demand for it, maybe I'll suggest to Veronica that she auctions it off. After all, maybe Harriet or Richard or Bridget would like a chance of reading it as well—"

"No," Jess protested. She leaned her head against the door, looking more tired than ever. "Please, Sally. It's absolutely vital that you don't show it to anybody else."

"Why?" Sally asked. "I don't understand—"

"Because if anyone sees it, they'll recognise it," Jess admitted bleakly. "It's a copy of the book I wrote myself."

"You mean — *you* are Mary Walter?"

"No. Mary Walter was someone I knew. She sent me the book to read not long after Miriam and I started Tales Out of School. She wanted advice on where she might find a publisher — the mainstream publishers had already lost interest in girls' school stories, and Vintage Child hadn't come on the scene back then. I didn't think I could help at all, but I enjoyed reading it — and I rang her up to tell her so, only when I rang she'd died. She'd been killed in a car crash."

"And so you passed the book off as your own?" Sally asked contemptuously.

"Yes. Not straightaway, but later, when Vintage Child started publishing. Please, Sally, don't tell anyone else will you?" Jess begged. "I'm not proud of what I did, but I couldn't bear the thought of everyone knowing. I've never told anyone — not even Justine, not even Miriam—."

"But Valerie knew, didn't she?" Sally asked. "That's why she was blackmailing you. That's why you gave her so many of your books."

"How do *you* know about—?" Jessica began, startled. Then she sighed wearily. "Yes," she admitted. "Valerie knew. Mary Walter's husband wanted to sell her collection of school stories after she died and contacted a book dealer. Valerie, of course, was the book dealer he contacted. When she was going through the stuff, she came across the carbon copy of the manuscript, and he told her she could keep it. She read it and liked it so much that she kept it. Then, when I got my contract with Vintage Child, and their website published some 'tasters' for the book, she recognised them as being from the manuscript she'd got. She kept quiet until the book was published, then the blackmail started."

It was hard, Sally thought, to decide who she felt the more disgusted with — Jess for passing off someone's work as her own, or Valerie for blackmailing her rather than exposing the plagiarism.

"Does anyone else know about this?" Jess demanded.

Sally shook her head.

"You won't tell anyone, will you?" Jess pleaded. "Please. I'm dying, Sally—."

"I don't know yet," Sally said. "But I am taking the manuscript, Jessica. I'm not letting you destroy it."

"That's what you think," said Jess, and, taking Sally completely by surprise, she made a sudden dive for the manuscript, tearing it from Sally's hands.

CHAPTER XXII.

ANOTHER CLUE — AND A QUARREL

"Sorry, Rebecca, I don't feel like any cocoa," said Sue, getting to her feet. "I'm going up to bed."

She went out through the door. Tish jumped up to follow her, looking annoyed. "Come back, Sue. Talk about it properly—"

Rebecca ... pulled her down into her seat again.

"Leave her alone, Tish!" she said. "You ... can see she doesn't want to talk about it any more tonight."

Anne Digby, *Second Term at Trebizon*, 1980

"JESS! Jess! Are you okay?" It was Miriam Lorrimer's voice; she sounded anxious, and no wonder, Sally thought, given the fact that Jess had looked so exhausted just fifteen minutes or so ago. Jess, for her part, froze, the manuscript still in her hands.

"*Jess!*" Miriam called. There was panic in her voice now, and Sally called out, "We're in here, Miriam."

The door opened and Miriam entered, looking concerned. "Oh, Jess, I thought you had collapsed or something—." She stopped abruptly, picking up on the tense atmosphere within the room. "What's wrong?"

"Oh nothing," said Jessica. "We were just talking — I'm fine, Miriam, don't worry."

"Actually," said Sally, "I was just saying to Jessica that I'm going to ask Veronica if I can have that old manuscript of Valerie's." She nodded towards the manuscript, which was still in Jessica's now trembling hands. "It looks really interesting."

And as Sally had guessed she would — for, after all, she wouldn't want to protest and risk Miriam asking to take a look at it — Jessica handed over the manuscript. "Take it, then. But I'd like to talk to you a bit more about — you know, what we were talking about."

"Well, so long as you're all right, Jess," said Miriam. "Don't wear yourself out now, will you?"

She turned to leave the room and Sally followed her. "I think I've said all I want to on that subject for now, Jessica."

"Please — Sally ..."

Miriam had left the room and was making her way downstairs. Sally turned round. "What?" she asked coldly.

"Please don't tell anyone."

"Well," said Sally, "that depends, doesn't it? I mean, if Valerie was murdered and you were being blackmailed by her ..."

"I wasn't even at the conference, Sally. And anyway, I thought the general feeling was that Valerie had taken a tablet inadvertently."

Sally shrugged. "I still think I should let the police know. Once they know that — and hear about the fact that your daughter arranged with another delegate to destroy some of Valerie's books ..."

Jessica sighed. "So Justine did have a hand in that — the practical joke. I was worried about that, from the minute Miriam told me about it. Justine knew Valerie had something on me, but I never told her what it was. The same with Miriam — she knows I was being blackmailed, but she doesn't know why."

"Sally!" It was Bridget this time, rushing up the

stairs. "There you are — we're all waiting for you. Are you ready to go to the pub?"

Sally nodded and followed Bridget downstairs, leaving Jessica Gibson staring miserably after her.

They didn't spend long at the pub — just enough time to enjoy a quick round of drinks. Sally had put the manuscript into the plastic carrier bag Veronica had given her for *The Vanishing Pony*. She knew exactly what Rhian would want to do with it — publish a piece on the school-story guru's plagiarism and the book dealer's blackmail. Sally sighed; it would all be so much easier to deal with if Jess Gibson *wasn't* dying ...

"If you want to leave now, I'll catch the train back with you," said Bridget, misinterpreting Sally's sigh as a sign she'd had enough of the pub.

There were goodbyes all round.

"I'd love to have everyone to dinner before you go back to Melbourne, Sal," said Richard. "Because I don't suppose we'll ever see you again."

"Well, not for a few years anyway," Sally smiled. "Trips over here are too expensive to manage on a regular basis."

"We could always come out for your conference," said Harriet.

"What did Miriam and Jess think of the idea?" Leonie asked.

"Oh, not interested," said Sally. "If there's to be a conference, I'll have to organise it myself."

"You should," Richard said. To her surprise, Sally realised that she was considering this as a real possibility. If she *could* get her bosses at *Australian Collector* interested, then it might well be possible to get something off the ground. It would be a lot of hard work, but ultimately rewarding, she was sure.

It was quite a chilly evening, as Sally found out when she and Bridget left the pub and walked along the quiet streets to the railway station. She buttoned her cardigan and wished she'd brought along a thicker jumper. Bridget, clad in a dress and a light jacket, shivered too. "Summer's over," she commented. "There's a definite 'touch of cold in the autumn night', to quote a poem I studied at school. Lucky you, heading back to the sunshine in a few days' time."

"Oh, Melbourne's pretty chilly this time of year," Sally said. "And September can be very wet."

"I've never been to Melbourne," Bridget said. "I went to Australia years ago — I spent most of my time in Sydney, but also went up to Queensland and to Darwin and the Kakadu National Park. But I never ventured down south."

"When was that?" Sally asked.

"Oh, way back — when I was doing my gap year between uni and starting work."

They arrived at the station only a couple of minutes before the train pulled in. They settled down opposite each other in the carriage. Bridget took out her *School Friend* comics and started chuckling over them. "Here — have a look," she said to Sally, passing one of the comics across to her. "The Silent Three are terrific."

Sally started reading, and was enjoying the comic when the train neared East Croydon station. Sally got ready to disembark, handing Bridget the comic she'd been reading. Bridget shook her head. "No — keep reading it. You're enjoying it, I can tell. Post it back to me when you've finished it. You've got my address."

"No, really, it's— "

"Please do. You'll probably never get another

chance to read one — how many of them do you find at car boot sales in Oz? And I know you'll return it — I trust you."

"Well, thanks." Sally had enjoyed the picture strips she'd read so far and was happy to finish reading a 1950s comic. "I'll post it back to you on Monday, Bridget. I'll package it up well for you so it doesn't get damaged."

"I know you will," said Bridget. The train pulled into the station and Sally rose to her feet. "Well, I don't suppose I'll see you again unless Richard does organise a dinner party and we both attend, but if this is goodbye, it's been nice knowing you, Sally."

"You too," Sally smiled. "Goodbye Bridget. And thanks again for this."

And the *School Friend* comic and *The Vanishing Pony* kept her happily occupied for the rest of her journey to Forest Hill.

Rhian wasn't home when Sally got back to the flat. Sally put the book, comic and manuscript in her bedroom, then went online to see if she'd received any emails. There weren't any, but Angus was surprisingly up and logged on to MSN, and she enjoyed a brief chat with him before he announced that he had to get off to school. Sally poured herself a glass of orange juice and settled down for a surf. She Googled on 'Jessica Gibson' and found several glowing reviews of her book; no wonder she didn't want other people knowing she'd not written it.

The Chalet Girls site had been busy, as usual — members were still discussing some of the talks that had been given at the conference, as well as today's auction. Several people were lamenting that the books hadn't gone more cheaply. Sally checked out some of the new threads — someone wanted to know how many words there had been in the average hardback Chalet School book. Leonie had responded — presumably from her room at the bed and breakfast — saying she thought that *Gay from China at the Chalet School* had been about 60,000 words long, and resurrecting an old forum thread on the same topic. Sally clicked on the link and found a thread dated two years ago; there seemed to be general concurrence that the average Chalet ran to 60,000 words. Bridget said she had picked a hardback off the shelf at random and had counted the number of words on one of the pages. If you multiplied that by the number of pages, she said, then— Sally frowned. Bridget had counted the number of words in one of her hardbacks. And the copy of *Lintons* that Margaret had stolen from Valerie's stall had had the number of words scribbled on one of the pages — did that mean that Valerie *had* been in possession of at least one of *Bridget's* books? Valerie had definitely had something on Bridget, that had been evident in their exchanges at the conference — but what?

Rhian clattered in at that moment. "Great night tonight," she said. "I went out with a bunch of folk from the paper, and had to drag myself away before I got hopelessly drunk."

"Oh, you should have stayed," said Sally. "Don't think you have to get back for me."

"Well, I wanted to get back because we're getting up early tomorrow," said Rhian. "I spoke to Fee this afternoon, and we thought the three of us could have a nice day out in Warwickshire. So we'll get up at the crack of dawn and drive up there. I've managed to get Justine Gibson's address from the electoral register, so I think we could pay her a visit."

"Okay," said Sally. "But I've got heaps to tell you, Rhee. Listen to what I found out at the auction!"

"Wow," said Rhian, when Sally had finished. "Plagiarism and blackmail — what a tale."

"I'll show you the manuscript," Sally said. She collected Mary Walter's manuscript from the bedroom, and Rhian examined it with interest.

"She begged me not to say anything," Sally said.

"But we will," Rhian said. "We have to. Passing off someone's work as your own is despicable. The person who wrote it originally deserves the credit, even if she is long dead."

"I know, but ..."

"But what?"

"She *is* dying, Rhian."

"And that makes it less of a crime? Don't be such a bleeding heart, Sally. She stole the work from someone who was dead, remember. It needs to be out in the open now — better than waiting till she's dead to say bad things about her ..."

"Yes, I know you're right, but?"

"But *what*?" said Rhian again, impatiently.

"Well, I'm just thinking that if any kind of charges were to be made, with Valerie dead and Jess dying, the ones who would get into trouble would be Justine and Margaret."

"And so they deserve to," said Rhian, crossly. "Theft. Criminal damage. Why are you feeling so sorry for them, Sally? They deserve whatever they get, in my opinion. Anyway, we'll talk to Justine tomorrow — see what she's got to say for herself. After what you've told me about the plagiarism, then it wouldn't surprise me if she *did* arrange to have Valerie bumped off. After all, once Jess dies, I guess Justine inherits any royalties she might get from that book. If the truth came out ..." Rhian shrugged.

"I don't know if the amount of money she'd get in royalties for a niche book like that would warrant killing someone," Sally objected.

"Well, we'll see what she has to say, won't we?" Rhian walked across to the CD rack and looked for something to put on. Sally sat quietly for a second, aware of the tension that had developed between them and feeling uncomfortable with it — after all, she was a guest in Rhian's home.

"I found out something else as well," Sally said, tentatively, as Rhian put on a Mozart CD.

"What's that, then?"

Sally told her about the thread on the forum, and how the book now in Margaret's possession might originally have been Bridget's.

"Could just be coincidence, of course," said Rhian. "If I had a valuable first edition, I don't think I'd go scribbling in it just to answer someone's question on the forum."

"Someone did, though," Sally pointed out.

"True. But it seems more the kind of thing a kid would do, not knowing that one day the book would become a valuable first edition. Which reminds me — there was nothing on Bridget Whodcoat on file at the *Clarion*. Though probably it's not so important to find out anything about her now. I'm pretty sure that if someone slipped a tablet to Valerie, it was Margaret acting on Justine's orders."

"Wouldn't a message have been placed in the forum, though?" Sally argued. "A Twenty Questions relating to someone who had died in a Chalet book. Why do it with the book burning and the office trashing if you don't do it with the murder?"

"Because news of Valerie's death would get out anyway? Justine would have heard quickly enough through Jess via Miriam ..."

"Maybe," Sally said.

"And the fact remains that, with her self-harm problems, Justine might well have had access to phenelzine. If we can find out that she's taken it at some stage ..."

Rhian's mobile rang at that point, and Sally was relieved when the caller turned out to be a friend; Rhian settled back in the armchair to chat for a while, and Sally retreated politely to her bedroom, taking Mary Walter's manuscript with her. She placed the manuscript carefully in a drawer, then got ready for bed. Much as she'd enjoyed her sleuthing over the past few days, she felt uncomfortable with Rhian's gung-ho approach to the case. Sally felt saddened as well as angered by Jess's plagiarism, and she knew that the collecting community, who had liked and respected Jess — and particularly Miriam Lorrimer — would be hurt by the revelations. Whereas to Rhian this was just a story — none of the protagonists were real to her. It was all about her research skills and her byline. Well, perhaps that wasn't *quite* true, Sally conceded — anyone who wrote for a living, as Rhian did, would be disgusted by plagiarism, and she was right in saying that credit for the book should go to its real writer. But Sally knew that the fall-out in the collecting world would continue long after Rhian's article had been printed, and she wondered just how her own part in the discovery would be received within it.

CHAPTER XXIII.

A DAY IN THE COUNTRY

"Hallo! She has done them well," said Rhoda to herself, pausing for a second to look. "But I wonder why there is an empty space here? It says 'Narrow-leaved hare's ear,' and there is nothing to be seen. Is it a kind of invisible plant, or has — well, I am sure there was something here once. You can see the mark of the stem, and the holes left where the thread went through."

Edna Lake, *Pamela of Peters'*, 1931

"IF we're driving through north London," said Sally the next morning, "would it be okay to drop this into Bridget Whodcoat's house at Hampstead Heath?" She waved the copy of *School Friend*. "I don't really want to trust it to the British post."

"That's fine," Rhian said, a little coolly. "We have to pick up Fee in Crouch End anyway, and Hampstead isn't far from there."

"What if Justine's not home?" said Sally. "It's a long way to go if she isn't."

"Then we enjoy a nice picnic and ramble in the country." Rhian grabbed a couple of bottles from the wine rack. "We'll get some food en route," she added.

Ten minutes later Rhian was weaving her way through the traffic and heading for north London. "I always think Melbourne traffic is bad," Sally commented, "until I come back over here and realise that, compared with London, Melbourne traffic isn't so bad after all."

It took them over an hour to reach Fiona's place in Crouch End. She was standing outside the terraced, 1930s house in which she owned the first-floor flat. "I was thinking we could have dinner at my place tonight," she said. "Sally hasn't seen my flat yet."

"Okay, good idea," Rhian agreed. "We can always stay over if we're too tired or too drunk to head back to Forest Hill. All right, Sally — whereabouts does your friend live?"

Sally gave her Bridget's address and Rhian checked it in the *A-Z*. "We can drop it round on the way home if you like," Sally said, "if we're coming back to Fee's."

"No, let's get it out of the way," said Rhian. "It's not far and I'm not tired now. I might be after we've been to Warwickshire and back."

Rhian drove out of Fiona's street and made her way east through Highgate to Hampstead. Bridget's house was in a street off Hampstead High Street, and the traffic was so bad that the women had ample time to gaze at the expensive shops and restaurants. No wonder Bridget can afford first editions if she lives here, Sally thought. Rhian was lucky enough to snag a parking space right outside Bridget's house — one of four attractive three-storey terraced houses, with mullioned windows, hanging plants, and an attic window. No garden, though, Sally noted, thinking how weird it must be to step right out of your front door on to the pavement.

Sally grabbed the comic, jumped out of the car and stepped up to the front door. A real bell was on the wall next to the door and Sally rattled its chain. The clanging of the bell brought a man to the door. He looked to be in his early forties — tall, blond, tanned and wearing jeans and a designer T-shirt.

"Hello," Sally said. "I've just brought this back for Bridget." She held out the comic.

"Oh," said the man, "she's just popped out for a moment, I'm afraid. But do come in — she won't be long. What about your friends?" he asked, looking across at Rhian's car. "Would they like to come in too?"

"We're actually going out for the day," Sally said. "I really can't stay."

"Ah, you must be the lady from Australia that she's mentioned. I'm James Whodcoat." He held out his hand and Sally shook it. "Look — she really won't be a moment and I know she'll be sorry if she's missed you. Why don't you go into the library and take a look at her books? That's what her collecting friends usually do."

"Well," said Sally, "just a quick look then." She signalled to Rhian and Fiona that she wouldn't be long, and then followed James inside. She found herself in a square hallway with gleaming wooden floorboards. A grandfather clock stood in the far corner, and an antique writing desk with stool was beside the staircase.

"Bridget's library is just in here," James said, indicating the door nearest the grandfather clock. "Can I get you a coffee or anything?"

"Oh no — I really mustn't stay. But thanks for the offer." Sally walked into the library and gazed around in awe. Three walls were lined with floor to ceiling bookshelves, and next to the door was a glass cabinet in which Bridget had placed some of her rarest titles. Sally moved closer to examine the bookshelves. Everything had been put in alphabetical order, so that the first set of bookshelves held Bridget's Enid Blyton books — a complete set of dust-jacketed Famous Fives as well as the Five Find-Outers, various other mystery series and, of course the three sets of school stories — her Angela Brazils and her Elinor M. Brent-Dyers. Sally looked admiringly at the perfect set of dustjacketed Chalet books, and then realised that there were some missing — no *Highland Twins at the Chalet School*, no *Changes for the Chalet School*, no *Redheads at the Chalet School* and, as Sally had suspected, no copy of *Lintons* ...

"I thought Bridge was finally losing her interest in this collecting lark when she started getting rid of some of the books," James commented. "But judging from her shopping expedition the other day and the auction yesterday, she's started buying with a vengeance again."

"Did she sell some on eBay?" Sally asked innocently, as she examined a beautiful first edition of *Lavender Laughs in the Chalet School*.

James chuckled. "Oh no. Bridge is much more at home spending money than making it. No, actually, she's given to one or two charity auctions, so I can't complain. Anyway, I'll leave you to look at the books. I know that's what you collectors like doing best. Actually," he continued, "you're the first member of the school-story brigade who's been round in ages. Bridge used to invite people round all the time to show off her books, but she seems to have stopped doing that."

"Oh," said Sally, lightly, "I suppose with the renovations you've had ..."

"Renovations?" he returned. "We haven't had any renovations."

"Sorry," Sally apologised. "I must have been thinking of someone else. I met everybody for the first time at last week's conference, and have probably mixed up more than half of what they told me."

James smiled and left the room. Sally carried on

examining the books, though her mind was only half on them. So Bridget definitely had been blackmailed ... and the whole story about renovations had been simply to keep people away from the house until she'd reacquired the collection.

She heard footsteps approaching the front door, and Sally half-hoped it was Bridget — it would be interesting to see Bridget's face once she realised Sally knew she had less than a complete collection of books and that there hadn't been any renovations. But when James opened the door, it was Rhian's voice she heard.

"—I know she'll be loving looking at the books, but we've got a really long drive ahead of us—."

"It's okay, Rhian," said Sally, coming into the hallway. "I'm coming. Tell Bridget I'm sorry I missed her," she added to James.

"I will," James said. "I can't think what she's doing — I expected her back by now."

"By the way," said Rhian, "what was Bridget's name before she married?"

"Emerson," said James, staring at her in surprise. "Why?"

"Oh," said Rhian airily, "it's just that a cousin of mine has a friend who went to Upland Park, so when Sally said she'd met someone who went there—."

"Yes, I suppose they might know each other," James replied.

"The friend's name is Catherine — Catherine Redmond, I think her name was before she married," Rhian frowned. "Not sure, though. Catherine anyway."

"I expect there were plenty of Catherines," said James. "Anyway, I'll ask her."

Sally said goodbye to James and followed Rhian down the drive to her car. "Do you really have a cousin with a friend who went to Upland Park?" she asked.

"'Course not," said Rhian scornfully. "I just wanted to find out what Bridget's maiden name was and that was a way of finding out. Like he said, there'd have been squillions of Catherines, so she won't suspect anything."

"Why did you want Bridget's maiden name?" Sally asked as they got into the car.

"So I can do a check for her in the cuttings file, of course — and on the internet come to that."

"Why? I thought Justine Gibson was your prime suspect," Sally returned tartly.

"She is. But if Valerie was blackmailing her too, then it's part of the same story."

"Bridget definitely *was* being blackmailed." Sally told Rhian and Fiona about the missing books and the fact that there *hadn't* been any renovations.

"I wonder what she was blackmailing her about?" said Fiona. "Do you think she plagiarised a book too?" Rhian had brought Fiona up to date with developments while they had been waiting for Sally in the car.

"Who knows?" said Rhian, driving off again. "Whatever it is, though, I'm determined to find out."

Justine Gibson's home couldn't have been more different to Bridget's. It was a two-storey house in a row of six — a 1970s-style terraced house, with no personality and thin walls; the three women could hear music thumping from one of the nearby houses. Rhian rang Justine's doorbell a couple of times and, when no-one answered, went next door to ask the neighbour if they knew where Justine was. The neighbour, a pretty blonde woman in her early thirties, with a toddler in tow, said she knew that Justine and the other two girls she rented the house with were all away for the weekend and, no, she didn't know where they'd gone.

"Wasted journey," said Rhian grumpily, as she returned to the car.

"You should have phoned first," said Sally.

"Yes, and then you get an answerphone and leave a message and then have no idea if they're away or just ignoring you," said Rhian. "I wish we had her mobile number. Could you get it from Jessica, Sally?"

"I doubt it," Sally returned.

"Miriam Lorrimer then?"

Sally shrugged. "No idea."

"Let's do something with the day now we've come this far anyway," Fiona urged them from the back seat.

"We're not far from Cotterford," Rhian replied. "We could go over there and take a look at the scene of the crime. Maybe even have a look in the manor house."

"There'll probably be a conference on," Sally pointed out.

"So what?" said Rhian. "We can bluff our way in."

Some twenty minutes later, Sally found herself once more in the drive of Cotterford Manor. That a conference was taking place there was apparent — several delegates, all sporting name badges, were standing around in groups on the steps and the lawns. She also spotted a familiar figure making her way down the steps. It was the young woman with the plait and nose ring that she'd overheard on the final night of the conference. Today she was wearing a jacket and had a bag slung over her shoulder, so presumably she'd finished for the day.

"We should talk to her," Sally said, getting out of

the car. She smiled at the approaching woman and said, "Hello. I was here for the school-story conference. Would you mind if I asked you something?"

"Depends what it is," the young woman returned, glaring at her.

"Are you Jo or Kate?" said Sally, remembering the names she'd overheard.

"Jo. Jodie."

Good, thought Sally. As Rhian and Fiona joined her, she said, "These are just friends of mine. One of them is a journalist and is writing a story about the woman who died at the conference."

"The one what committed suicide?"

"Is that what you think happened?" Rhian asked.

Jodie shrugged. "Dunno. The cops haven't been back, so it doesn't look like they think it's murder."

"On the last night of the conference," Sally said, "I overheard you and your friend talking about some spinach rolls that went missing before the folk dancing. Could you tell us something about that?"

"Is this for your paper?" Jodie demanded, looking at Rhian.

Rhian shrugged. "I don't know. Depends on how significant what you have to tell us is."

"Do I get paid for it?"

"No," said Rhian, firmly.

"I thought—."

"Well, you thought wrong. If I use what you say, I'll quote you. Your name will be in the paper. But I can't pay you, sorry. I work for the *Clarion* and, believe me, they take their sweet time about paying *me*."

Jodie looked disappointed. "Oh, well," she said. "It isn't anything much. The police didn't think so."

"What was it, anyway?" Rhian asked. "You never know — I might think it's more significant than the police do."

"Well, there were a hundred delegates, and I had to make a hundred spinach rolls, and a hundred of virtually everything else. Anyway, when I was laying the food on the trolley outside the kitchen, I put the spinach rolls on four large plates, twenty-five on each. Then I went back to the kitchen to prepare something else. And when I came back, there seemed to be space on one of the plates, and I counted the rolls and there were only twenty-three. And so I counted the other three and they all had twenty-five on them. So someone had taken them."

"How long before the dance was this?" Rhian asked.

"An hour or so. We put everything on the table in the conservatory before the dancing, so they could eat during the break."

"Did you hear anyone while you were in the kitchen — or see anyone?" enquired Sally.

"I actually did think I heard footsteps, but thought nothing of it," said Jodie. "I told the police that — I just thought that if there was a chance this woman was murdered, then someone could have taken the rolls and put poison in them and somehow put them on her plate. But everybody thinks I watch too many whodunits on the telly. Most likely someone just felt peckish, saw them and grabbed them. Look, I've got to go," she added. "I've arranged to meet my boyfriend down the pub."

"What's your name?" asked Rhian. "In case I need to quote you?"

"Jodie Bennett," Jodie returned, and headed off down the drive.

The conference delegates had all gone back inside Cotterford Manor. Rhian looked wistfully at the main entrance. "Let's go in and have a look around."

"And what do you think you'll find?" scoffed Fiona. "Antidepressant wrappings in somebody's waste paper basket? Come on — let's go and have lunch somewhere. Can we picnic in the grounds?"

"I don't know," said Sally, "But let's do it anyway."

They locked up the car and carried their picnic down to the rose gardens, where they settled down to eat.

"Has Bridget written any books that she might have plagiarised?" Rhian asked Sally, as she lay on her side on the grass and sipped wine.

"No. I'm surprised she hasn't written any books about school stories, actually, because she's very knowledgeable," Sally said.

"So what secret about her might Valerie have found out?"

"She knew something," Sally said. "She made a few pointed remarks at the conference."

"In relation to what?"

Sally was silent for a few moments as she recalled the altercations. "Well, she made a couple of remarks about the school Bridget attended — Upland Park ..."

"Maybe it's in connection with that?" Rhian suggested. "Maybe Bridget got expelled or something — something that she doesn't like people knowing."

"Bridget's views are very left-wing," Sally said. "I doubt she'd care two hoots if she'd been expelled from an establishment like Upland Park. In fact, from what I've read about her posts and seen of her personally, she'd be proud of it."

"It's a starting-point, though," said Rhian. "Tonight we can take a look on Friends Reunited, and maybe contact a couple of her friends through them and try to find out something more about her."

Fiona finished her wine, reached for another sandwich, and said, "Given you're going to do that tonight, can we *please* have a break from talking about Valerie, Justine and Bridget now? It's all you two have talked about all day and it's getting really tedious."

"Sorry," Sally apologised. She was tired of it too, despite her curiosity about the blackmail, and had been wishing Rhian would give it a rest for a while.

"Oh, all right," said Rhian, good-humouredly. "I can see you've had enough of it, Fee. Let's talk about something else instead."

CHAPTER XXIV.

THE MYSTERY UNRAVELS

The vase and photos of her parents which had stood on the mantelpiece were lying inside the fender and the ink-bottle had been turned upside down over them. The ink was meandering across the hearth and some had even seeped through under the fender and was staining the pretty hand-made wool rug she had done herself with such pride.

All in all, short of a tornado or an earthquake, only a cageful of monkeys from the Zoo could have made as much havoc.

Elinor M. Brent-Dyer, *Bride Leads the Chalet School*, 1953

IT was around nine o'clock when Rhian pulled up outside Fiona's flat that evening. After the picnic, they'd gone on a long walk through the Warwickshire countryside, then Rhian had driven back to London. Once back, they trooped up to Fiona's flat, where Fiona immediately set about ordering takeaway pizzas and garlic bread and Rhian examined the small wine rack on the kitchen bench for a suitable bottle of wine.

Sally spent a few minutes exploring Fiona's flat. The living room was quite large and Sally guessed that it attracted plenty of sunlight during the day. The prominent features of the room were a widescreen TV, Fiona's extensive DVD and CD collection, and a couple of bookcases filled with literary fiction and light whodunits. Fiona didn't have a spare room, but there were two sofa-beds in the living room that meant they would be able to stay overnight if they wished — Sally, watching Rhian pouring generous glasses of wine, guessed that they would definitely be staying.

"Can I check the internet?" Rhian asked Fiona, while Sally browsed the bookshelves.

"If you like. I'll fetch my laptop," Fiona said. She disappeared for a moment, returning with her laptop computer. "I'm still on dial-up, I'm afraid. I don't use the internet all that much — I use the computer enough at work!" She fired up the laptop and connected to the internet. "I suppose we're back to sleuthing now."

"Just a bit," Rhian said, with a grin.

Sally stood behind Rhian's chair as she went to the Friends Reunited website and keyed 'Bridget Emerson' into its search engine. There were no entries, so she searched for Upland Park school. "Which year would Bridget have left school?" she asked Sally.

"Not sure. She's in her mid to late thirties, I think," said Sally doubtfully.

"We'll look in about 1987, then," Rhian said. A long list of old girls appeared for that year. Rhian sighed. "She could probably have left school at any time between 1986 and 1990 — would girls from that type of school know pupils who were in different years?"

Sally shrugged. "I knew kids who were the year above or the year below me, but only if they lived nearby — not through school. But I don't know how somewhere like Upland Park would work."

"Oh well," said Rhian. "I'll pick someone at random then and email them." She chose a name, Katie Bellfield, from the 1987 leaving list and wrote an email to her saying that she was organising a 'This Is Your Life' presentation for Bridget Emerson's upcoming birthday and understood that Bridget had attended Upland Park school at some stage. Since Bridget didn't talk about schooldays much, any information on things she'd got up to back then would be most welcome. If she'd picked someone from the wrong leaving year, she apologised, and could Katie suggest another contact.

"She'll think it's odd you're organising something for her birthday and don't know which year she left," Sally commented.

"True," Rhian acknowledged. "What shall I say it's for then?"

"What about a work leaving party?" Fiona suggested.

"OK," Rhian nodded. She changed the wording and hit the send button.

"Fancy you being a paid-up member of Friends Reunited," commented Sally. "I've never felt compelled to part with the money just to be able to email someone from the past or have them email me."

Rhian shrugged. "It's useful for things like this."

The doorbell rang. "That's the pizza," said Fiona, hurrying to the stairwell to collect it.

Rhian disconnected the internet, and the trio hungrily tucked into garlic bread and pizza. Fiona was about to re-fill their wine glasses when Rhian's mobile rang. She didn't say much on the phone, but the other two noticed that a frown had appeared on her face, followed by an expression of anger.

"That was my neighbour," she said when she'd finished the call. "She just got home and noticed that my front door's been vandalised and it looks as if someone tried to break in. Sorry to break up the party, Fee, but I think I'd better get back."

"I'll come with you," said Sally straightaway. She had a strange feeling that somehow the vandalism was connected to the case. Of course, Rhian was a top national journalist and no doubt stepped on many people's toes, but for her flat to be targeted now, when they'd uncovered so much about Valerie Teague's blackmail and her victims, seemed to be too much of a coincidence.

"Oh no, Sal, you stay here and enjoy a night with Fee," Rhian said. "There's no need for you to come — really."

"I'd much rather. Your place might be a bit of a mess — you don't want to face that on your own, Rhian," Sally said.

"Perhaps I should come too," said Fiona. "I'll never settle down to anything here, wondering what's happening at your place, Rhian."

So in the end both Sally and Fiona travelled back to Forest Hill with Rhian, Fiona taking a change of clothes so she could stay overnight and turn up reasonably dressed for work the following day. Rhian drove quickly, weaving her way across London with an ease that Sally envied. Sally tended to stick to tried-and-tested routes in Melbourne, and felt that she would never have dared to drive across London.

Rhian's neighbour greeted her when she got back. She was in her late twenties, with long dark hair. "I don't think anyone got into your place, Rhian," she said, as Rhian got out of the car, "but they certainly tried. I didn't see anything, unfortunately. It happened after it got dark, and we had the curtains drawn. We heard a noise, and Steve took a look to see what was happening, but the person had gone by then."

"Thanks, Sarah," Rhian said. Once Sally and Fiona were out of the car, Rhian locked it, and turned towards her flat. The window in the door had been smashed. Someone had spray-painted the door: "Keep your noses out."

Noses, not nose, Sally thought. That seemed to indicate that the vandalism was related to the Valerie Teague case and not to something that Rhian was working on on her own.

Rhian, with Sally, Fiona and Sarah close behind her, turned the key in the lock. As she opened the front door, the women noticed smashed glass all over the small hallway. There was a large stone on the lowest step of the staircase that led up to Rhian's flat; Rhian trod gingerly over the glass, then picked up the stone. Someone had attached a message to it; white paper was held on the stone by an elastic band. Carefully, Rhian turned the stone over to read the message. "Stop poking your noses in where it's not wanted," she read. "We know where you live."

"Something to do with your work, then, Rhian?" suggested Sarah. She looked at the glass-covered floor in dismay. "I do wish we'd seen who did this."

"That's okay, Sarah. At least you heard them and were able to alert me. It wouldn't have been much fun coming back to this with no warning."

"Well, I'm sorry it's happened," said Sarah. "Do you want me to help you clean up or anything, Rhian?"

"It's alright," said Sally. "We're staying with her tonight. We can give her a hand."

Sarah nodded, said goodbye and left.

"Will you call the police, Rhee?" Fiona asked.

"Yes, for what it's worth. I doubt they'll come out tonight, though. But I'll ring them and we can get things cleared up later." Sally and Fiona followed Rhian upstairs; fortunately the person hadn't managed to get into the flat; everything in there was intact. All the same, Sally went straightaway to check that the manuscript was where she'd left it. It was; she breathed a sigh of relief.

"I'm so sorry, Rhee," she said, coming back into the living room. "What's happened must be to do with me and the Valerie Teague case."

Rhian nodded. "I agree. Interesting that Justine Gibson wasn't at home today. She has a nice line in vandalism, as we know. Or I suppose Margaret Wilks could have done it. She lives close enough."

"How would they know your address?" Fiona wondered.

"I'm afraid I gave it out to a few people in case they wanted to catch up with me after the conference," Sally said apologetically. "I gave Rhian's address and phone number, plus my own email address."

"Did you give my address to Margaret, then?" Rhian asked.

"I don't think I did, but she could have got it from quite a few people. Or Justine Gibson could have got it from Miriam Lorrimer."

Rhian phoned the police and gave details about the vandalism and veiled threats. As she'd predicted, a broken window and graffiti did not rate highly enough in the London crime stakes to bring the police out that night. They took the details from her, and suggested she kept the stone and paper and left the graffiti in place for them to see when they did come round. So Sally and Fiona helped Rhian to clean up the broken glass, and to board up the window. When that was done, they went back up to Rhian's living room, where Rhian decided that the occasion called for something stiffer than wine and opened a bottle of whisky.

"Not long now, Sal," said Rhian, as they all sat in her living room sipping whisky and trying to put the vandalism out of their minds, "and you'll be heading back to Oz. Any idea when you'll be back here?"

Sally shook her head. "It's so expensive to come out here — even with you kindly providing free accommodation for me, Rhian, it's prohibitive. What with the cost of the flight and then getting around here. ... We only get about 40p for our dollar, and everything that costs a dollar in Australia seems to cost a pound here. No, next time you want to see me, you'll have to come to Melbourne."

"It's time that's the problem for me," sighed Rhian. "I know it's a lot cheaper for us to come to you than for you to come to us in terms of cheaper air fares and better exchange rates, but really it's not worth going to Australia for less than a month, and getting a month off work in one hit ... Well, it's not a goer at the *Clarion*, unfortunately. Last time I came out, I was between jobs so it worked out okay, but I can't see myself managing another trip in the near future. How d'you manage to get a month off from your job?"

"So many Australians have family or friends overseas or interstate that there's nothing unusual in taking four weeks' holiday," Sally told her. "Mind you, I ended up doing about a month's work in my last week before flying out, because they don't bring anyone into cover for me."

Rhian glanced at the clock and rose from the sofa. "Nearly time for bed. What a day. I'm knackered. I'll just check my email, then I'm hitting the hay."

"Leave your email if you're that tired," advised Fiona, yawning. "I'm ready for bed myself."

"You use the bathroom first then," said Rhian. "It won't take me long to check my email. There probably won't be anything for me anyway."

Fiona, who was spending the night on the sofa, headed obediently to the bathroom. Sally disappeared to her own room to get undressed. She'd just got into her nightshirt when Rhian came darting into her room.

"Sally! Sally! Come and look at this — you're not going to believe it." She grabbed Sally's arm and pulled her towards the living room.

"What?" Sally asked. "Let go of me, Rhian — you're hurting me."

"Sorry," said Rhian, carelessly. "Just look! There — at the email on the screen." She nodded towards the computer screen. "I'll just call Fee." She banged loudly on the bathroom door. "FEE! Come out here and look at this."

Sally sat down and read the email in shock and disbelief.

Dear Rhian,

Thank you for your email regarding my old classmate Bridget Emerson. I think, however, you must be thinking of another Bridget Emerson, because the Bridget I was at school with died in a climbing accident in New Zealand in 1990, during her gap year after university. I don't recall another Bridget Emerson attending Upland Park — at least not during the years I was there — so the one you're searching for must have attended another school. I wish you luck in tracing her and good luck with the This is Your Life presentation.

Kind regards,

Katie Bellfield

"That must be her secret," said Rhian excitedly, behind Sally. "She's not Bridget Emerson at all ... That must be what Valerie found out about her. No wonder she was being blackmailed ..."

Sally frowned. "So if she's not Bridget Emerson, who is she then? It doesn't make sense."

"What doesn't?" asked Fiona, coming up behind them, wearing her dressing gown. She read the email. "God. How weird."

"Let's Google on Bridget Emerson and see what comes up," said Rhian. The search engine showed up nothing.

"1990 was pre-internet," said Sally. "Someone who died then wouldn't show up, unless their death was controversial for some reason."

"What time would it be in New Zealand, Sal?" Rhian asked.

"I think they're four hours ahead of Australia, so ..." Sally looked up at the clock. "It would be about one o'clock in the afternoon there. Why?"

"I've got a friend who used to work for the *Clarion*," said Rhian. "She works in New Zealand now, for a newspaper in Auckland. They'll probably still have something on the cuttings file about Bridget Emerson. I'll phone her and see what I can find out. In the meantime, try Googling on James Whodcoat and see what you can find out."

Rhian disappeared into her bedroom with the phone. Fiona dragged up a chair beside Sally and watched as her friend keyed 'James Whodcoat' into the search engine. He turned up in a small number of entries — he was a financial consultant and gave regular seminars on all aspects of finance. A short biography on a programme for a seminar he'd given earlier in the year said that he had been educated at Eton and at Christ College, Cambridge.

"I wonder if he's really who he says he is, or if he's

pretending to be someone else like Bridget," said Sally.

"Or perhaps Bridget faked her own death in New Zealand for some reason," Fiona suggested.

"Maybe some insurance scam, do you think?" said Sally. "It's possible." Her eyes fell on the next entry for James Whodcoat. "Oh, that's interesting, look — this entry mentions that James has a brother called Robert, who's a psychiatrist. I wonder if he lives near Bridget or if she sees him regularly?"

"Why d'you ask that?" Fiona asked.

"Because," said Sally, "if James's brother is a psychiatrist, then he'd be able to prescribe phenelzine. And if Valerie discovered that Bridget wasn't who she said she was, then ..." She remembered the night of the folk dancing, how Bridget had been first to tuck into the buffet, and how she'd hung around the table while Valerie, in common with others, had temporarily left her food in order to dance. She would have had ample opportunity to take the spinach rolls — already containing the phenelzine — from her bag and swap them for the ones already on Valerie's ... "Well, if the Whodcoats know that Bridget has stolen someone's identity, perhaps Robert Whodcoat was more than happy to prescribe phenelzine to stop Valerie blackmailing her. And if they didn't know, well, if Bridget was happy to steal someone else's identity, then I doubt if she'd baulk too much at stealing from her brother-in-law's prescription pad."

It was a couple of hours later when Rhian's contact in Auckland finally rang her back, having checked her newspaper's cuttings file. While they waited for the return call, Rhian had topped up the whisky glasses and read the entries that Sally had found about the Whodcoats.

"I think we're really on to something here," she said happily. "I think whoever this person who calls herself Bridget is *did* assume Bridget Emerson's identity and somehow Valerie found out. And I think she did get hold of the phenelzine, knowing that Valerie had been given phenelzine in the past. You said, didn't you Sal, that those who were regulars on the conference circuit seemed to know about that?"

Sally nodded. "Richard and Harriet certainly did, and I should think Bridget knew as well. She's a close friend of theirs."

"Well," said Rhian, "tomorrow, in my capacity as *Clarion* health editor, I shall phone Robert Whodcoat and ask if he's had any prescriptions go missing. It happens a lot — I doubt he'll be surprised that we're running yet another story on prescription theft."

"We're going to have to tell the police about this now, aren't we?" asked Fiona.

"Absolutely — once we're one hundred per cent sure that we're right," said Rhian. "And I am almost — I just want to hear what Lynne turns up from Auckland."

When Lynne phoned back, Sally and Fiona strained their ears trying to hear what she was telling Rhian. But they couldn't catch much of what she said, and had to wait until the phone call had ended before Rhian could tell them what they wanted to know.

"Lynne found the cuttings on Bridget Emerson," said Sally, her eyes sparkling. "She was backpacking in New Zealand, and went climbing in the South Island and ended up falling. At the time, she was travelling with another girl from England.

They hadn't known each other in England, but had met in Australia and were travelling back home together from there, via New Zealand and Fiji. The other girl wasn't out climbing with Bridget — that was a genuine accident. Anyway, Lynne says one of the cuttings had a photo of Bridget and this girl together. She's going to photocopy it and email it through to me." She clicked on her email. "Ah, here it is now."

Rhian clicked open the attachment, and Sally's eyes fell on a photo of two girls in their early twenties — one, Bridget Emerson, short and plump with long dark hair, and the other tall and blonde. The caption called her Lorraine Wilson, but the photo was definitely of a younger version of the woman Sally had come to know as Bridget Whodcoat.

CHAPTER XXV.

SALLY IN PURSUIT

"I see," said Daphne. "But I'm worse than you think, Miss Grayling. I haven't only stolen — I've told lies. I said I'd never been to another school before, because I was afraid the girls might get to know I'd been sent home twice from schools. I pretended my people were very rich. I — I had a photo on my dressing table that wasn't my mother at all — it was a very grand picture of a beautiful woman ..."

Enid Blyton, *Second Form at Malory Towers*, 1947

"I WONDER if we should go to Robert Whodcoat with this?" Rhian said.

"Don't you think we should just go straight to the police?" Sally responded. "I think we've got enough here for them to be able to question Bridget — or Lorraine, rather — about Valerie's death."

"And Robert might well be involved," said Fiona. "It's probably not a good idea to visit him, Rhee. If the Whodcoats did kill Valerie, then he might decide to kill you."

"I think James and Robert probably aren't involved," said Sally. "Well, Robert might be, but I doubt it. James certainly isn't. If he'd known about the blackmail and about Bridget killing Valerie — if she did — why didn't he stick to the same story she'd been giving about renovations when I visited? But I don't agree with you that we should go to see his brother, Rhian."

"Well, let's sleep on it," said Rhian. "None of us is going to be able to get up in the morning, it's so late. And Fee and I have to get to work. Lorraine Wilson — I wish we could find out more about her, but there'd be way too many in the world for us to be lucky enough to hit on the right one."

Sally went to bed, worried that Rhian would wake up still determined to visit Robert Whodcoat. It was true, she knew, that they still didn't have all the pieces to the puzzle — did Robert Whodcoat know the true identity of his sister-in-law? *Had* she stolen a prescription from him in order to get hold of phenelzine? — but Sally would have felt more than happy to let Steve Arrowman and his team finish off the investigation.

When the three women got up the next morning, it was immediately apparent that Sally's fears were well-founded. Rhian had been online and discovered that Robert Whodcoat practised in Kensington, just off the High Street. "I'm going to go and see him," she said. "Once I've heard what he has to say, we can get on to the police."

"Well, I can't come with you — I've got to get to work," Fiona said. "I think what you're doing is stupid, Rhian, to be honest, but—."

"Honestly, Fee, almost every day of my life I have conversations with people that they might object to," said Rhian. "I can drop you off at a convenient tube station on the way. What about you, Sal? Coming with?"

"Oh, all right," said Sally, gloomily. "I agree with Fee, but I don't think that you should see Roger Whodcoat on your own — I'll come."

They skipped breakfast and Rhian drove across to West London. Fiona stayed in the car all the way to South Kensington, where she could hop on the Piccadilly Line and get to work. Rhian drove down bustling Kensington High Street, already crowded with shoppers, and found the road where Robert Whodcoat's practice was located. "Must be our lucky day," she grinned, as she snagged a parking space right outside the house where he practised. "Come on, let's see if he'll see us."

They walked into the building and found themselves in a small waiting room. A counter, behind which sat two receptionists, took up most of the available space. Both receptionists were young; one of them, with a long, fair pony-tail, looked up and smiled at them. "Do you have an appointment?"

"No," said Rhian, "but we're here to see Robert Whodcoat."

"Mr Whodcoat's busy until three," the receptionist returned, looking down at the diary.

"Could you tell him that this is urgent family business?" said Rhian.

"You're family?" the receptionist asked doubtfully.

"No — but we've come in connection with his sister-in-law, Bridget."

"I'll just tell him," said the receptionist. "Take a seat." She disappeared up the stairs, leaving Rhian and Sally to join the two patients who were sitting in the waiting room. The receptionist returned a couple of minutes later and said, "Mr Whodcoat will be down in a minute."

Robert Whodcoat, when he came downstairs, looked very like his brother, with his blond hair and sun-tan, though he was a little older — perhaps mid- to late-forties. He shook hands with Rhian and then Sally, and asked, "What's happened to Bridget?"

"Can we go somewhere private?" Rhian asked.

"Of course." He led them up the narrow staircase and into a small room that seemed crammed with heavy furniture. He sat down in a big green armchair and motioned the two women over to the sofa. Before she sat down, Rhian took the cuttings from her briefcase and handed them over to him.

"I'm actually a journalist," she said, "investigating a story about blackmail. One of the people being blackmailed is your sister-in-law, and it seems that this is the reason why."

Robert read through the cuttings, a deepening frown on his face. "I can't get my head around this," he said, perplexed. "Surely there's some mix-up. The wrong names under the wrong faces in the caption?"

"But the other cuttings have photos of Bridget Emerson too, and clearly refer to her being the girl who died," Rhian pointed out.

"Yes, I can see that, but it makes no sense. I've known Bridget for fifteen years." He ran his hands through his hair. "It's impossible that she's someone else."

"How did your brother meet her?" Sally asked, curiously.

"He met her in Canada," answered Robert. "He was working for a financial institution and they sent him over there for a year for overseas experience. Bridget was also working there. They dated for a while, then got married quite quickly."

"Have you met her family?" Rhian asked.

"No — never. Bridget said both her parents were dead. She said that was why she'd spent a year out travelling after university — that her mother had died when she was small, and her father had died just before her final exams. She had no other family. James and Bridget got married in the Caribbean and she became friends with his friends. They've been very happy together." He looked down at the photo of the real Bridget Emerson again. "I'm sorry — this really doesn't make any sense."

"You've never met any of her friends from Upland

Park?"

"No — she had no friends there. She always said she hated the school and had a dreadful time at it. Have you spoken to James about this? Or to Bridget?"

"Not yet," said Rhian. "I just have one more thing to ask you, Mr Whodcoat — do you have a prescription pad on your desk?"

"No," he said. "I print out prescriptions from the computer and sign them. Why?"

"It's just that—." Rhian hesitated, then decided to tell the truth. "It's possible that the person who was blackmailing Bridget — or rather Lorraine — was murdered last Saturday. She was given phenelzine."

"Well, Bridget was certainly round here the week before that, but I've no idea if she printed out a prescription," said Robert. "I honestly can't imagine her killing someone."

"But until a few moments ago, you couldn't have imagined her not being Bridget Emerson either," Rhian pointed out. "Did she have access to the computer — was she alone with it at any time?"

"Oh yes. She came and helped me with some filing. She rang up and offered to do it, out of the blue. I was very grateful. One of my staff has been off sick for a while and there was a backlog of filing."

It really wasn't looking very good for Bridget, Sally thought, as Rhian took back her cuttings and thanked him for his time.

"I'd better be getting to work," Rhian said, when they returned to the car. "I'll give Arrowman a call too. What are you going to do, Sal?"

"Not sure," said Sally. "To be honest, I feel a bit too unsettled by all this for sightseeing."

"I know what you mean — I'm glad I'm going into work. Would you prefer to ring Arrowman yourself?"

"No — you can do it," said Sally. "It'll sound more

reliable coming from you. He thinks all school-story collectors are nutters, so probably wouldn't take me seriously anyway."

Rhian was about to drive off when her mobile rang. She answered it, then said to Sally, "It's the police saying that they can call round to the flat this afternoon at about two about the vandalism. Would you mind going back there, Sal, to show them? I won't be able to get away from work."

"Sure," Sally said, glad of something concrete to do. "I'll start heading back now." She glanced at her watch; it was ten-thirty. It would take a couple of hours easily to get back to Forest Hill. She decided to get off the bus in East Dulwich and take a look at Enid Blyton's birthplace in Lordship Lane. She had her camera with her, so she'd be able to take photographs of the plaque.

In the end, the journey was quicker than she'd anticipated. She caught the tube to Victoria, and then a bus that took her right to Lordship Lane, a long stretch of mostly restaurants, cafes and wine bars that started almost at crime-ridden Peckham and finished almost in expensive Dulwich Village. She found the shop that had been Enid Blyton's birthplace, took a photo of it, asked a passing pedestrian if she'd take a photo of her standing outside it, then waited for a bus to Forest Hill. She still had one-and-a-half hours until the police came; she thought she might read until then, or perhaps get all her laundry done — it wasn't long before she was due to leave England, after all.

As she turned the corner towards Rhian's flat, she could hear raised voices, and spotted Sarah, Rhian's neighbour, struggling with someone. Thinking the vandal must have returned, Sally broke into a run. As she did so, she saw Sarah fall back, and her assailant take to her heels. She instantly recognised the woman who was running towards her. It was Bridget Whodcoat.

When Bridget recognised her, she turned and started running in the opposite direction. Sally ran after her; as she did so, Sarah yelled out that she was phoning the police. Sally hadn't thought of herself as being particularly fit, but Bridget was no doubt tired from her earlier struggle with Sarah and Sally found herself gaining on her. Bridget stopped, out of breath.

"I do wish you'd kept out of it," she gasped. "James and I were happy. Valerie made a lot of people miserable — not just me. Why couldn't you have left well alone?"

Sally looked around. The street was quiet, but no doubt there were people behind at least some of the windows. Bridget wouldn't harm her, surely? She'd poisoned Valerie, not shot or knifed her. So she was probably safe to question her. "How did Valerie find out about you, Bridget?"

"She bought some books from a woman who'd been to Upland Park school — her mother had died and had a load of G.O. titles. When Valerie asked her about someone called Bridget who'd been there in the 1980s, the woman could only think of Bridget Emerson and told her that she'd died. Valerie did some more investigating, then she came to tell me what she knew and said if I didn't pay her in books, she'd tell James."

"James didn't know, then?"

"No. No-one did. I was travelling with Bridget when she died. We were the same age and met up in a hostel in Australia. We got on well, despite the differences between us. She'd had everything I ever wanted — boarding-school, horses, the lot. I'd only ever read about those things. My parents died when I was a kid — I grew up in foster care." Bridget leaned against a wall, looking weary. "I didn't have a bad childhood, but it wasn't the sort I wanted. I left school with just a few GCEs, worked in odd jobs for a while ... I hated it. The day Bridget was killed, she'd left some of her stuff at the hostel — not her passport or driving licence, but her certificate from university, and some references from her lecturer and someone she'd worked for during holidays. I kept them. I thought I might be able to use them to get a well-paying job while I travelled. When I got back to England, I got her birth certificate from St Catherine's house. Then I got a passport in her name — it was easier to do that sort of thing back then, because the sort of technology we have today just wasn't around. So I went to Canada and started a new life as Bridget Emerson. Then I married James, had the children. It was all fine until Valerie found out. I hadn't harmed anybody — all I'd done was take advantages of the opportunities that automatically came the way of someone from a privileged background. Opportunities I'd never have had if I'd stayed as Lorraine Wilson."

"Wouldn't it have been better to confess what you'd done than to kill Valerie?" asked Sally.

"I couldn't — not after all those years. I just couldn't bring myself to tell James and the boys. If Valerie had just accepted the books I gave her I'd never have harmed her. But she didn't stop. She just wanted more and more things. James would have become suspicious. I had to get rid of her." Bridget stopped leaning against the wall and said, "Well, now you know everything, Sally. Congratulations on your sleuthing — yours and your friends'. Very 'girls' own'. But the police won't catch me. I'll be out of here before they'll believe your story."

"I don't think so," Sally said, as the police car, siren screaming, came flying round the corner.

CHAPTER XXVI.

SALLY UNFOLDS A TALE

"Oh, you!" he said, with affectionate scorn. "You think the school couldn't get on without you! You're a wife and a proud mamma, but in a good many ways, Jo, you're still nothing but a schoolgirl."

"You've missed out the chief part of it," she said. "I'm still, in part of me, what I shall always be — a Chalet School girl."

Elinor M. Brent-Dyer, *The Chalet School and the Island*, 1950

"HERE we are," said Sally. "Looks nice, doesn't it?" They had pulled up in the lane by Richard's picture-book thatched cottage in a village just outside Ludlow. It was just two days before Sally was due to depart from Heathrow, and he'd decided to throw a dinner party in her honour. Having heard about the part that Sally's friends had played in the arrest of the woman he'd known for over ten years as Bridget Whodcoat, he'd magnanimously invited Rhian and Fiona as well. They all clambered out of the car, and Sally pulled on the bell that hung beside the stable-style door. Richard opened the door and greeted Sally warmly, exchanging pleasantries with Rhian and Fiona.

"You're the third, fourth and fifth to arrive," he told them, showing them into an elegantly appointed living room, with antique furniture, shelves crammed with books at each side of an enormous fireplace, and a huge grandfather clock in the corner. Sally spotted Harriet Lenton, clad in a plastic apron depicting old manuscripts, standing in the doorway to what appeared to be the kitchen, and an uncomfortable-looking Leonie Carr perched on the edge of an armchair in the corner of the room. Sally kissed Harriet and Leonie, then introduced Rhian and Fiona.

"You make yourselves at home," said Richard. "Drinks? There's Scotch, gin, vodka …"

"Man after my own heart," said Rhian, with a grin. "I'd love a Scotch, thanks. Just neat, with ice if you've got any." The trio had booked rooms for the night in a hotel in Ludlow; if Rhian had too much to drink, they had thought, they could easily take a taxi.

Sally and Fiona accepted gin and tonics. Richard poured the drinks. "Jolly good sleuthing, you three," he commented. "Worthy of Nancy Drew herself."

Leonie grinned. "So which of you is Nancy, which is George and which is Bess?"

The reference was lost on Rhian, but Fiona said regretfully, "Bess is the fat one, isn't she? I must be her — I'm a bit plumper than these two."

"What a pity our Bridget turned out to be a murderer, though," said Harriet. "I'd much rather it had been someone I didn't know. I always *liked* Bridget."

"I liked her too," said Sally. "Well, until I realised what she'd done." She felt sad that someone she'd warmed to and who had been so welcoming to her had turned out to be the murderer. She would have to scrap Bridget's comments from her still-to-be-written article too; she'd already arranged on email with Maria Laker for some comments to replace them.

"I *adored* her," Richard said. "By God, we must be

bad judges of character." He passed a neat whisky to Rhian.

"I don't think it makes you bad judges of character," Rhian said, sipping it. "Bridget was, after all, a conwoman — it's what she was good at. It's no wonder people believed her and liked her."

"It's her husband and children I feel sorry for," said Leonie. "Imagine coming to terms with the fact that your wife or mum is not only a murderer, but that she's never been who you've always thought she was."

Sally thought of Bridget's sons, still in their early teens, with their mother on remand in prison and likely to be convicted of murder. She shuddered at the thought of how they must feel being separated from their mother, and how Bridget must feel being separated from them. It was *awful*.

"I wonder what'll happen to her books," sighed Richard. "She had a *divine* collection."

Sally smiled faintly at his thinking of Bridget's books before her family. "Yours isn't so bad, Richard," she said, going over to examine the bookcases. There was shelf after shelf of 'boys' own' books, including series she recognised like Biggles, Jennings, Billy Bunter and Just William, and lots of books and authors that she didn't, with wacky titles like A *Duffer at Drinan's* and *Six Stout Fellows and Me*. Then there were boys' annuals, heaps of them, and girls' annuals too, all containing stories by the writers who Richard specialised in. The other shelves, on the far side of the fireplace, contained classics — Dickens, Hardy, D.H. Lawrence and many more.

The doorbell rang and Richard went to answer it. Leah Brindsley and Sue Parkinson entered; Richard poured them drinks while Sally introduced Rhian and Fiona to them. "I'd better get back to the kitchen," Richard said. "Coming, Harry?"

"Oh well, they're still an item," Leonie said in low tones, when Richard and Harriet had disappeared into the kitchen. "It's actually quite a long relationship for Richard — what's it been? More than two weeks."

Richard served up soup and garlic bread as a starter. They all sat around the large oak table at the far end of the room. "So," Richard said, "I wonder what will happen to Bridget? I suppose I should call her Lorraine, but I can't get used to that. I assume she'll get life, and be released in — what? — fifteen years?"

"How did she actually manage to kill Valerie with the antidepressants?" Leonie asked. "Did she doctor her food somehow?"

"Yes," said Sally. "She hasn't said so, but from what we've worked out, she grabbed a couple of spinach rolls from the trolley prior to the folk dancing and then injected crushed phenelzine into them. She knew from previous conferences that Valerie used to pile her plate high with food and eat the lot, but that she'd leave her food occasionally for dancing. So when Valerie left her plate unattended, Bridget swapped the spinach roll on her plate for one of the ones in her bag."

"Or perhaps both of the rolls on her plate for both of the rolls in her bag," Fiona cut in.

"She's lucky no-one saw her," sighed Leah.

"Or Valerie was unlucky," Harriet said.

"You never are looking at what people are doing with food when you're dancing or watching dancing or stuffing your own face," Leonie commented. "Bridget probably thought she'd easily get away with it."

"What an idiot," said Leah. "Fancy being so stupid as to let yourself be blackmailed. You'd think she'd have had the guts to tell her husband rather than give away countless valuable books and then poison the blackmailer."

"Well, Bridge wasn't the only one being blackmailed," said Richard. "Tell them, Sally."

Sally told them about Jessica Gibson's plagiarism and Justine's revenge. Rhian had written her story about plagiarism and blackmail in the 'girls' own' world; it was due to appear in the next day's *Clarion*. She had offered Sally a share of the byline, but Sally had, somewhat reluctantly, turned it down. A byline in the *Clarion* would be brilliant and look good on her CV, but in the end she was part of the school-story collecting world and wanted to remain so — she couldn't have written it and continued to be accepted by the fans. But she had, she realised, enjoyed the sleuthing. Perhaps, if the opportunity arose to write an investigative piece on something for her magazine, she might have a go at it herself instead of commissioning someone else.

Sue sighed. "I can hardly believe it of Jess Gibson. She always seemed such a lovely lady. Miriam's going to be so disappointed in her when she finds out."

"It's rather a shame it has to come out when Jessica's dying," Harriet commented.

"Well," said Rhian, defensively, "I think it's better that it comes out when she's alive rather than just having people saying bad things about her when she's dead."

"Maybe you're right," said Richard. "And she must have known the truth would come out one day. I suppose that's why she threw the first edition Rosalie into Valerie's grave? Because Valerie had taken everything else of value from her?"

"What a fool she's been," Leah said. "All for having her name on a book cover."

"Goodness," sighed Harriet. "Rhian and Fiona must think that the G.O. world is full of villains."

"It certainly seems like it," Rhian grinned. "A blackmailer. A plagiarist. A conwoman with a nice line in vandalism. A vandal. A firebug. A thief."

"What d'you mean about a conwoman with a nice line in vandalism?" Sue Parkinson enquired.

"Oh, Bridget put a stone through Rhian's door on Sunday night and left nasty messages to warn us off," said Sally. "And after she heard that we'd visited her brother-in-law and given her away, she drove over to Forest Hill to do some further damage to Rhian's place. Fortunately Sarah, Rhian's neighbour, spotted her and was brave enough to tackle her and prevent it happening."

"Lucky she was spotted, really," said Rhian. "We were actually blaming Justine Gibson for the vandalism up till then."

"But I checked with someone who knows her in Haweshill and Justine's been at a conference in Birmingham all weekend," put in Fiona. "So we'd probably have remained puzzled about the vandalism if Bridget hadn't been caught in the act."

They finished the soup and Richard produced the main course — a chicken and mushroom pie with chips and salad. He opened a bottle of red wine.

"So when do you go back to Australia, Sally?" he asked.

"In just two days' time."

"Have you had a good time?"

"Well, overall, yes. It's been different to what I imagined it'd be," said Sally with a grin.

"It's the shame the conference was marred by all this business," said Harriet. "Don't let it put you off coming over for another one, though, Sally. They're usually tremendous fun. And to be honest, without Valerie Teague around, they'll be even more fun."

"Harriet!" chided Richard.

"She's right," said Leonie. "I don't think anyone really got along with Valerie."

"Well, apart from you, Richard, at that conference last year," said Harriet, slyly.

"Please don't remind me of that little indiscretion," Richard shuddered. "All I want to do is to forget it ever happened. Anyway, my dear, I think you got off very lightly yourself. If Valerie had lived, she might well have started blackmailing *you* — first edition Chalets or she'd tell Charles all about your raunchy nights with me."

Harriet made a face at him. "What's raunchy about them?"

"Something else you can do, Sally," said Sue, diverting attention from Richard and Harriet, "is to come over in 2010 for the Passion Play at Oberammergau. A group of us who are Chalet School fans are going — we went in 2000 and had a fantastic time."

That sounded wonderful, Sally thought, remembering the events in *The Chalet School and Jo* where the Chalet girls visited the Passion Play at Oberammergau during half-term. "I'll think about that seriously, Sue," she said. "That sounds like a great idea. It all depends on cost, though. Flights from Australia can be expensive, and I don't suppose the Passion Play is cheap either. But like I say, I'll think about it." After all, she realised, the kids really would be off her hands by then; any money she earned would finally be all hers, to do exactly what she wanted with.

"Bear in mind, though," said Richard, "that anyone who does go will have to dress up as Red Indians like those naughty Middles did. Everyone ready for pudding?"

There was treacle tart and custard for pudding,

followed by coffee and cheese and crackers. Richard also offered liqueurs, which everyone declined. Those who were driving didn't want extra alcohol, and those who weren't were already feeling the effects of the wine and aperitifs.

They talked about the murders and the conference a little more, then Sue and Leonie rose to leave. "Sorry to have to go so soon," said Leonie, "but it's a long drive and unfortunately both of us have to work tomorrow. 'Bye Sally, it was nice too meet you. You too," she added to Rhian and Fiona.

They all said goodbye and Richard showed them out. "We'd better go too," said Sally, sensing that the other two had perhaps had more than enough 'shop' talk. Harriet, it appeared, was staying the night.

"Before you go, Sally," said Harriet, "I was just wondering if you'd given up on the idea of a school story conference in Australia."

"What's this?" Rhian asked.

Sally enlightened her. "I haven't really given up on the idea," she said. "I think it would work. There's plenty of interest out there. When I get back, I'm going to talk to my bosses about having the magazine organise and sponsor the conference. There are people in Australia who would make good speakers, I'm sure."

"Good for you," said Harriet, approvingly.

"If you do go ahead," said Richard, "give me a call. I'm sure I could manage to combine a trip to your conference with something else for work and give my services free of charge. If you're happy to have me as a speaker, that is."

"More than happy. I'll let you know if I do get it up and running, Richard," Sally promised warmly.

"And I might think about coming out too," said Harriet, quickly, and Sally caught Rhian and Fiona exchanging quick grins; it hadn't taken them long to pick up on Harriet's jealousy as far as Richard was concerned.

They said goodbye to Harriet and Richard and went out to the car. It was a chilly night; autumn had definitely arrived. Sally shivered, glad that she'd be going back to spring.

"It's been great having you over, Sally," said Rhian as she beeped the horn in farewell to Richard and Harriet and drove off towards Ludlow. "And it's been fun sort of working together, hasn't it?"

"Yes," said Sally. "When I came over for the conference, I never thought I'd end up investigating a murder."

"Never mind investigating," said Fiona. "*Solving* a murder is what you did."

"And now you're going to organise a conference of your own," said Rhian. "Perhaps you'll have a murder to solve there too."

"I hope not," laughed Sally. "Organising a conference is something I never envisaged myself doing, let alone solving a murder."

Fiona laughed. "And just think," she said. "You'd never have done either of those things if, when you were a little girl, you hadn't become a fan of the Chalet School."